It was refl

My mind must have registered the movement an instant before the window disintegrated. I don't remember doing it, but I wrapped an arm around Megan's waist and dove to the left, pulling her off the stoop. My shoulders hit the driveway. Her head snapped back, catching me on the chin. The back of my head kissed the pavement, and I saw stars. She slid off me and banged her head on the driveway.

She rolled left, aiming her weapon and rising to her feet in one smooth motion. Movement in the street caught my attention. One of the troopers who had been on the surveillance assignment had moved to the sidewalk, directly in front of the picture window to back us up. I saw his legs go out from under him, and he clutched at his thigh. His partner rushed over, used a parked car as a shield, and dragged him back. In the distance, I could hear sirens. Somebody must have called it in. This whole thing made no sense. We had a warrant to search the place, and we were going to bring him in for questioning. What triggered this attack? I swung my gaze back from the street.

"What the fuck?" Megan's face was filled with rage.

Before I could respond, we heard gunfire coming from the rear of the house. Myers must have company, or he'd been waiting for us.

"Front door?" Megan hooked a thumb at the stoop.

"Damn right."

Praise for Mark Love

"If you're looking for a riveting police procedural, pick up Mark Love's new murder mystery."

~M.S. Spencer, author of Lapses of Memory

~*~

"Mark Love's gripping murder mystery winds and twists and leads the reader down a maze of dark alleys as a team of hardened detectives pursue a slippery serial killer with a maddening penchant for taunts and teases."

~Teresa Rose, author of River of Gold

~*~

"*WHY 319?* is a page-turning who-done-it…The story is crisp and well-paced with just enough strategically placed misdirection to keep the reader guessing."

~Mark Pople, author of Roger's Park

To Elizabeth,
What's life without
a little mystery?

Enjoy!

Why 319?

Mark Love

by

Mark Love

A Jefferson Chene Mystery

Why 319?

Cover Art by *RJ Morris*

The Wild Rose Press, Inc.
PO Box 708
Adams Basin, NY 14410-0708
Visit us at www.thewildrosepress.com

Publishing History
Previously published by Black Rose Writing, 2014
First Mainstream Thriller Edition, 2017
Print ISBN 978-1-5092-1450-1
Digital ISBN 978-1-5092-1451-8

A Jefferson Chene Mystery
Published in the United States of America

Dedication

For Travis and Cameron,
my pride and joy

Prologue

It was almost becoming too easy. They were everywhere. One plain Jane after another kept crossing my radar screen. Some nights it was like shopping for bananas, and they were visible in bunches.

Tonight was one of those nights. It was as if someone were holding up a sign, steering them in my direction. Like right now. Off to the left at one of those elevated stations, where you had to sit on a barstool in order to reach the table, were two perfect physical examples of the ideal target. Four women, each in their early to mid-twenties were crowded around the postage stamp-sized table. I ruled two out immediately. They were chunky, flashing lots of cleavage with large breasts. For a nanosecond, I wondered if the flesh was real or the results of surgical enhancement. It didn't matter. They were unworthy of any further consideration.

But it was the other two who caught my eye. The one on the right was a bottle blonde, which was obvious by the dark roots showing and the dark eyebrows. The other was a brassy redhead. She was tiny, almost doll like. I was in a perfect position to observe her. She was wearing high-heeled red boots that came up over her knee, sassy-looking things that accentuated her legs. Her black skirt barely touched the middle of her thighs, but it might have been longer if she was standing up.

She wore a heavy ivory-colored wool sweater that covered her from the throat to the waist. It was loose enough to keep the goodies beneath it a well-guarded secret. With the boots and the short skirt, she was almost too good to be true. And upon reflection, I realized she was.

Her attitude was a turn off. This was a girl who flaunted the little bits she had. As she sat on the stool, swaying to the background music, she kept crossing and uncrossing her legs, putting on a floorshow of her own. Her hands were constantly in motion. Now they were slowly, seductively sliding down her arms, dropping below the table into her lap. They lingered for a moment, then skittered down her legs to tug at the bottom of the skirt. This was no timid child. She was well aware of her body. By the way she was moving, she knew how to use it.

My focus returned to the bottle blonde. This one had potential. Her wardrobe was the polar opposite of the redhead. Loose-fitting slacks, with low heeled shoes that would have been rejected by a nun with an orthopedic condition, she wore a blouse buttoned to the neck and a jacket to help conceal her. The only thing that broke the mold for this plain Jane was the hair color. Upon a closer look, it was blonde highlights swirled in with the natural brown, a shade best described as mousy brown. Perhaps she was letting it grow out after getting it dyed for the holidays. What would she look like, sprawled naked on a bed, unable to resist, unable to stop, unable to do anything at all?

My body began to respond.

My heart rate kicked up a notch. A warm glow started in the pit of my stomach and eased out in every direction. I basked in the tremors of anticipation. My cheeks flushed with beads of perspiration.

Yes, she could very easily be the next one.

But first the stage had to be set. And it was a time for patience. The plans were perfection, which was evident by the lack of awareness of the public or any progress by the police. Those bumblers in blue would never put it together because of the meticulous planning. If by chance they somehow managed to get a clue, the misdirection was already in place. So there could be no deviation from the plan. It had taken weeks of study, of strategizing each and every move. Every step was plotted out. Every move was a smooth, choreographed motion. Every action triggered the next in a series of reactions. Just reflecting on the past efforts was enough to make me smile. The memory of my last victim, her limp body slowly cooling as the life force ebbed away was enough to bring a smile of triumph to my lips.

"What the hell are you grinning at?" The band's drummer, Malcolm, asked as he stepped up.

"Just thinking about how good a night this will be," I said.

"I don't want a bumpy ride tonight."

I turned and looked him right in the eye. "You got nothing to worry about, man. Everything will be smooth."

Malcolm hesitated a moment as he studied me, then nodded in agreement. "We can't ever be too smooth."

My smile widened. "That's me, man, I'm too smooth."

****

I am elusive. I'm a cold, calculating, efficient

machine. No computer can analyze my moves and predict when and where the next victim will be found. No one can determine the motive that lay beneath the actions. Only someone who has lived in my body, had the same experiences, the same influences, the same events coursing through their veins would have even the slightest glimmer of a possibility of figuring this out.

"I'm too smooth," I said softly, closely studying the reflection in the mirror. "That's smooth spelled with seventeen Os."

Everything was moving forward according to plan. The next victim was being developed, that timid one with the blonde highlights from the bar last week. She was so uncertain of herself, it was as if a strong wind could change the direction of her focus. Her name was Melissa. She was a preschool teacher, helping four- and five-year-olds learn their colors and the alphabet. For a moment, I wondered if that had been the extent of Janet's own knowledge. She certainly hadn't appeared to be experienced in the ways of the world when it came to dating. Of course, she needn't worry about dating any longer, now that she was dead.

It had almost been too easy to cut her from her small group of friends at the bar. With the crowd noise, the interactions of both men and women reveling in the music, the booze, the pheromones, and the physical contact, it was only a matter of paying attention, of waiting for the right moment to pick her off. Each of her three friends was drawn to the dance floor, where the press of bodies was intense.

"Melissa, my dear, you are about to discover the world of excitement. The world of romance, of passion, of intensity that you could never imagine is waiting for you. And I intend to be the one to introduce you to it."

I spun from the mirror and snapped off the lights. Game on.

Chapter One

You never really get used to the smell of a dead body. It's that thick, ghastly odor that attacks the nasal passages and stubbornly clogs the back of your throat and just hangs there. It lingers, waiting, like some sadistic culinary delight that you really don't want to sample. The temperature in the room was hot, which would expedite the decomposition process. The gases inside the body were already starting the decay. That was the stench that assaulted me the second I crossed the threshold of the motel room.

Two crime-scene technicians were already at work. One was busy with a video camera, filming the details. The other was making notes and dusting surfaces for fingerprints. Standing in the outer hallway were two uniformed police officers and a detective in a gray flannel suit. As I was taking in the details of the room, I felt a finger prod my spine, just below the shoulder blades.

"Hey, Koz," I said, without flinching.

There was a chuckle in the deep voice behind me. "Damn, Chene, you must be a great detective. You never even turned around."

I inclined my head toward the small oval mirror on the opposite wall. "Sometimes you make it too easy. Anyone else get the call?"

"Nah. You figure it's the same guy?"

"Hard to say. But it's got the right feel to it. They haven't given the media the specifics yet, so we can rule out a copycat."

Koz nodded as the guy in the gray flannel appeared in the doorway. The suit was badly wrinkled. The guy was in dire need of a shave. He was about five foot ten, with curly black hair framing his head. We followed him across the hall to another room and waited while he closed the door behind us. Koz slumped into one of the upholstered chairs. I leaned against the wall.

"Name's Costello. I was just going off duty when we got the call from the hotel manager. I've got two detectives on a stakeout, one on vacation, and another out with appendicitis. This just isn't going to be my day."

We did the business card exchange. His had the Bloomfield logo in the background. Sergeant Norman Costello. I doubted that the State of Michigan shield on our cards impressed him. I didn't really care. He gave the cards a quick once-over, then looked up quickly. "Jefferson Chene. Isn't that an intersection downtown?"

Reluctantly, I nodded. "I'm Chene. That's Kozlowski. Koz is easier on the tongue. What made you think to call us?"

Costello pulled a pack of cigarettes from his shirt pocket and looked at us briefly. Koz raised his hands palms up. I merely nodded. It took him three tries to get a match lit. He took a deep drag before answering.

"Saw the notice from the top yesterday. There have been two other killings in the Metro area in the last two months. Both fit the same description. Young females, slender build, with no evidence of drug use. Both found nude, spread-eagled on the bed. Sexual activity evident, but it's uncertain as to whether it was pre- or postmortem, or both. Cause of death appears to be suffocation." Costello rubbed his left hand across his face. "It looks like he used the pillow. No apparent struggle. No signs of forced entry."

"How long you been here?" Koz asked.

Costello checked his watch. "About forty-five minutes. We're lucky that the room is on the end of the hallway. I put one uniform on the door, another at the end of the corridor to keep any guests out. Called for the evidence techs, then called you guys."

"Who's the top?" I asked.

"That would be Chief of Police Ryun. Him and the lady mayor notified us yesterday. She wanted to make it abundantly clear that we contact the state police immediately. It's almost like she expected us to be involved."

"This scumbag has committed two other murders, one each in Wayne and Macomb counties. Stands to reason Oakland was due," I said.

"Yeah, but why couldn't he pick something like Troy or Southfield? Or even Royal Oak where all the trendsetters are," Costello grumbled.

"Just lucky I guess," Koz said.

"No offense, but we'll have our forensic team join the party. We'll need copies of whatever reports you generate from this investigation."

An inch of ash teetered on the tip of Costello's cigarette. He looked around the motel room for an ashtray, then gave up and cupped his palm beneath it. He took another long drag and walked into the bathroom. I could hear the hiss of the ember hitting the water, then the toilet flushed as he got rid of it. He came back in the room, brushing ashes off his hands.

"You smoke much?" Koz asked as he rose from the chair.

"I gave it up three years ago, used to do two packs a day without even thinking about it."

"So what's with today?"

Costello gave a reluctant shrug. "First homicide I've seen in years. Most of what we get is home invasions. Maybe some snatch and grabs, DUI, that kind of stuff. To make matters worse, she looks like a girl that works as a babysitter in our neighborhood. We don't get homicides out here in the suburbs."

Koz gave him a single nod of understanding. "You do now."

We gloved up and went back into room 319. Costello remained in the hallway. The room was average size for a motel, but not big enough for half a dozen people to be moving around inspecting a crime scene. He conferred with the two uniformed guys out in the hall. Koz and I took a quick look at the body while the techs hung back.

She was a plain girl. Not gorgeous, not pretty, but plain. Average looks, the kind of girl you would pass in a store or on the street and wouldn't glance at twice. Once upon a time, she'd had large dark green eyes. Thick brown hair extended just beyond her shoulders. She had a straight up and down figure, a size one or maybe a size two, with small, almost nonexistent, breasts and a narrow waist. I guessed her to be about five foot three, maybe ninety pounds.

I picked up her wrist and slowly rotated the hand. Her skin was clammy in the overheated room. Koz instructed one of the techs to turn off the heat.

"Nails were cut. Just like the others."

He nodded. "Not the type of girl to bite them. Check out the polish. Same shade on the toes, and it looks recent. Spent some time making herself look good."

"Pro?"

"Doubt it. She's probably a career girl. We'll know more from registration. I'm guessing we'll find a car in the lot."

I leaned back on my heels, studying her. I knew it was the same guy. It had to be the same guy. I glanced at Kozlowski. He was looking at the wall above the bed. The cream-colored paint and wallpaper were immaculate. No splatters of blood. Death must have been quick. No bruising on the body. He was neat and tidy, just like before.

"I'm guessing he used a douche on her too. Makes sure he doesn't leave any DNA." Koz shook his head in disgust. "Guy even shaves off her bush, so he doesn't leave any of his hair behind."

"You never know. Some girls prefer the smooth look."

He snorted a laugh. "Yeah, like hookers trying to pass for thirteen."

"You check?"

"Nah. Go ahead."

I walked into the bathroom, flicking on the light with the back of my knuckle. It was on the mirror. The message was written in lipstick, the smeary letters almost a foot tall. Acid built in my stomach as I studied the riddle.

WHY 319?

I don't normally spend time gazing upon my

reflection in the mirror. But as I stared at the message and the light-skinned black man staring back at me, I noticed it was written fairly high up on the glass. It was just about eye level on me, so maybe this was a clue to our killer's height.

My gaze flicked down. Lying on the counter was the lipstick container. During the investigation, we would learn it was hers. Victim number three. I hadn't asked her name yet. But in the next few days, I would strive to learn everything I could about her. Leaning out toward the room, I hooked a finger at the tech with the camera equipment.

"Don't forget the bathroom," I said. "Get the whole room."

Kozlowski was waiting for me in the hallway, snapping off the latex gloves and stuffing them in the pocket of his coat. His blue eyes were cold and hard as he stared past me into the motel room.

"Same message?"

"Yeah."

"This guy is starting to piss me off."

"Me too. You call for Rudy?"

He nodded. "Fen's going to do the autopsy himself. He's bringing the crew to do the evidence sweep. I asked Costello to get the manager and the details."

We turned to see Costello walking down the hall, escorting a very pale and timid woman. It was obvious that she was unaccustomed to dead bodies in her motel, and that the last place she wanted to be was anywhere near the victim. Unfortunately, she didn't have much choice.

Chapter Two

The four of us gathered around a table in the center of a small banquet room. The manager didn't want to even be on the same floor where the body was. Costello collected a dirty coffee cup to use as an ashtray on the way in and was a few feet apart from us, firing up a fresh smoke. He was trying to explain the situation to the manager. According to the shiny brass tag on her blazer, her name was Elise Woods. She was having a hard time following the conversation. Koz caught my eye and inclined his head slightly. I nodded once, letting him take the lead.

He slid his chair a little closer to her, then gently reached over and took her hand. From the moment of physical contact, her attention was locked on Kozlowski.

"Ms. Woods." He spoke in his low, deep voice. "What happened here is a tragedy. It's something that should never happen, but it does."

She gulped and nodded, her eyes focused on his face. With her free hand, she swept a lock of hair back off her forehead.

"The person who did this needs to be stopped," Koz continued. "They need to be punished. But in order for us to catch them, we need all the help we can get. And that starts with you."

"I understand." Her voice wobbled. She cleared her

throat and tried it again. "I understand."

"We need to know everything you can tell us about room 319."

Without letting go of his hand, she flipped open a folder that was on the table before her. "She checked in yesterday after six. The room was guaranteed with a credit card. It was only booked for one night."

She pivoted the folder around so Koz could see it easier. I knew he was a pro at reading documents upside down, but he gave her a soft smile at the courtesy. His eyes flicked over the registration documents, then up to me.

"The room was paid for with a Visa card in the name of Janet Calder. Indicates a four-year old Honda," Koz said.

I turned to Costello. "Anything in the lot?"

He gave his head a brisk shake. "We checked it out right away. Every car accounted for. No Honda registered to the victim."

"Check it again. Could be a lease unit, or registered in the name of relative."

"You think the killer took the car?" Costello asked.

"You get a lot of homicides tied to a car booster?"

"Guess not."

"Check the lot."

Koz maintained contact with Elise Woods. Still keeping his voice low, he continued with his questions. If she had heard any of my exchange with Costello, she was ignoring it now. I caught the end of his latest question.

"Anything else you can tell us about the young lady when she checked in?"

"I was off duty. I wouldn't be called unless there

was a problem. But we can check the security cameras. They are aimed at the desk. The disks aren't due to be switched yet," Elise Woods said.

Koz shifted his eyes to me. "It looks like we're going to instant replay."

Leaving Kozlowski and the manager, I walked out into the cold March rain and stood beneath the canopy that covered the main entrance, watching two uniformed cops slowly check each car in the parking lot. It was a lot easier once they knew the type to look for. I turned my attention to the main road, watching the late morning traffic go by. Small curtains of spray flew behind some of the cars, like hydroplanes on the river.

The two cops were headed back toward the lobby. Neither had spotted a car that matched the description on the room registration. I noticed a few cars were parked in the adjacent lot. It was a steakhouse, part of a regional chain that was usually jumping from lunch until closing time. Most of the cars were by the rear of the building. They probably belonged to the prep crew, getting the kitchen ready for the day. One car was near the front.

I walked past the cops. Neither one stopped until they reached the shelter of the canopy. The small strip of grass that separated the two parking lots was the consistency of a swamp. I lengthened my stride just before the curb and hurdled the grass. The car at the front of the lot was a Honda. The license plate matched the registration card. I was looking through the driver's side window when the two cops joined me. One went around the other side to get a better look.

"You're thinking she was in the steakhouse before she went to the motel," said the cop beside me.

"Anything's possible." I checked the nameplate on his uniform jacket. Winston. I jerked my thumb at the kitchen. "You mind checking with the prep crew? Find out when the manager comes on duty, and have him get in touch with us."

Winston nodded. The hair that was visible under his hat was jet black. His nose was bent and crooked, as if he'd been rapped there more than once. Scar tissue had built up beneath his left eye. I got the sense we were sizing each other up. "Boxer?"

"Hockey. Local league made up of a bunch of wannabes."

"You the enforcer?"

"When I'm on skates, I'm more of a klutz."

I glanced at his partner, who was still on the far side of the Honda. Winston caught the look and intervened.

"Terry, stay with the car. Nobody touches it or tries to move it. The forensic guys will probably want to check it out first before it's towed."

"Great," Terry muttered. "I get to stand out in the rain and wait."

Winston rolled his eyes. "Don't be a schmuck. Get the squad car and park behind the Honda. Grab a cup of coffee from the hotel. I'll wait until you're in position."

Terry brightened and started to run back toward the motel. He stepped in the grass median and immediately sank up to his ankles in the mud. Cursing, he pulled himself free, leaving one of his shoes in the muck. He almost fell on his ass pulling it loose.

Winston slowly shook his head. "Rookies."

****

Back in the motel, I found Kozlowski with Elise

Woods. They had migrated to her office, a small room behind the reservation desk. Koz looked impassive as always. At six and a half feet tall and three hundred pounds of muscle, he can be the most intimidating person I've ever known. Yet he can be the voice of serenity when it fits his needs. This was one of those times.

"I just don't understand it," Elise said, opening a cabinet beside the desk. She ejected a disk from a video machine, checked the label and picked up another one. She examined that one, replaced it, and reached for another.

"What's wrong?" I asked.

"Disk is missing," Kozlowski said.

"It's got to be here. It's always here." Elise kept sifting through the stack of disks.

Koz filled me in. "They have two dozen digital disks. Each one is good for eight hours. That works out to three per day, with three spares. If something's going to happen, they figure it will be within the week. The one labeled for last night's time frame is missing." The look on his face was a mixture of disgust and admiration.

"Guy's thorough."

"So what do we do, Chene?"

I told him about the car next door. We were debating how to continue when our forensic team arrived. Rudy Fen, the coroner, would oversee the crew. He gathered them in the lobby, waiting for instructions. Two technicians were sent out to examine the car. The other two followed us up to room 319.

"Any observations, gentlemen?" Rudy asked. A Chinese American, he had attended medical school at the insistence of his parents. His mother wanted him to be a surgeon. His father wanted him to discover the cure for the common cold. Rudy couldn't stand the thought of treating the ill. In reality, he wanted little if anything to do with people in general. The living annoyed him. Only the dead ones captured his interest.

"I'm thinking cause of death is suffocation," Koz said. "One of the cleanest corpses I've ever seen."

Rudy flicked his eyes to me. "How about you, Chene? Care to second guess the medical expert?"

"My money's with the giant. But I'm going with the idea of something in her system, drug or alcohol that would eliminate much resistance."

Rudy gave me a look that clearly said "amateur," but he had the common sense not to utter it. Instead he resumed his professional persona. "Who gets the reports, you or Cantrell?"

"Send them to me. We're going to need the full boat, Rudy. And fast."

He fluttered a latex covered hand in my direction. "Yes, yes. Toxicology, complete autopsy, fingerprints, hair and skin residue. I'll provide you with the 'full boat,' Chene. Now leave me to my work."

Koz and I were walking down the hall to the elevators when my cell phone rang. Cantrell's name flashed on the ID screen.

I answered, moving away from the elevator doors. Kozlowski stepped into the opening and propped his back against the doors to hold them open. If anyone else was in a hurry for the elevator, I doubted they would complain.

"Whatcha got, Chene?" Cantrell's scratchy country voice drawled in my ear. I could hear the exhalation of breath and knew he'd be working on his second pack of cigarettes by this time of day.

"Looks like our boy struck again. Fen's just arrived with his crew. The locals are being very cooperative."

"Y'all better come in and gimme a rundown. The giant with ya?"

"Yeah. I'll leave him to wrap here. I should be at the squad within an hour."

"Make it thirty. We got a different kinda trouble brewing."

"Later." I broke the connection and looked at Kozlowski.

"I'll cover the saloon next door and get the locals to secure the crime scene. Forensics should have her car out of here by now," he said. "Anything else?"

I was silent as we rode the elevator down to the lobby. I wanted to put a face and a name on this taunting killer. Three identical homicides were getting out of hand. We had to find this guy and stop him before there was a fourth. I looked at Kozlowski as we walked into the lobby.

"Talk to the manager again. Get the locals to pull the victim's photo from her driver's license and get color copies. Let's circulate her picture among the staff. If there are any guests still here, check them too. See if she's been here before. Do the same next door at the saloon. Maybe she was a regular. Maybe somebody knew her."

"And maybe somebody saw her last night," Koz said. "And saw the wonderful guy she left with."

"We should get so lucky."

Chapter Three

Captain Prescott "Pappy" Cantrell was in his office when I arrived. The fluorescent lights were off, but the brass floor lamp in the corner was lit. Behind him, a window was always cracked open, no matter what the weather. Despite the state law banning smoking in public buildings, Cantrell continued to light up whenever the mood struck. As a chain smoker, he was perpetually in that mood.

He was tipped back in his chair, gangly legs crossed at the ankle. The bottom drawer of his desk was open, allowing just enough space to prop his feet. In faded khakis and a blue checked shirt, Cantrell looked nothing like the stereotypical police captain. Maybe that was part of the reason he was so successful.

Taking a seat on the other side of the desk, I waited for him to start.

"Crime scene look the same?"

I nodded. "From the photos we viewed last week, it looks identical. No signs of a fight. No struggle. The victim was on her back. No splatters. No bruising. The girl was spread-eagled. It was like she'd been posed, as if she was waiting for her lover to arrive. For all intents, she could have been asleep."

"Same message?" Cantrell worked a pen across the back of his knuckles. This was an old habit. He claimed it helped him concentrate.

"Yeah. Didn't measure it, but I'm sure Fen will include that in his report. Lipstick will probably be the victim's."

"Y'all got a name?"

"Janet Calder. She drove a four-year-old Honda. We found it in the saloon parking lot next door. She checked in after six. Room had been reserved with her Visa card."

"What else ya got?"

I checked my notebook. Koz called while I was on the way back with more details. We had yet to find her purse or wallet, but he'd pulled the information from the driver's license when the Bloomfield cops brought the copies.

"She was twenty-five. License shows her at five foot three, with green eyes. She was tiny. Nails polished, some makeup, but not overdone. She fit the profile of the other victims."

"Clothes?"

"None at the scene just like the other two. The killer strips them down to nothing. Think he keeps the wardrobe as mementos."

"Jewelry?"

I shook my head. "Her ears were pierced. She had two holes in the right lobe and three in the left. But she wasn't wearing earrings. There were indentations on her right hand, fourth and fifth finger, that were probably rings. It looked like thin bands that would have been more evident in the summer time if she was tanned."

"Family notified?"

"Not yet. Koz will call me when he's leaving the motel. We'll meet up at the address on the license. I think it's an apartment building. The car registration has a different address. That could be her parents."

Cantrell paused to light a fresh smoke. "Tell the giant to give y'all the details. Ah pulled Megan off the chop shop surveillance. Take her with ya."

I hesitated, trying to follow the logic. "You got something against Koz?"

"You two can look about as copasetic and unnerstandin' as two linemen going after a quarterback's fumble in overtime. It won't hurt to have a woman there."

I chewed on that for a moment. "You're pulling in the whole squad, Pappy?"

By tilting his head back, Cantrell was able to blow a plume of smoke directly at the opening of the window. Like an ancient signal, it drifted quickly through the screen. "Yep. We got the green light. It comes all the way from the capital."

Our involvement in this case was a fluke. Normally, we only get a case when it crosses into multiple jurisdictions, at the invitation of a city when their own investigation has stalled, or when we get orders from the governor. Our cases tend to be complicated.

Pappy happened to be having a drink with the chief of police from Warren last week. That's when he heard about their unsolved homicide. Something about it rang familiar. Cantrell had an eidetic memory. He could remember details from files he'd read five years ago. He had a special flair for homicides. The motel room number stuck in his head. It took him less than an hour to recall where he'd seen it before. There was a homicide in January, in a hotel room in Plymouth. He offered the squad's assistance on an unofficial basis. He'd notified his boss in Lansing about what he'd stumbled on. It was passed up the chain of command. Our governor frowns on serial killers.

"So Laura and Barksdale?"

"Ah put out the calls. They'll join Kozlowski at the scene. Megan's on her way. Y'all notify the family, then we'll caucus."

"You decide how we should handle the investigation?"

"Ah'm working on it. Y'all better clear your social calendar. Ah think we're going to be very busy for the next few weeks."

I slumped lower in my chair. "Or longer."

****

After getting the address information from Koz, I called Megan to meet me there. It was a small apartment building in Berkley, one of the suburbs just west of Royal Oak. It was a quiet community, filled mostly with older homes built in the fifties that were used to raise families—affordable bungalows and colonial houses, not nearly as expensive or upscale as the northern suburbs were. I waited until Megan pulled up behind me before getting out of my car.

"You look like hell, Chene."

"Good morning to you, too." I jerked a thumb at her Mustang, which was parked within three inches of my rear bumper. "Still don't know how you can afford the insurance on that thing, let alone the gas and the monthly payments."

"Don't pick on my baby. I've wanted a Mustang since I was ten years old. I think you're just jealous that I finally got one." She patted my arm, like an

22

exasperated mother trying to explain something to a six-year-old boy. "Leasing, Chene. Nobody buys cars anymore. They lease them."

"So you basically rent the vehicle, making the same monthly installments you would if you were buying it."

"It's more complicated than that."

"But that doesn't explain why you picked yellow?"

The exasperated look returned. "You're so out of it, you'll never understand."

It was my turn to pat her arm. "Just admit it's a chick thing." I had to take a step back before she popped me on the chin.

Our conversation was simply a stall tactic to prepare for the meeting. "You ready for this?" I asked.

"Yeah. I got the basics on the phone. Do you want the lead?"

I nodded. Chances were this was the victim's apartment. We'd probably have to repeat this process with her immediate family, once we learned more.

The apartment was on the second floor. The mailbox at the entrance listed the tenants as Calder and Bettencourt. We climbed the interior stairs, looking for the right number. The place was small but well maintained. The halls had been painted recently, and the carpeting was in good shape. Megan stopped beside the door, pausing to shake some of the excess rainwater from her coat. Inside, we could hear music and voices. I rapped on the door. Before I could count to three, it opened. We both stood there waiting, dripping water on the carpet.

Standing in the opening was a young black woman who obviously wasn't expecting visitors. Her thick black hair was running in a thousand different directions. She had soft brown eyes with little flecks of gold in them, but they were rimmed in red. Circles surrounded her eyes, as if she hadn't slept for a day or two. She was dressed in baggy sweatpants and one of those large gray T-shirts that read "Property of University of Michigan Football." Her feet were bare.

"Hi," she said in a strained voice. Her gaze flicked back and forth between us. "Did something happen to Janet?"

"Are you Janet Calder's roommate?" I asked softly. She nodded. "May we come in?"

She didn't hesitate, just stepped aside and waved us in. "Is Janet all right?"

Megan took her by the elbow and steered her toward the couch, introducing us on the way. Newspapers and magazines were scattered across the floor. The couch was large and plush, a shade of blue that had been stolen from the sky on a clear summer day. A pair of matching rocking chairs sat across from it. On the table beside the couch were a coffee mug and a plate of muffins. Steam rose from the coffee, warming the room. I inhaled the aroma of the fresh baked muffins, blueberry, or maybe raspberry. Megan got the girl settled on the couch, then slowly turned to me.

"Have you known Janet long?"

"Yes. We've shared an apartment for a few years. We were in the same dorm room together at college." She started to reach for the mug, then pulled her hands back into her lap. "It's bad, isn't it?"

"I'm afraid so, Miss Bettencourt. There's no easy way to tell you this. Janet's dead."

I was expecting tears, perhaps even wailing or

denials, or maybe something getting thrown. What I wasn't expecting was the menacing stare of those brown eyes as they drilled into me. Or the three little words that followed.

"I knew it."

Megan and I exchanged a confused look. For a moment, I wondered if I had misinterpreted the comment.

"What do you mean, you knew it?" Megan said.

Bettencourt shook her head vigorously, sending her hair flying. "I can't explain it. We were close. Like sisters. Sort of knew each other in high school. Then we ended up rooming together in college. We shared an apartment when we left the dorms. Drifted apart for a while, but always came back together. We were tight."

"So you knew each other well, Miss Bettencourt?" I asked.

"We didn't keep secrets from each other. Although lately, our schedules were so busy, we hadn't been able to spend as much time together as we like. We always made it a point to meet for lunch or drinks once a week. And Saturday mornings were special for us. We always found time for Saturday mornings."

She pushed off the sofa and went to the stereo. A deep masculine voice was introducing a musical guest when she lowered the volume.

"What about Saturdays?" I asked.

She moved slowly from the stereo, stopping to open the blinds on the gray morning. Looking out on the cold rain, she resumed talking.

"Janet is the quiet one. I'm Miss Rowdy. Love to party, love to get crazy, and love to dance all night long." She might have given her shoulders a little shrug, but the movement was lost inside the oversized T-shirt. "Janet is always reserved. She is…careful. She doesn't rush into anything. And she's a bit naïve when it comes to some things, especially guys."

She turned to face us. She was holding a picture frame in her hands. Hesitantly, she stepped forward and handed it to me. I glanced at the shot. It showed the two women, arms around each other's shoulders, smiling for the camera. Bettencourt was turning all her warmth and charm on the photographer. Janet Calder was smiling, but it looked like she was holding something back. I passed it to Megan. It was her first glimpse of the victim.

"Janet rarely dated in high school. Most of the guys our age only had two things on their mind: drinking and sex, and not necessarily in that order. She usually stayed close with a couple of other girls. Some kids thought the group was stuck up. In reality, they were just shy and maybe a little bit afraid.

"In college, Janet started dating a little. Usually older guys, those who were a bit more mature. She went with one guy for a couple of months before she gave it up." Bettencourt came back to the sofa and sat beside Megan.

"The relationship?" I asked.

Despite the sadness of the moment, a laugh escaped her lips. "The virginity." She turned to Megan and gave her head a little shake. "Men."

I ignored the dig. "When was the last time you saw Janet?"

She raked her fingers through her hair, actually pulling it into some semblance of order. "Wednesday night. She was here when I came home from the bar. I stopped off for a couple of glasses of wine with some people from work. We talked for a little, then she crashed. She was gone for work Thursday before I got up."

"You didn't see her Thursday night?" Megan asked.

"No. I didn't come home until early this morning." She turned those brown eyes on me. I got the feeling she was daring me to ask where she'd been. So I did. There was anger in her voice as she answered.

"I had dinner with my mother Thursday. I ended up staying the night. I had a date after work Friday. It was a group thing. We went to a concert and then a bar afterwards. I got home around three. I've been waiting up for her since then."

"So why did you say you knew she was dead?" Megan asked.

"Because I saw her die."

Chapter Four

From that point forward, her eyes were always on mine. I could have made a list of all the emotions pouring out of those orbs, but it would have never been complete. Anger, denial, resentment, frustration, sadness, and guilt all seemed to be taking turns. And those were just the ones I could think of.

She didn't answer Megan right away. She pushed off the sofa and walked into the kitchen. I started to follow, but Megan waved me back into the rocking chair.

"Give her a minute."

We could hear cupboards being slammed and chairs thumping on the tile floor. We waited. On the stereo, the deep voice I'd heard before began telling a story about a guy who owned a record store that specialized in classic rock. The story was just getting interesting when she came back in the room. She was carrying a tray with two mugs of coffee. Little eddies of steam were swirling above them. She offered them to us then gestured at the muffins on the table.

"It was part of our Saturday morning routine. We'd crawl out of bed around nine. Brew a huge pot of coffee. Sprawl at opposite ends of the sofa and catch up with each other. Then we'd listen to *The Vinyl Café* and slowly plan our day."

Megan nodded toward the stereo. "Is that *The Vinyl*

Café?"

"It's a Canadian program, featuring a lot of eclectic music and great stories, with plenty of gentle humor. Janet's dad got hooked on it a few years ago. Says the narrator reminds him of Jimmy Stewart. We listen to a podcast every Saturday."

I tested the coffee. It was strong without any frills. Megan added a couple scoops of sugar from the tray. She preferred coffee with enough sweetness to make ice cream. "Let's get back to your comment that you saw her die," I said. "Because earlier you said you didn't see Janet yesterday."

"I didn't physically see her. But I saw the image of her being killed as I was coming in the apartment."

"Look, Miss Bettencourt…"

"Simone. Please, just call me Simone."

"Okay. Simone. Can you describe what you saw?"

The eyes burned into me for a second. Maybe she thought I was just humoring her. Maybe I was. But she seemed serious. There was no harm in letting her explain.

"Janet and I developed this over the years. It's not uncommon. Usually it happens with people who spend a lot of time together, like married couples, close friends. They say it's really strong in twins. We could finish each other's sentences. Complete each other's thoughts. It was sort of a combination of déjà vu and telepathy."

"Can you give me any examples?" Megan asked.

"One time, Janet was running late. Suddenly, I had the image that she was in a car accident. Not five seconds later, my phone rang. She'd been rear ended less than a mile from here. She was okay, but her car was a mess."

"Any others?" Megan asked.

"Once I left the oven on. There was a towel stuck in the oven door. It started to catch fire. Janet sensed there was something wrong and came home. She pulled it out just before the whole stove was burning. We used to laugh about it.

"But it wasn't something predictable. I think it was really triggered by the emotions. Maybe it's tied to adrenaline when it enters your system."

I took a second before asking my question. Megan sipped her coffee, then absently broke an edge off a muffin and popped it into her mouth. Simone kept watching me. "Give me an example of the emotions. You talked about the accident. Were there any others?"

"Yes. Janet was stronger. She could sense things happening to me more frequently but didn't talk about it. I didn't get the images of her as often. When I did, they were usually very intense. Then it would fade out quickly. Like the night she lost it. Her emotions were running wild. She was nervous, anxious, excited, scared, and aroused all at the same time."

Before she could continue, Megan leaned back so she was no longer in Simone's peripheral vision and mouthed the word "sex." I had already figured that one out.

"Did she mention a new boyfriend?" I asked.

"No. She'd broken up with Tony, the guy she'd been involved with, about six months ago. His job got transferred out of state. There was no way she'd consider moving. Besides, he wasn't that good to her. Janet complained that he only wanted to do it one way. He wasn't even open to discussing other positions." She gave her head a little shake. "What an ass."

I'd waited long enough, so I rephrased my earlier question. "Okay. Describe the image you saw last night."

Simone took in a long, slow breath. "It looked like a hotel room. Cream-colored walls with cheap artwork, like a seascape. There was one large bed. Janet was sprawled across it. She was naked. She was having trouble focusing and breathing. She couldn't move her arms and legs much. It was like she was very, very drunk. And then there was the pillow."

"What else?" I asked.

"All of her attention was on the pillow. It came down slowly, covering her face. But it slipped, leaving her right eye exposed. She could see a blurry image. But she couldn't do anything to stop him."

Megan cleared her throat. "Could you see him, enough to describe him?"

"He was smooth. All I can tell you is that he was really smooth."

****

Megan and I met with Simone Bettencourt for more than an hour. We went over her account of the vision she'd had several times, trying to see if there were any other details she could recall. I knew this was not something that would ever be used in a trial, and it wasn't the same as eyewitness testimony. But for a reason I couldn't put my finger on, it wasn't something I could easily dismiss.

We ducked into Megan's car for a moment before heading back to the squad.

"Are you considering sharing this with Cantrell and the crew?" she asked.

"And risk getting sent for a psychiatric evaluation? No, thank you."

"What did you make of her visions?"

I thought for a moment, listening to the rain pound on the roof of the Mustang. "I've read about this type of thing before. I haven't personally experienced it. Kozlowski told me about a homicide case he'd worked, where there was a telepathic connection between two sisters. He couldn't explain it, but he couldn't explain it away either."

"What was the outcome?"

"They busted the killer. The cops followed up on a bunch of clues, put things together. Standard police work. When they made the arrest, the sister came in and freaked the guy out. They weren't twins, but they looked like it. Guy ended up confessing to everything. The sister even prompted him with a few details to get him started."

"So you think Cantrell wouldn't accept this?"

I shook my head. "Let's focus on the normal processes. We really didn't get much from her anyway. Everything boiled down to the fact that the killer is smooth. Guy's pulled off three identical homicides without so much as a clue anywhere. You're damn right he's smooth."

"At least we got the parents' information. Simone said they're out of town until the first of the week, but she'll try to reach them. Should we head to the squad?"

I nodded. "Cantrell will have everyone assembled by now."

I climbed out of the Mustang and watched her pull away. As I opened the door to my car, movement caught my eye. I looked up to see Simone watching me.

Even though the rain clouded my vision, I sensed her tears had returned. I raised a hand, then ducked into the car. Cantrell was waiting. And he was not a patient man.

****

The six of us were gathered around the conference table. Before each place were copies of the investigative work done on the first two victims. Everything from crime scene photos, autopsy reports, and interviews was arranged in neat, chronological order. Some departments call it the murder book. Every detail is logged in, with every tip, theory, clue, and idea jotted down. Some are more thorough than others. I was hoping these were the former.

Cantrell rolled an unlit cigarette across his knuckles. "We need to do this fast. Like the poet once said, timing ain't waitin' for no one."

Despite his butchering of quotations, we all knew what he meant. We only had so much time to figure this out and find the guy before he struck again.

"We need to determine the common denominator," Megan said. "There's got to be something that all three of our victims shared. We just need to look at them closely and let them tell us what that is."

Barksdale made a derisive snorting noise beside her. "Just how do we do that, McDonald? Call the psychic hotline? Break out the Ouija board?"

"We look at the evidence," she said with a sneer.

"We look at the evidence," Barksdale mimicked, waving his hands like a cheap carnival magician.

"Knock it off," I said. "Megan's right. We have to go through every bit of information we can find on the victims. That means reviewing the files, repeating every

33

single interview. We have to take the investigation a step further. If the locals talked to three coworkers, we need to talk to six. If they interviewed one neighbor, we interview five."

Barksdale turned his scowl to me. "So how are we going to do that before this pervert strikes again? We got other cases going."

"Not no more, ya don't," Cantrell said. "As of right now, this un is your one and only. And Ah hate to ruin your Saturday, but there ain't no days off until we crack it. Y'all need to break it down and find the pattern."

If Cantrell expected any grumbling from the squad, he would be disappointed. Even Barksdale held his tongue for a moment.

"So how you figure we're going to do this, Pappy? That's a lot of territory to cover, no matter how you cut it," Barksdale asked.

Cantrell shifted his gaze to me. "Whatcha think, Chene?"

"We could break it into sections. Laura could delve into their background. Barksdale could handle the autopsies. Koz could focus on the departments…" I stopped when I saw Cantrell slowly shaking his head.

"Y'all need to move faster."

Laura spoke up for the first time. She was the newest member of the squad and still getting accustomed to Cantrell's laid-back management style. "So how should we handle it, Pappy?"

"Y'all break into teams. Boy and girl on each. We got three homicides *that we know of*, so each team takes one. Y'all start from the ground up."

Megan pointed out the obvious. "You do realize we're a girl short."

Cantrell checked his watch. "Bloomfield's offered up one of their detectives to work the investigation, so Ah agreed. She'll be here shortly."

This was highly unusual. Cantrell was always adamant about keeping our investigations within the house. He never wanted outside agencies involved. Once we took over a case, he didn't give it back until it was closed. Then the top brass would hold a press conference, explaining how the local department, working diligently with the state police, had solved the crime. It made for great public relations and even greater politics.

"When?" The anger in my voice surprised me. It was obvious to the rest of the squad that I didn't like this sudden change in Cantrell's policy.

"Maybe twenty minutes." He glanced at the clock on the wall.

Koz caught my eye. Without missing a beat, he pushed back from the table. "Guess I'll grab a coffee while we wait. You did want to wait until the other detective got here before proceeding, right, Pappy?"

Cantrell tucked the cigarette into the corner of his mouth and snapped a flame with his lighter. "Yep."

I waited until everyone else filed out of the room. Cantrell let his eyes close as if he were meditating. With the smoke curling up around his head, he looked like something out of a Tennessee monastery. The Art of Zen, courtesy of Jack Daniels.

"Well?" he muttered without opening his eyes.

"When were you going to clue me in on this plan, Pappy?"

"Y'all weren't ready."

I didn't try to keep the anger from my voice.

"Bullshit. I've been the lead on ninety percent of the investigations we've handled for the last three years. You know it. I know it. The whole freaking squad knows it."

He took a long drag and pulled the cigarette from his lips. "But not everybody likes it."

I didn't even have to think about it. "You mean Barksdale. The guy's a dinosaur."

"Would that be a triceratops?"

I was surprised he was able to name one, but then, Cantrell could be full of surprises. Like this new plan. "So how do you see this?"

"We split into three teams, just like Ah said. We put Koz with the new girl, Laura. Give them the oldest case, the Wayne County. You and Megan take the Macomb one. Bloomfield will want their girlie working their crime. We stick her with Barksdale."

"So why didn't you tell me before?"

"You all right, Chene, but you ain't no actor. Ah wanted everyone to know this was a surprise, even you. It made your reaction real. You gettin' pissy 'cause Ah didn't tell you about it first."

I considered it for a moment. The old bastard had it down cold. Barksdale would have pitched a holy fit if I'd made the decision to split the team by case and assign him the outsider. He and Megan could barely stand each other. Laura was too new to stick with him. That left the Bloomfield detective. Since the orders were coming down from Cantrell, there was no way he'd argue it. Especially when it appeared that Cantrell did not trust me to make the call. It was a stroke of genius, pure logistical genius. I told him as much.

"'Tweren't nothin. You might have figured it out in

a couple of days."

"Don't be so modest, Pappy. You know how to manipulate him."

"Uh huh."

It took me a moment to admit the rest. "And me too."

He nodded slowly. "Hell, Chene, if Ah can't ever manipulate ya, y'all ain't no good to me."

Chapter Five

We reassembled in the conference room. Cantrell and I had walked out for coffee and returned to find everyone else grouped around the table. The female detective from Bloomfield was sitting in Cantrell's chair. No doubt at the direction of someone trying to be cute. Nobody ever sat in Cantrell's spot. She looked about as tall as Laura, maybe five eight, with hair as dark as midnight that fell to the shoulders. No rings or jewelry. Gray eyes that kept flicking around the room.

Pappy didn't even hesitate but took the empty seat between Laura and Megan. He introduced himself.

"Tess Jarrett." She passed a stack of business cards around. "My cell phone's always on. In case something breaks, I thought you guys would want it."

Cantrell nodded. "You aware of the situation, Tess?"

"Yes sir," she said with a sharp nod. I noticed the black hair bounced in front of her eyes when she did that. She swept it back subconsciously and hooked it behind her right ear.

"No sirs here, missy. Y'all call me Cantrell or Pappy. We don't stand on formalities. We focus on gettin' the work done and puttin' the bad guys away."

"Okay, Pappy." She didn't look comfortable with that, but Cantrell had a tendency to grow on people.

He introduced the rest of the team: Cameron

Kozlowski, Megan McDonald, Dennis Barksdale, and Laura Atwater. He described the plan to split the investigation in three. He named off the pairs and the counties. Kozlowski and Laura would take the first homicide. Mary Rosen was found in a Plymouth hotel. Plymouth is one of the western suburbs, on the outer edge of Wayne County. She was a bookkeeper for a veterinary clinic. Twenty-eight years old. She lived alone in an upper flat in nearby Redford. Cantrell pointed to her picture on the bulletin board. Her hair was light brown and sparse. There was a bend to her nose, as if it had been broken when she was young and never properly reset. She might have been attractive, but no one outside of her family would have ever called her pretty. The photo showed no effort to smile, the eyes downcast and timid. This was obviously not a party girl. I made a few notes to follow up on with Koz.

Next was the victim found in Macomb County. Her name was Stephanie Grange. She was twenty-four years old and worked as a waitress. Stephanie was five foot six, with dark brown hair. Like Mary Rosen, she was thin, almost painfully so. Her expression was sullen. There was no sparkle in the eyes, no trace of humor or excitement. I had to remind myself that these were not autopsy photos that Cantrell put on the wall. These were copies the investigators obtained from the families. There was something wrong with this case, something odd. Megan and I would soon become very familiar with Stephanie Grange.

Now Cantrell was talking about our latest victim. Barksdale and Jarrett would be investigating the death of Janet Calder. He gave the details we had gathered so far and pointed to a picture. Megan had borrowed one from Simone Bettencourt, with the guarantee that it would be returned. I looked at the light brown hair and the soft features. My memory called up the shot we'd seen just a few hours ago, of Simone and Janet together. This picture didn't do her justice. The other one showed a bit more personality. Not a lot, but a glimmer or two was there. Megan relayed our conversation with Simone, excluding the details about her vision. Knowing now that Barksdale would be interviewing Simone, I planned to call her and tell her to keep that part of the conversation to herself. Barksdale would be quick to discredit her, and it could have a negative impact on the investigation.

"Y'all better take the time to review each case. See if there are any details that trip your trigger, before you go chargin' off to start." He paused to cast a steely glance around the table. "No shortcuts or bullshit. Y'all need to do this un by the numbers. But y'all better find this sumbitch soon. Questions?"

There was a lot of head shaking, then Barksdale said something that had been obvious to all of us.

"This sure isn't a bunch of beauty queens. I wonder if this guy's got a thing about homely girls."

Megan and Laura looked ready to slap him. Tess was too new to know if he was joking or not. Barksdale wasn't politically correct, but he'd nailed it. This was what all three women had in common. They weren't gorgeous or famous or worth millions. They were just three plain women, similar in age, all with variations of brown hair. Was that the connection?

Cantrell reminded each team of their assignments. Tess didn't flinch when she was linked with Barksdale. I kept a scowl on my face, so Barksdale would know my feelings about the assignment. At least, the ones I wanted him to feel. Pappy jerked a thumb in my direction.

"Chene here has the lead. Y'all are gonna go through each and every item, every interview, every report. You gonna know everything about the victims. I wanna know things they wouldn't share with their mommas. I want y'all to talk to their doctors, their preachers, and their lawyers. I wanna know where they went, who they met, what they did. If they farted from eatin' Chinese food, I wanna know."

I looked at Tess and Barksdale. "The little bit we know about Janet Calder is in the reports from Kozlowski. Fen is doing the autopsy and running the forensic reports. As soon as they hit, you'll have them."

She nodded vigorously, shaking the hair loose again.

"You ever work a homicide before?" Koz asked.

"I've done every type of investigation. I've worked forensics, hit and runs, manslaughter, domestic assault, prostitution. I've done some small scale drug wars and drive-by shootings."

"I'm impressed," he said. "I didn't think Bloomfield got that much action."

"Oakland County Sheriff's Department for six years. I got passed over for detective three times in OCS. Bloomfield looked like a good career move."

"We'll see if you still believe that when we get into this case," Dennis Barksdale said. The guy not only looked like a dinosaur, he sounded like one. He was shaped like a lumpy bowling ball. He favored polyester slacks, short sleeve dress shirts with narrow ties and polyester sports coats. He had three, one brown, one black, and one blue. Of the entire squad, he was the only one who wore a coat and tie on a daily basis. Cantrell loathed them. If the investigation warranted it, or if we were appearing in court, we wore suits. Otherwise, it was casual. That was just one of the perks of working for Cantrell.

"Welcome to the party," Koz said.

Everyone filed out of the conference room. Cantrell hung back, watching me. He was having a difficult time keeping the smirk off his face.

"Something on your mind, Pappy?"

"Nope. But don't let Barksdale get ya. It kinda makes his day when he sees y'all gettin' irritated. Boy's a pain in the ass, but he can be a good cop."

"You're right."

Cantrell squinted at me. "Y'all think he's a good cop?"

"No, but he is a pain in the ass." I hesitated, then looked at him. "There's something else, isn't there?"

"Yup."

I walked over and closed the conference room door. Dropping into the chair closest to it, I rocked back and propped my feet on the table. He'd tell me when he was good and ready.

"Y'all need a grouper."

"A what?"

"A lister. Somebody to stack all the facts, see if there's a pattern."

It took me a second to get it. We needed an analyst. Somebody who could make sense of the reams of paperwork we were about to start churning through. Ideally, it would be a cop, someone who understood the process, someone who could objectively look at things.

"Got anyone in mind, Pappy?"

"Nope, just making an observation. Y'all got three different homicides, each with its own truckload of clues. Somebody's gonna have to put it all together. It can't be you when you're neck deep in your own work.

"And don't give me that bullshit that y'all can do it in your sleep. We both know ya barely function some days as is."

"Thanks for the vote of confidence," I snapped.

He glared at me. "Shut up, Chene. You a good cop. Best I got. I don't want this thing getting away from ya."

"I'll keep it in perspective."

I was about to rise when something occurred to me. Something he'd said during the earlier meeting. I let it roll around in my head for a moment, trying to recall it. Cantrell just sat there quietly, watching me. At length, it clicked in.

"We're working three separate homicides. Each team is covering a different county. Are we being arrogant?"

Pappy's face twitched with a scowl. "The hell you talking about, Chene?"

"You said there are three homicides that we know of, Wayne, Oakland, and Macomb. But what if this guy's gone beyond our territory? Is it that much of a stretch to think he might have killed other girls outside the tri-county area?"

Cantrell's chin dropped. He jabbed a narrow finger at my chest. "Y'all thinkin' there's more than three victims?"

"It's just a guess. Maybe he's done the same thing in Washtenaw, out by the universities, or up north, in

Genesee County. Hell, he could have even gone across the river and gotten his kicks in Canada."

He mulled it over for a moment. "If there are more cases, there's more of a chance of trippin' this bastard up. More chances of findin' the…whaddya call it…"

"A common denominator."

"Yeah, that. Ah'll reach out to the other areas. Quiet like. Maybe we get lucky. Good thinkin', Chene."

"Thanks, Pappy. For the victims' sakes, I hope I'm wrong." I stood to leave.

"This could be one of those times where ya hate it when you're right."

****

Years ago, Megan commandeered two desks that faced each other in the bullpen, hers and mine. Other cops would come and go, but she always had the desk across from me. It was as if she wanted to keep an eye on me. She was already poring over the paperwork on the Macomb County case. I started with the crime scene reports while she reviewed the autopsy.

For the next three hours, we didn't speak. I was beginning to feel like my bones were permanently attached to the chair. Finishing the last report, I closed the file and pulled over a legal pad. During the course of my review, I'd made several notes on things I wanted to follow up on. I started adding a few more points on the list when Megan groaned in disgust.

"I need a break," she said, glancing at her watch.

"Food?"

"Yeah, and lots of it. Other than that muffin, it's been a coffee day. I'm fried. And we need to formulate a plan."

I stacked my copies of the investigation inside a

44

briefcase and struggled to close the zipper. Eventually, I'd make it home. I knew I'd spend at least another couple of hours going over the material again.

"Sharkey's?"

Megan hesitated for all of two seconds before her face split into the first honest smile I'd seen all day. "Are you buying?"

"Nah, Ted's buying. Bring your hot rod. We'll eat and plan out tomorrow, then call it a night."

She locked up her copies, grabbed her purse, and was out the door before I pulled my jacket on. Food can be a powerful motivator. I noticed the other two teams had already left, whether to strategize or to begin their own investigations, I didn't know. In that regard, I followed Cantrell's management style. Get the best detectives you can. Give them the case and let them develop it in their own methods. Micromanaging didn't work. Maybe that's why Cantrell had such a high success rate of clearing cases.

Before heading out the door, I pulled three glossy photos from a folder and pinned them to the cork board on the wall. There was one for each victim. It may have been an unnecessary visual reminder, but I didn't want any of us to forget why we would be devoting every waking hour from this day forward to two things: finding this gruesome son of a bitch and stopping him before he struck again.

Chapter Six

Megan was already at a booth in the corner by the time I got to Sharkey's. Squeezed in beside her was a man in his fifties. He had a full head of wavy silver hair that still showed faint traces of blond and a neatly trimmed goatee. Blue eyes sparkled beneath his bushy brows. Although a couple inches shorter than Megan's five six, he appeared physically fit and ready to take on the world. Megan was laughing at some comment he made when I sat on the opposite bench.

"She's a bit young for you, old timer."

"Nonsense, she's over the age of consent. A beautiful woman is always fair game for the art of romance. Just look at her! Those luscious curves, that flirtatious smile, the wavy blonde hair...What man in his right mind wouldn't want to flirt with her?" His voice was low and husky from too many cigarettes and too much scotch.

"Try romancing me, old man, and you'll end up in the hospital," Megan said with an affectionate grin.

He turned his attention to me. "You look like hell, Jeff. Is the insomnia still knocking you down?"

"Yeah, Ted. I figured a meal here and some of your scintillating conversation would put anyone to sleep."

He wiggled a thick finger at me. "You better respect your elders, or I'll report you to the nuns." Then he shifted his gaze back to Megan. "And that goes for you, too. I've got enough dirt on the two of you to send those penguins to an early mass grave."

"How about bringing us some food, old man?" I asked, trying my best to change the subject.

"It's a lousy night. Cold, damp rain all day long, you need something hot, something filling." He winked at Megan. "You trust me?"

"Occasionally."

Ted considered it for a beat, then smiled broadly, a lecherous gleam in his eyes. "Hell, that's better than I usually get. Leave it to me."

With that, he slid out of the booth and headed for the kitchen. In less than a minute, one of the wait staff returned with two steaming bowls of Italian wedding soup and a bottle of Riesling. Until the food was in front of me, I didn't realize how hungry I was. Megan tasted it, then closed her eyes and sighed contentedly. "God, he can be a nuisance, but I really love that man."

"Quickest way to get rid of Ted is to mention love."

She shook her head. "We both know better than that."

We ate the rest of the meal in silence. After the soup, we had mushroom caps stuffed with crab meat, then grilled scallops in lime sauce. I didn't remember drinking the wine, but the bottle was empty as we finished eating. Megan ordered coffee and sat there watching me savor the last few ounces of wine.

"How many years have you known Ted now?"

I did the math. "Sixteen. It was in the summer."

"Yeah, back when you were a badass street kid, living the life of crime." A wide smile split her face and she rocked back and forth in her seat. "Until you got busted by that old man."

"He wasn't that old back then. And he could move pretty quickly."

She shook her head slowly. "Good thing I'm the only one who knows this story. Guys like Kozlowski would never let you live it down."

Megan and I attended the same elementary and high school. She was the first person to befriend me, and we'd been close ever since the third grade.

"You think Koz never committed a crime when he was a kid?"

A condescending look crossed her face. "I'm not talking about the crime. I'm talking about getting caught."

She could be so annoying when she wanted to be. I ignored her.

"You really should go get some rest, Chene. We'll probably be on the run most of the day. How do you want to begin?"

"We'll start with the Warren detectives. Then I want to go back to the scene, even though it is a month old. Let's see if we can view the room, maybe talk to the staff and get a feel for the layout of the place. Then we'll move on to the family and friend interviews. Monday, we'll start with the employer, coworkers, and contacts."

Megan drained her coffee, then checked her watch. She raised her eyebrows at me, her face bearing a quizzical expression.

"You got a date?"

"Sort of. We talked about meeting in an hour."

"And?"

"And I'd like to go home, freshen up, put on

something frilly, a splash or two of perfume, and go jump his bones." She batted her lashes at me and tried to appear innocent. It didn't work.

"You're such a romantic. You realize that's a lot more information than I need."

She slid from the booth and grabbed her jacket. "I'm just trying to give you ideas, Chene." With that, she leaned over and gave me a sisterly kiss on the cheek. "I'll be at the squad by eight. Thank Ted for dinner."

Just that quickly she was out the door, leaving me with a lecherous old saloonkeeper and the dregs of the wine.

I sat there for a while, listening to the rain, staring out at the lake, and slowly twirling the wine glass. I tried not to think about serial killers and young women ending up dead. It didn't make it any easier that they were a trio of plain Janes. Watching Ted work the bar reminded me of the thousands of hours I'd been under his tutelage. I realized how much I missed it.

I was fifteen when we met. I'd been going into restaurants, having a meal, then sneaking out without paying the bill. I'd leave a paperback book or a newspaper on the table, as if I'd simply gone to the bathroom. It worked for weeks, until I walked into Sharkey's. Ted caught me trying to slide out the door at the end of the lunch rush. He'd given me three choices. Pay up, work it off, or he'd call my parents. Rather than go into details, I opted to work it off.

Within a week, I came back twice more. Scrubbing dishes in exchange for a free meal led to a regular job. It was an arrangement we maintained all the way through high school and college. I ended up tending bar when I was old enough, then managed the place occasionally. I have no family. Although I thought of Ted as a surrogate father, he preferred the favorite uncle approach. I caught a glimpse of his reflection in the window as he slid onto the opposite bench.

"Tough case?" He brought a pot of coffee and two glass mugs. "It's decaf. The last thing you need is caffeine at this hour."

"Homicides. Young women." I took a mug and sipped it. Ted was known to lace his coffee with Bailey's Irish Cream. I wasn't disappointed. It went down easy.

"Don't know how you can do that, Jeff. Looking at innocent people who got killed, then trying to work backward to catch the bad guys."

I shrugged. "It's from all those mysteries I read when I was a kid. I figured if I could solve one of those, real crimes would be easy."

"And is it?"

I gave him another shrug and stifled a yawn. The effects of the wine, the food, and the warm booze coffee were catching up to me. "Sometimes. Often with a homicide, we find out they are committed by someone the victim knows. Maybe it's the result of a crime of passion, anger, money, or jealousy. You just never know what will tick somebody off. Push them over the edge."

"Is this one like that?" He was leaning forward, his elbows propped on the table, palms cupping his chin. It's the pose he takes when he's concentrating, giving anyone else his full attention. Ted can block out the rest of the world that way.

I thought about it for a minute. "No, this one's

cold, calculating. Son of a bitch knows exactly what he's doing. He's deliberate. He's…taunting."

"Taunting? Like egging you on?"

"Uh huh. This guy is making it into a game. Sort of like, catch me if you can."

Ted stared right through me. "You gonna catch him?"

"We're sure as hell gonna try."

****

Cantrell had given me a directive. He didn't like to call them orders, and he certainly wasn't one for rules. He liked to think of them more as guidelines, which might seem odd for a guy who would always follow the letter of the law. But rules could annoy the shit out of him, like the one about no smoking in public buildings.

He was right. With three separate investigations going on, I needed someone who could analyze all the data, log it, tag it, cross-reference it, and look for a connection. Laura was pretty sharp with the computer, but there was no way I'd pull her off the investigation with Kozlowski. I needed someone I could trust with sensitive material. No civilian would pass muster with Cantrell. He rarely let anyone into his domain, beyond the crew in Squad Five, which handled explosive devices and firearms.

I was heading out of Sharkey's when inspiration struck. Actually, it was a crutch that struck, right in my shin. I was slow moving aside as one of the regulars, a muscular guy on crutches with a bulky knee brace, hobbled past.

"Sorry about that. I'm still learning how to walk with these damn things."

"No sweat." I pointed toward his knee. "Skiing

accident?"

He shook his head with a laugh. "Like I'm going to race down a snow-covered hill on a couple lengths of fiberglass? I wrenched it playing rugby. Doc tells me if I stay off it, I'll be able to play in three weeks."

"The sport of gladiators."

"Damn straight. I'm trying to get Ted to sponsor the team."

"Good luck with that."

I watched him swing to a booth and slide in. As he got settled, the idea hit me. I waited until I was in the quiet confines of my car before pulling the cell phone from my pocket and calling dispatch. The desk sergeant was able to fill in the blanks for me. Two calls later, I was on my way.

****

Donna Spears met me at the door to her condo. She greeted me with a firm handshake and jerked a thumb at the sofa. I moved inside and got settled while she maneuvered to an upholstered chair with a matching ottoman.

"You look like shit, Sarge."

"So everyone's been telling me. How's the knee, Trooper?"

"Hurts like hell some of the time. If I keep it elevated and packed in ice, I can make it through the day."

Donna worked on one of the patrol squads. She had been at the scene of an accident two weeks ago when she had to jump out of the way of a passing car. She'd landed funny and snapped the ACL in her right knee. She was out on a medical leave for at least another eight weeks. We met years ago when she'd first joined up. Donna is more tomboy than sorority girl. She played all kinds of sports through high school. She's short and solid. She's a good cop. Only a few of us know about her personal life and her preference for an alternative lifestyle. Her lover is a young female schoolteacher in Grosse Pointe, who also teaches yoga. It was difficult picturing Donna doing yoga.

"Going stir crazy yet?"

"If it weren't for the sports channels, I'd go nuts during the day with nothing to do but watch talk shows and soap operas."

"What would you say if I had some work for you that would help pass the time?"

Donna banged the stool with her crutch. "I can't be on my feet. Not only will the doctor give me grief, the pain is a bitch. I've got another two weeks before I'm supposed to get reevaluated. God only knows when I'll be able to start physical therapy."

"What I've got in mind you could do from the comfort of your chair."

She gave me a stern look. "I'm not looking for charity, Sarge."

"There's nothing charitable about this. I need help. What if I told you this could be an important part of a homicide investigation we're working on?"

"You've got my attention." She let the crutch fall to the floor and sat up straighter in the chair.

I described the situation, with the mountain of files, the need to analyze and review each investigation. The details had to be cross-referenced. I needed someone to search for similarities.

"Are you taking pain medications?"

She shook her head. "Only at night, so I can sleep.

Damn things make me too groggy during the day. I feel like a freaking zombie. My mind is still sharp, Sarge. It's my knee that's giving me fits."

"I talked to Cantrell. He can grease the skids with the insurance company and the union. You'd get your regular pay, and it won't impact your injury claim. We can have you work from home. If you want this, I'll arrange to have a computer brought here. We'll set you up with a secured password and remote access to the server. Copies of the original files will be brought over, along with whatever reports each team generates."

"Chene, you know every cop worth a shit wants to be a detective." There was an excited expression on her face. "I'd do anything to help out on this case."

"You understand this is only for this investigation. Don't get me wrong. This role is going to be crucial. But I can't guarantee anything beyond that. And the clock is ticking. We need to find this bastard before he kills again."

The expression shifted to determination. It was as strong as any one I'd ever seen. "I want it, Chene. I want to help nail this guy."

"As Kozlowski says, 'welcome to the party.' I'll have a set of files delivered to you tomorrow morning."

Chapter Seven

Say what you will about Cantrell. He certainly knows how to get things done. I'd called him on my way home from Donna Spears place to tell him she was now part of the team. Before nine Sunday morning, he had a computer installed at her house, and copies of all the case files. There was almost glee in her voice when she called to let me know she was ready to get started.

"How do you want me to organize this?"

"Begin with the first homicide. Mary Rosen. I need you to read every scrap of paper in that file. Study it like it's the cheat sheet for the sergeant's exam. When you've got it cold, then move to the next one."

"Will do, boss."

I cringed. That term always frosted me, for reasons I've never been able to determine. "Don't call me boss. Chene works just fine." My voice was harsher than I intended.

"Got it," Donna said cheerily as she broke the connection.

"Well, why don't you just bite her head off and shout down the hole?" Megan said tersely. She was sitting beside me in the Pontiac, staring glumly out the window.

I glared at her. "Kiss my narrow black ass."

"My rosy lips are never getting close to that part of your anatomy." She was as cranky as I was. "Rough night?"

"Usual. I slept for about three hours. I spent most of the night reviewing these case files, looking for something that got missed. How was your evening?"

Megan shuddered and looked out the window. "Think I've awakened a monster. This joker wanted sex all night long. Not the soft, tender, cuddling stuff, but constantly banging away. Then around three, he wants me to get rough with him, use my handcuffs, and slap him around."

I glanced over to see if she was kidding. She wasn't.

"Like I need that! I was just looking for a little passion, a little something to appease my urges, and a warm body to snuggle with on a cold night. Instead I get some insatiable pervert."

"Where'd you find this Romeo?"

She turned and looked at me with a stare that could penetrate steel. "He's an accountant. The guy does my taxes."

The laugh jumped out of my throat before I could stop it. "You're kidding me."

"Who would expect a bean counter to get kinky? I had to kick him out to get some sleep. And if you breathe a word of this…"

"Not me. Besides, who would believe you and an accountant?"

The scowl on her face summed it up. "Screw you, Chene."

"Now there's the Detective McDonald we all know and love."

Earlier, I filled Megan in on Donna Spears and the duties she would perform. Megan nodded in agreement.

"She is a good cop. She's observant and dedicated. And she can handle the confidential part. She's definitely not a blabbermouth. I mean, there are maybe three of us who know she's a lesbian. That's no easy feat."

"If she can help us crack this case, Pappy wouldn't care if she was a stripper after hours. He just wants results, and he wants them fast."

We were on our way to meet with the detectives who originally handled the Stephanie Grange investigation. Megan called late yesterday and told them we'd be by this morning. Warren is another suburb, not far from the post. There are a lot of comfortable homes in the residential neighborhoods, but there's a fair amount of industry in the city as well. General Motors has a large technical center that's been a cornerstone of the city for years. It's seen better days, but the same could be said for all of us.

I swung into the parking lot behind the police station on Van Dyke. At least today, the rain had stopped.

"Ready to go?"

Megan snorted. "Sure, I love interviewing cops who screwed up the investigation."

"Maybe they didn't screw it up. Maybe they just needed our help."

She scowled and kicked open the car door. Her eyes were stone cold, and whatever warmth she possessed vanished from her face. "Hey, Chene?"

"Yeah?"

"They screwed it up, and another girl is dead. As far as I'm concerned, that's one girl too many. So pardon me if I'm less than pleasant to these guys. But if you don't like it, you can kiss MY lily-white ass."

It was going to be a very long day.

****

The Warren detectives were in their bullpen. Neither one complained about meeting on a Sunday morning. I recognized one guy, a stocky fellow with a shaved skull named Williamson. Our paths had crossed a few times before. He was just finishing up a call when we approached. He nodded once, then jerked his thumb at the conference room. I knew from past experience it was also one of their interview rooms. The other cop stood and walked us to the door. He was olive skinned with a full head of thick black hair. He was leaner than Williamson, but no taller than Megan.

"I'm Benedetti. You guys want coffee?"

I shook my head. "Not for me. Name's Chene. This is McDonald."

"How fresh is the coffee?" Megan asked.

"About ten minutes old. Some French roast crap Williamson got hooked on." He glanced over his shoulder, making sure Williamson was still on the phone. "It ain't half bad, but I'd never admit that to him."

"I'll give it a try," Megan said.

I dropped the case file on the table and slid into a chair while Benedetti led her to the coffee room. Williamson entered, and we shook hands.

"It's been a long time, Chene."

"You ain't looking any better, Paul. I see you gave up on the Rogaine."

He grinned and ran a palm across his bald plate. "What can I say? The chicks dig the freshly shaved look."

"And all these years, I thought that meant facial

hair."

We settled across from each other as Megan and Benedetti returned. I introduced Megan. I was hoping the caffeine would improve her mood.

"Are you guys still working the Grange case?" she asked.

Williamson and Benedetti exchanged a look. I already knew who was in charge of this pair. Williamson shrugged and rolled a pencil between his thumb and forefinger. "Officially, our captain instructed us to hand it off to you guys last week."

"And unofficially?"

"Unofficially, I keep reading through it," Williamson said. He nodded at his partner. "Him too. We're busy here, but we don't get many homicides. Lots of burglary, simple assaults, home invasion shit, but not murders. I'd like to think this is a fairly quiet city, you know."

"So where did you hit the wall?" I asked.

"We didn't have many clues to start with," Benedetti said, "and whatever leads we had seemed to run out pretty damn quick. I still don't know why we had to kick it over to you guys. We could have probably solved it in a couple more weeks."

"We don't have a couple more weeks," Megan snapped. "We've already got another dead girl!"

Benedetti sat back as if she'd slapped him. "What the hell are you talking about?"

I studied Williamson for a moment. When we worked together before, he seemed pretty straightforward. I sensed I could trust him. I wasn't sure about Benedetti. I pointed at the mirror. "Anybody behind the glass?"

Benedetti gave me an indignant stare. "Hell no! It's a Sunday morning, for chrissakes! You're lucky to get the two of us in here. What's going on, Chene?"

I looked at him for a moment, then back to Williamson. "You vouch for him?"

"Yeah, no worries. Will one of you tell us what the hell is going on?"

"This doesn't leave this room. Grange was the second victim of a serial killer. The third girl was found dead yesterday morning."

"Aw shit!" Benedetti threw his coffee mug against the wall. The ceramic cup shattered and rained a few drops of coffee to the floor. "We fucked up and another girl dies?"

Megan nodded. "I'd say that about sums it up."

****

We spent the next several hours going over the case file with Williamson and Benedetti. It was an exercise in futility. They had worked the case just last month, spending nearly three weeks chasing leads and trying to find someone who would have a reason to kill her. Stephanie Grange was a bland girl. The closest thing to trouble they could find was several speeding tickets, two ounces of marijuana in her medicine cabinet, and a lot of medical receipts.

"There wasn't much in Artie's background that gave us any leads," Benedetti said, flipping back through his notebook.

"Who's Artie?" Megan asked.

Benedetti actually looked embarrassed. "Sorry, that was the nickname I gave her. This girl must have had issues. Autopsy showed she had breast implants, although you could hardly tell by looking at her. She also had some liposuction on her ass, her teeth done, and her hair bleached. A couple of tattoos on the hips, and a tramp stamp just above the ass. This girl really was artificial. It's like she was trying to assemble the perfect body in pieces. And she was a fake baker."

My head came up at that one. "A what?"

"Fake baker," Megan said. "She went to a tanning salon."

"We pulled everything we could think of on this girl," Williamson said. "She went to three different colleges in as many years. She kept changing her major. We found pay stubs from half a dozen different jobs. She didn't keep any of them longer than two months." He spread a number of photos on the conference room table. They showed Stephanie Grange at different ages. She looked like an unhappy girl. Williamson and Benedetti had interviewed everyone they could think of. Two weeks later, the trail ran cold, and they still had no suspects.

She lived alone in a small upper flat in Roseville. Her parents lived only a few miles away. Apparently she wanted her independence but wasn't willing to completely cut the cords. Megan sat there tapping her thumb on the case file.

"Did you interview her doctors?"

Benedetti nodded. "We tried. Not much help there. Surgeon wouldn't talk to us without a warrant. Internist wasn't much help."

"You find her datebook?" Megan asked.

The two cops exchanged a glance. Both shook their head no.

"How about her cell phone?"

"Never recovered it," Williamson said.

Megan smiled thinly for the first time today. "Gotcha."

****

We were on the way to the motel where Stephanie Grange had been found. Thanks to Benedetti's comment, we were now referring her as Artie. Some cops did that as a defense mechanism to help deal with the stress of the job. I knew homicide cops who challenged each other to come up with the most creative nicknames.

"A twenty-something girl like that had to use a cell phone," I said.

"Please. Eight-year-olds get cell phones. Artie probably lived in a dump but bought the latest phone gadget available. I'll bet she could access her email, take pictures or videos, and play games simultaneously."

I considered it for a minute. "And chances are she used that as her calendar too."

"Got it on the first try," Megan said sarcastically. "Give the sergeant a prize."

"Shut up," I muttered. "Artie must have had the phone with her when she was killed. I'll bet he scooped it up along with all her other possessions for his treasure chest."

Megan nodded. "Yeah, but we can still get her phone records. We'll need to talk to her parents and get the number, along with the service provider. Then Cantrell can get a judge to sign the warrant. With luck we can have her records within a couple of days. And we can have the service try and locate it if it's still turned on."

"You're pretty smart for a girl," I said playfully.

"Fuck you, Chene. And I'm a woman, not a girl." There was a glint of laughter in her eyes as she said it.

"Still can't take a joke. Call Laura and Barksdale. Have them get the details on their victim's cell phones."

Megan pulled her phone from her jacket. "And by the way, I can so take a joke. I work with one every day."

"Damn, baby, that's cold."

"Not as cold as our victims are," she said quietly.

****

The motel manager was less than enthusiastic. After all, it was early Sunday afternoon. There had been a couple of wedding receptions the night before, and many of the guests were lining up for an elaborate champagne brunch. There was bright sunshine streaming through the windows of the restaurant and the lobby. Megan had her back to the reception desk, elbows propped on the edge. I could see the handle of her gun dangling from the shoulder holster inside her leather jacket.

"You sure you're all right?"

Megan gave me her steel-melting glare. "Don't I look all right to you?"

"No, you don't. You look mad as hell. Normally, you never lose your cool."

She started to give me a sarcastic response, then pulled it back. I watched her gnaw on her lower lip for a moment. Then she shrugged and looked up at me. "Guess this guy is hitting too close to home. I could have been one of his victims."

"Not a chance."

"Why not?"

"Several reasons immediately jump to mind."

His face darkened quickly. "Such as?"

"First, this guy is into plain Jane girls." I waved off her attempt to interrupt. "Not only are they all plain in looks, but in their attitudes as well. I'll bet as we dig we'll find out each one was a bit of a mouse. Naïve, like Simone said about Janet. Low self-esteem, with very little confidence."

"Just like Artie."

"Exactly like Artie. And you are the polar opposite of these women. So don't take this the wrong way, but you're not this sick bastard's type."

She brightened for a moment. "But you never can tell about people until you get them behind closed doors. Like last night."

"We've all had dates that didn't exactly work out the way we imagined them."

"Guess you're right. But I really want to nail this son of a bitch before he kills again. And if I happened to castrate him in the process, that wouldn't be so bad either."

I shook my head in mock disbelief. "If the nuns could hear you now, they'd be bringing tanker trucks of holy water to your apartment."

Megan was about to respond when the manager finally appeared. His name was Ellsberg, and he reluctantly led us to an office down the corridor away from the registration desk. Although his charcoal gray suit was neatly pressed, he himself appeared washed out, as if he never saw the light of day. He had the nasty habit of speaking as if he were more than one person. His voice was a nasal whistle.

"I don't see how we can be of service. It's been weeks since that terrible incident occurred. We've already started renovating."

"Has the room been used since the murder?"

"Good heavens, no. We closed it off. We decided it would be best to completely refurbish, paint, carpeting, bedding, everything." His hands fluttered about like two frantic birds.

"So there's no one we would be disturbing by looking at it," Megan said.

Ellsberg crossed his arms and huffed out a breath. "We can't have our guests being bothered by the police."

I nodded to Megan. She stepped forward and placed both hands on his shoulders and drove him into the wall. Shock registered on his face as she brought her nose within an inch of his. Her voice was low and guttural.

"Look. I'm going to use small words so I'm sure you'll understand. We are investigating a murder. It happened here. We want to look at that room. No one needs to know we're cops. Just let us in. Shut the door. And. Shut. Up." She released his shoulders and took a step back, but the glare on her face had the same intimidating impact as physical contact.

He was shaking as he found his voice. "Okay. I'll take you to the room."

"Cooperation is always the best approach," Megan said as she watched Ellsberg hurry down the hall.

"Very tactful."

She shrugged. "I learned it from you."

Chapter Eight

After Ellsberg let us into room 319, I pulled the crime-scene photos from my briefcase. From a cost perspective, I didn't see the need to completely refurbish the room. There was little evidence that a murder had taken place. From the photos, it was no different than the Calder murder. Stephanie Grange had been suffocated. There was no blood evident in the photos. It was probably no worse than someone having a heart attack. It certainly wasn't like a homicide at an airport hotel a decade ago, where a flight attendant had been brutally murdered and the entire room sprayed with her blood. So why would they go to the trouble and expense of refurbishing?

Megan voiced the same question. "And if they are going to do it, what's taking so long? It's been a month since Grange was killed."

We moved slowly around the room. The evidence techs from the Warren Police Department had been thorough. There were still traces of fingerprint residue on the counters in the bathroom, the table, chairs, and lamps. Even the message on the mirror remained. Housekeeping had probably never been allowed into the room. Management must have decided to gut it and start fresh. Some hotels do that on a rotating basis, upgrading a certain number of rooms annually, so there is no huge expense in any one year. I wondered if that was the case here. After all, it was one of a large chain of hotels, and they always seemed busy.

Megan sat on the edge of the bed and nervously jiggled a leg. "It's a waste of time, Chene. Let's get on with the interviews."

"Want to do them in here?"

"Hell, no. Ellsberg was setting up a conference room. Why would we want to question staff in here?"

"We could do it for the shock value."

She shook her head in disgust. "You can be a morbid son of a bitch, Chene."

"Yeah, but I don't go around threatening hotel managers."

"You don't need to when you got me with you." She pushed off the bed and started for the door.

"Good thing you didn't decide on a career in politics."

Megan looked over her shoulder and batted her lashes at me. "You smooth talker, you. Let's go grill some employees. Maybe we'll find a clue."

"With any luck at all."

After the shock had worn off from his initial conversation with Megan, Ellsberg was very helpful. He reviewed the list of employees who had previously been interviewed and identified those on duty. Megan and I talked to a maid, the desk clerk, and two waiters before taking a break. Something felt wrong. I looked over the list again and still couldn't put my finger on it. Megan took it away from me.

"Williamson and Benedetti interviewed all these people. You've read their reports. So what's with the disgusted look?"

"We're missing something. I just can't figure out

what."

She studied it for a minute, then smiled. She asked one of the housekeeping staff to send Ellsberg in. When he returned, he remained on the other side of the conference table. Obviously, he had learned to keep a little distance from her.

"According to the report, one of the housekeeping staff first found the body. Corazon Smith. We'd like to interview her as well."

Ellsberg cleared his throat and tugged at his necktie. "Ms. Smith no longer works here. She left shortly after the incident."

"Because she was upset by what she saw?" Megan's glare was boring holes in his chest.

"Yes, I mean, no."

"How about maybe?" I asked.

His eyes jumped from Megan to me and back again. "I'm not at liberty to say."

"We need a straight answer. And we will talk with her." Megan rose smoothly from her chair, placing her palms on the table and leaning toward him. "Are you familiar with obstruction of justice, Mr. Ellsberg? How about interfering with an ongoing police investigation? You can't get much more important than a homicide investigation. Would you like to spend a few days in the Macomb County jail, to see what happens to people who break the law?"

He nervously leaned back. "I didn't break the law."

"Where is she?" Megan snapped. "Who is she?"

"She quit. She left. She didn't want to work here anymore." The words were practically flying out of his mouth.

Megan kicked the chair out of the way. She

reached across the table for his lapels. Ellsberg's face grew so pale his skin was practically transparent.

"She was illegal!"

Megan kept a smoldering gaze on the hotel manager. Once he started talking, it didn't take much effort to keep him going. It turned out that the housekeeper was an illegal alien. Ellsberg had gotten mixed up with some people who would provide him with workers smuggled into the country from Canada. They had no visas, no work papers. They spoke enough English to get by. They came from Croatia, Poland, Hungary, and any number of other countries in Europe. They did the work and kicked a large portion of their pay back to their handlers. Ellsberg didn't profit directly from their efforts, but it helped cut down on his gambling debt. Apparently, he was a favorite of the casinos. He played often but not well.

From the employment records, we got the address and phone number of the mysterious Ms. Smith. The phone was not in service. The address turned out to be nonexistent. It wasn't much of a lead, and it fizzled out quickly.

"You don't really think this maid had anything to do with the killings?" Megan asked as we cruised back toward the post.

"No. I'd say what she saw spooked her. Maybe it reminded her of something from her homeland. Maybe it was more than she bargained for. I'm guessing she took one step into the room, saw Grange's body, and freaked out. The other people we did talk to who were working that day make it seem likely."

"So what do we do now?"

Megan called a friend who worked for ICE, the

Immigrations and Customs Enforcement agency, the division of the government that was formerly the Immigration and Naturalization Service. Agents would be visiting Ellsberg and his hotel to audit his records and interview the staff. Megan had a list from the management staff at the hotel of all current employees. She also had details on anyone who had left the job, for whatever reason, during the last year. With only one irate stare in Ellsberg's direction, she had also received a comprehensive list of all employees who had been working either the day before or the day of the Grange homicide.

We needed time to regroup.

But how much time did we have?

****

Back at the squad, I was debating my next move over a lukewarm cup of coffee. We had conducted a briefing with all the teams and Cantrell. Not much progress had been made today. Cantrell pointed out that since it was St. Patrick's Day, many people were out celebrating in one form or another. We should have better luck tomorrow. He explained to the others about Donna Spears and her duties. The three teams were able to identify the victims' cell phone numbers and the carriers. I generated the request for a warrant for the records from each provider. Pappy approved it and sent it along to a judge who took a very dim view of murder. We expected to have it back by Monday afternoon. Cantrell was going to have the cyber unit handle it and get us the results.

The other teams had departed. Cantrell was headed for his favorite Irish pub for a dinner date. Megan was checking her messages. I noticed the light on my phone blinking rapidly. Somehow, I sensed it wasn't good news. Four calls: Fen from the coroner's office, Cantrell, Ted checking in, and Simone Bettencourt. I called her first.

"I wanted to let you know I was able to contact Janet's parents. They're on their way back now. They should be in town by six." Her voice, although clear, was devoid of any emotion. She sounded exhausted.

"Have you slept?"

"I can't sleep. Every time I close my eyes, I see Janet being smothered by that pillow."

I glanced at my watch and realized it was almost six. Megan was rubbing her eyes as she cradled her phone.

"Are the Calders coming to the apartment, or going to their house?"

"I don't know. They didn't really say," Simone said.

"Would you mind if I stopped by, in case they come over? I'd like to talk to them."

Her voice remained a dull monotone. I wondered if she had taken a sedative or something to ease the pain. "That would be fine."

I ended the call and looked at Megan. She smothered a yawn, then cupped her chin in her hands, propping her elbows on the desk.

"I need rest, Chene. A warm bed, thick blankets, wool socks, and flannel jammies." She batted her lashes at me for incentive.

"Call Fen. He left me a message while we were out. See what he's got. Then you can split."

"What about you?"

"I've got to talk to Pappy. Then I've got a couple

things I want to go over. We can meet here in the morning."

She was already dialing Rudy Fen's number before I finished speaking. I hit the speed dial number for Cantrell's cell phone. He answered by the third ring. Briefly, he told me that he'd reached out to his counterparts in Washtenaw and Genesee counties, along with the Ontario Provincial Police in Canada. Each response had been negative. There were no homicides that fit our pattern. By the time I finished the conversation, Megan was nothing but a memory. I pitched the coffee and headed for the door. I knew the Calder case technically belonged to Barksdale and Tess Jarrett, the Bloomfield detective. But if there was a chance her parents could give us a clue, I wasn't going to get hung up on technicalities. I could always relay the information to them. Was there another reason I wanted to stop at the apartment? I pushed that thought away and tried to concentrate on the case.

****

Simone Bettencourt must have been watching when I arrived. She was waiting at the door before I finished climbing the stairs. Her hair was brushed and she was wearing jeans and a lightweight yellow cotton sweater. This outfit was much more flattering than the sweats of yesterday, making her slender figure evident. Her feet were bare. It was easy to see the toenails had been recently polished. I caught a faint whiff of perfume as I approached.

I was almost to the door when I noticed her lips trembling. Her eyes were red and puffy. Before I could say a word, tears overwhelmed her again. I stood there for a heartbeat, uncertain what to do. All the years on the job and this was still one of the most difficult parts of it, dealing with the survivors.

Simone might have reached for me. Or I might have reached for her. It was one of those things that I could never definitively answer. All I know is that one moment I was standing in front of her, the next she was in my arms. She buried her face in my chest and started sobbing. Somehow, I guided her back into the apartment and closed the door behind us.

I don't know how long we stood there. It was a lot more than a moment but less than an hour. Periodically, little tremors ran through her. After a few minutes, I began to feel foolish standing there. Well, foolish isn't the right word. Uncomfortable was more like it. I tried to ease her back, but she clung to me tighter. The scent of her shampoo filled my head, or maybe it was the slight fragrance of her perfume. I tried to think of other things, non-female kinds of things, with her body pressed close to mine. I tried hockey games, motorcycle races, golf tournaments, and high school debates, politics, old movies, and football. Bad guys I'd put in jail. Dead comics whose humor I'd enjoyed. It didn't matter. Nothing was working.

At some point in time, Simone seemed to slowly run out of tears. She pulled back a little, wiping her face with her fingertips. Her body was warm. I could feel it through the thin material of the sweater as my hand slid slowly up and down her back. She started to turn away and stumbled. I caught her around the waist and steadied her. I was surprised at how little she weighed.

"I should be all cried out by now." Her voice caught. "You must think I'm some kind of basket case."

"Not at all. People deal with grief differently.

Some never let it out. Others get angry, resentful. Some seek vengeance." I realized I was still holding her. It took some difficulty, but I guided her over to the sofa. She collapsed onto the cushions.

"Janet's parents called just before you got here. I think they're still in shock. Her dad sounded wooden, as if it wasn't really him speaking."

She told me they wouldn't be coming over. They couldn't. They were at their home but didn't want to see anyone, least of all the police. They were exhausted. A neighbor who was a doctor had come over and sedated Janet's mother. Her father was numb. Nothing would be gained by visiting them tonight. I would let Barksdale and Tess deal with them in the morning.

I went into the kitchen. The muffin tin she had used yesterday morning was still sitting on the counter, residue from the batter stuck hard to the surface. There were four fingers worth of cold coffee in the pot. I sensed she hadn't eaten since we'd been here.

Back in the living room, Simone stared vacantly at the windows. I'm no therapist, but even I could tell that her body would start shutting down if she couldn't get past this point. She would also need fuel in her system. I turned back to the kitchen to check the supplies.

What the hell was I doing here?

The kitchen was surprisingly well stocked. I would have expected two young, single women sharing an apartment to eat out frequently. Apparently, one of them liked to cook. I found some boneless chicken breasts in the refrigerator, along with a fresh box of mushrooms. There was a lemon just starting to shrivel and a bottle of Chardonnay already opened. Hunting around, I discovered a bin with flour and some linguini noodles. I got started.

After slicing the chicken into thin strips, I dredged it in flour. The skillet was heated with a chunk of butter slowly melting in the center. I added the chicken and sliced the mushrooms. While it was browning, I found a pot for the pasta and got that boiling. With the chicken brown on both sides, I added the mushrooms, the juice from half the lemon and a generous glug of wine. I found a small skillet and used it to sauté some onions and minced garlic in a few spoons of olive oil. When the pasta was done, I drained it, then tossed it in the oil mixture. I was serving it onto a platter when Simone appeared in the doorway.

"You're cooking?" Her voice was incredulous.

"Somebody's got to. I'm betting you haven't eaten since Friday night."

She shrugged. "I haven't had much of an appetite."

I guided her to the table and set a plate in front of her. She looked at me suspiciously.

"It's comfort food."

"What is it?"

"Chicken *piccata* and pasta with olive oil and garlic."

Simone tentatively tried a bite. I poured her a glass of wine and set it beside her plate. She chewed thoughtfully, then washed it down with a sip of wine. I didn't say a word while she speared another piece of chicken. I tested it, then watched her try the pasta. Apparently, her body was responding to the food.

"This is really good. I wouldn't have expected a cop to cook."

It was my turn to shrug. "I like to eat. Restaurant food gets boring all the time."

It took a while, but she ate everything I'd put in front of her. She drained the wine, then sat back, looking at me.

"You're not like most cops."

"You know a lot of cops?"

While eating, her hair had tumbled down over her eyes. She brushed it back now before answering. "I know a couple. They are real macho men. They come around to some of the clubs we go dancing at." A glimpse of a smile crossed her face, then faded. "Janet used to make fun of them. Said maybe someday, they'd grow up to be real people."

"You can't judge all cops by a couple of cowboys."

"I know. It's just fun sometimes."

Simone sat there and watched while I cleaned up the kitchen. I stacked the dishes in the dishwasher, despite her protests that she could take care of things. She didn't argue very much. I noticed she refilled her wine glass. With dinner over, we moved back to the living room.

She sat gingerly on the sofa as if afraid it wouldn't support her meager weight. Simone looked at me once, then looked away. For an instant, my mind flicked back to the case and the paperwork I should be reviewing again. Involuntarily, my eyes went to the clock on her stereo. It was getting late. I was about to move when her voice stopped me.

"I have no right to ask you this. I don't know you. I don't know anything about you. But there's really no one else."

"Go ahead." She had my curiosity now.

"Will you stay?"

The question nearly knocked me off the chair.

"Look, Simone..."

"But there's no one else I can ask. I don't want to be alone again. I just want someone to hold me, like you did before. That's the first time I haven't been seeing the image of that pillow on Janet's face. Please." Her face was starting to crumble again. "I'll give you sex, if that's what you want. Please, just stay."

I took a moment to absorb it all. I moved to her on the sofa and wrapped her in my arms. "No sex. And just tonight, okay?"

She shuddered and slumped against me. "Okay."

What the hell was I doing?

Chapter Nine

In a strange way, it was a comfortable night. After reassuring Simone that I would in fact stay with her, she dragged several fluffy pillows and a thick down comforter out to the sofa. I pulled off my boots. My gun and shoulder holster were slipped inside my jacket while she was out of the room. I even switched the cell phone to silent mode.

The sofa was wide, deep, and surprisingly comfortable. I took the inside, fully expecting to spend most of the night watching Simone sleep. Maybe it was the wine. Maybe it was the warmth of the room. Burrowed under the comforter, with only her head peering out, Simone suddenly looked like she was thirteen.

"You're sure about this? I mean, the bed is a whole lot roomier."

"This is fine." If we were in her bed, I couldn't guarantee there would be no sex. The last thing I needed was to get involved with someone while in the middle of a homicide investigation. At least, that's what I kept telling myself.

She yawned several times, then curled against me. And just like that, she fell asleep. There was enough light coming in the windows for me to see her face. Slowly, her features softened. With some recuperative sleep, the dark circles and worry lines would fade. I realized that somehow my left arm was around her shoulders and my right hand was pressed against the small of her back, keeping her close. She was still wearing the jeans and sweater. I listened to her slow, deep breathing.

What the hell was I doing?

She moved slightly, and I felt her hand come to rest on my hip. I tried to think about the case. I tried to think about work. I tried to think about Sharkey's. I tried not to think about the way her head was tucked beneath my chin. I tried not to think about the warmth of her. I tried not to think about the soft scent of her perfume. I wasn't very successful. There was no mistaking the physical effect she was having on me. As if on cue, she pressed a little closer and mumbled contentedly.

The perfume was the last thing I remembered when I too fell asleep.

****

Megan was already at the squad when I arrived. She had a smug look on her face. There was a cardboard cup of coffee on my desk blotter. Even before I picked it up, I knew it would be cold. Without tasting it, I walked down the hall to the kitchen and warmed it in the microwave. Her expression was still in place when I came back in and sat down.

"Thanks for the coffee."

"I figure I still owe you for dinner the other night."

I nodded. She was waiting for an explanation. She would be waiting for a very long time.

"Any calls?"

"Just Fen. He finished the autopsy late yesterday. Toxicology reports should be in this morning." Megan cupped her chin in her hands, as she had done last night. I've seen this pose so many times before that I knew exactly what it meant. It was the old "I'm not budging until I get what I want" look that she'd been displaying since the fourth grade. Nice to know some things never change.

"Cause of death?" I asked.

"Asphyxiation. Rudy said it's consistent with the other victims based on the autopsy reports he read. He also confirmed there was sexual activity prior to her death which matches the other autopsies."

"What about the other toxicology reports? Was there anything that could give us a lead?"

She slowly shook her head. "There were various amounts of alcohol in their systems, but nothing significant. I'm still betting on the date rape drug. You're a little late today."

"Traffic was heavy."

"I hardly ever beat you to the squad."

"It must be that ugly yellow Mustang." I sipped the coffee and leaned back in my chair. I knew better than to start talking about last night. If I did, Megan would never shut up. That's why, even though it cost me twenty minutes, I'd swung by my place for a quick shower and a change of clothes. Simone was still curled on the sofa when I'd left. I felt a little lethargic, having slept for more than six hours. I also felt a little guilty, remembering where my hands were when I awoke. We were like spoons. Her bottom was pressed against my groin. My face was buried in her hair. One of my hands was cupping her breast. Simone must have removed her bra when getting ready for bed. I could still feel the sensation of the warm softness of her breast through the thin cotton sweater. My other hand had been draped across her waist, the fingertips resting on her bare flesh where the sweater had ridden up. Somehow, her hands were clasped to mine, mirroring the positions.

I was also feeling guilty about my body's response to the proximity of this soft, fragrant young woman wrapped in my arms. Yes, I was still dressed. And so was she. But even through the layers of clothes she had to feel my arousal. And I felt hers as well. The swell of her nipple, poking through the sweater against my palm, was no accident. She certainly couldn't claim to be chilled, burrowed beneath the heavy quilt, pressed tightly against me. Even now, the memory warmed me. I wondered if it would have same effect on her.

When I'd awakened, I slowly moved my hands. Shifting around, I was able to slide out from my spot against the back of the sofa. Sitting on the edge of the coffee table, I'd yanked my boots on, then pulled on the shoulder holster and shrugged on my jacket. I was about to rise when I realized she was awake, watching me.

"Thank you for everything." Simone's voice was a sleepy, seductive octave lower than normal.

"You're very welcome. It's early. Go back to sleep."

She pushed the quilt down and reached for me with both arms. My body responded before my mind even had a moment to consider it. The next thing I knew, I was kneeling beside the sofa, holding her close once again. Simone pressed her lips to my cheek. A throaty whisper reached my ear.

"Can I see you again?"

"Yes."

I lowered her back to the sofa, pulled the quilt up

to her chin, and knees creaking, got to my feet. I made sure the door was locked and ran out to my car. Twice, I started to turn around and go back to her. But if I had, there's no telling where it would have led. I certainly wouldn't have been to work yet.

It almost took a physical movement to shift my thoughts from her back to the case. Megan remained before me, a petulant look on her face.

"You gonna join me in this conversation, or is it gonna be a monologue?"

"I thought you needed jokes for a monologue. You're just doing a soliloquy."

Her face twisted with disgust. "Did you even hear what I said?"

"Sorry. I checked out for a moment."

"I said that I might have a new angle on finding our killer."

So the smug expression was the result of more than just my late arrival. I tipped my chair back and put my heels on the desk.

"You have my undivided attention. Go."

"Actually, it's something Ted mentioned the other night," Megan said.

I tried to recall the conversation, but there were too many topics covered for me to narrow it down without help. I raised an eyebrow over the coffee cup and told her so.

"It was just a snide comment. Ted said if we didn't behave, he'd report us to the nuns. And last night driving home, I started thinking about them."

"I haven't thought about the penguins in years."

Megan rocked her eyes and gave her head a little shake. "Well, unlike some people, I still go to the church where we grew up. So I started wondering about the message our killer keeps leaving." She paused, looking around to confirm we were still alone.

"Yeah, the room number is too easy. It's got to mean something else."

Megan pulled a three pound book out of her drawer and dropped it with a thud in the middle of my desk. I barely glanced at it. Judging by the heft and the worn cover, I knew what it was.

"You think our guy's following instructions from the Bible?"

She raised her palms. "We don't know what the hell it's about. What if he is referring to a particular chapter or verse?"

I let that simmer for a minute. At this stage, I wasn't going to rule anything out. I let my boots fall from the desk and leaned forward. "You're not seriously expecting me to dust this off and start reading?"

"You? Chene, I love you like the brother I never had, but interpreting the good book would not be something you could do. I'm thinking we already know an expert. And he'd probably jump at the chance to help us."

"Oh, hell no. I'm not—"

"It's Monday. He'll be finishing up with the seven o'clock service by the time we get there."

"You're not even sure—"

"I called. He's expecting us." She was already getting out of her chair and reaching for her coat.

"Son of a bitch!"

Megan was quiet on the drive there. Even though the day was overcast, she was wearing her sunglasses. I guessed she was trying not to make eye contact with me. She probably wouldn't have been able to keep a straight face.

I parked in the lot. The buildings were gigantic, early-twentieth-century stone structures. To the south was the school, where even now rows of children were lining up outside. To the east was the convent, which in the past had also housed the small dormitories of the orphanage. On the west side of the quadrangle was the rectory. And the most dominating building, the church, was immediately in front of us, facing north. As we sat there, two of the massive oak doors swung open and a handful of people, mostly elderly women, began streaming out into the crisp air.

"Showtime, Chene."

"One of these days, McDonald, I will get even with you for this."

She laughed out loud and imitated one of the nuns in a high, squeaky voice. "God loves you, Jefferson."

It was difficult to keep the disgust from my tone. "God must have a warped sense of humor."

We walked up the big stone steps and into the vestibule at the back of the church. Only now, in the dim light did Megan remove her shades. Our heels sounded like gunshots on the thick marble floors as we moved up the aisle between pews. My eyes went to the gigantic stained-glass windows that lined the walls, reaching to the heavens. Their beauty was diminished on this overcast day. A boy, probably no older than ten, dressed in a cassock and surplice, approached the altar and began solemnly to snuff out the candles. He paused at the center of the altar, bowed his head, then resumed his duties.

"Bring back fond memories?" Megan whispered.

"Memories, yes, but they are not fond."

A deep voice boomed behind me. "Well, I see some things haven't changed. I'm surprised you remembered the way in, Jefferson."

We turned around to face him. Just at that moment, the skies briefly cleared and a beam of sunlight shot through the stained glass, casting him in a rosy hue. He had removed the vestments from the morning Mass and was wearing his customary black slacks, with a black long-sleeved dress shirt and the white cardboard collar at the neck. A small wooden cross on a leather cord dangled from his neck. I always pictured him as a giant, so it surprised me to realize that he was only as tall as Megan, with a chunky frame. I could see the broken veins in his cheeks and nose, the sign of a heavy drinker. But his eyes were still sharp and black as coal. The gaze was piercing, giving you the impression that not only could he read your mind, but he'd edit your thoughts before putting them back.

"Hello, Father," Megan said warmly. She stepped forward and hugged him.

"It's good to see you, Megan. How's the prettiest policewoman in the state?"

She actually blushed. "I'm good, Father Dovensky. How are you?"

"God's work keeps me busy," Dovensky said. He released her and turned his attention back to me. "You're too big and too old for an embrace, Jefferson, so I suppose a handshake is in order."

We clasped hands for a moment. I almost expected him to grind my fingers together as a form of penance for my absence. He didn't, but I was willing to bet he wanted to.

"You look good, Father D."

He shrugged it off with a quick grin. "Megan tells me you have a problem with a case that I might be able to assist you with."

My eyes flicked around the great open space of the church. I remembered how sounds could carry here. "Perhaps there's somewhere else we could talk, Father."

"Is this something you're uncomfortable discussing in God's house, Jefferson?"

I cut Megan off before she could respond. "We're trying to catch a serial killer, Father. He is brutally slaying young women."

He considered that for a moment. "Perhaps you're right. Let's go to the rectory."

Chapter Ten

We were settled in Dovensky's office. It looked the same as when I used to visit while a resident of the orphanage. Except instead of a typewriter on the desk, there was a computer. Otherwise the clutter of books, photos, and sports memorabilia crowded every flat surface. I glanced at the spines on the bookshelves. Many of the old literary classics were mixed in with a few psychology books. There was nothing recent. A housekeeper brought in a tray with coffee and condiments, along with a large plate of freshly baked cookies. There was a basket of scones on the desk and a bowl with apples, oranges, and pears. Dovensky looked longingly at the cookies, then reached for an apple.

"Dieting, Father?" Megan asked as she plucked a warm chocolate-chip cookie from the plate.

"I gave up sweets for Lent. No cookies, baked goods, or candy. The staff seems determined to test my resolve."

Megan passed me the plate of cookies. I took three and put them on the napkin beside the mug of coffee. "I'll savor these for you, Father."

"I'll bet you will," he said with a chuckle. "So tell me how I can help with your investigation."

Megan and I took turns explaining the case to him. We made certain he understood the need for confidentiality. The press was not aware of the fact that the three killings were related. We were hoping to keep it that way. The last thing we wanted to do was panic the general public. But if we didn't turn up something soon, we might not have a choice. Dovensky would treat it like a parishioner in the confessional.

He was sitting behind his desk, giving us his undivided attention. He rested his left elbow on the blotter and struck a pose that brought an onrush of memories. He hooked his thumb under his chin, then curled the middle three fingers across his mouth. His pinky rested alongside his nose. Those dark eyes flicked back and forth between Megan and me while we wrapped it up.

"So what makes you think I can help?"

"Actually, it was Megan's idea. All three victims have been found in motel rooms, number 319. And the message on the mirror refers to that."

"I'm wondering if there is some significance in the Bible that might give us a clue," Megan said. "And who better to ask about the Bible than my favorite priest? There's a chance the number refers to a particular chapter and verse."

Dovensky leaned back and sipped his coffee. His eyes went to me. "How are the cookies?"

"Delicious. I'm getting just a hint of walnut."

He sighed. "Marie takes great pleasure in tormenting me. Last night, it was glazed blueberry scones with my tea." He pushed the basket across the desk to Megan. She didn't hesitate to pluck one from the stack. I watched her bite into it and widen her eyes.

"Nice to see the help still has a sense of humor," I said.

"Indeed. And it is many long days until Easter."

We were quiet for a while. I couldn't think of anything else to add. I was still debating whether this was such a good idea. Maybe we could have gotten Donna Spears to read through the Bible.

"So will you help us?" Megan asked.

He hesitated, letting those black eyes flick back and forth between us for a moment. "If it might stop another murder, I'll do the research."

****

Megan smiled all the way back to the squad. Not only did she succeed in getting me in front of Dovensky, but she'd also walked out with the basket of baked goods.

"So, should we tell Cantrell and the crew about this angle?"

I shrugged. "I don't see why not. It might spark something along the way. Now I'm wondering if there is any religious connection between the victims."

We agreed that at this stage, we couldn't take anything for granted. There had to be something the victims had in common. Even though they lived in different cities, perhaps they belonged to the same faith. Pappy had left word that we would meet late each afternoon to regroup and update the others. With that in mind, Megan called the other teams and instructed them to find out about any religious affiliation of the victims. Since we had to go past the post to get to our appointment with the Grange family, I decided to brief Cantrell personally. Megan graciously left the baked goods in the squad room.

Now I was wondering about the religious angle. Maybe there was a recent worship event all three attended. Or maybe it was something simpler. Maybe all three wore a cross. Maybe that was enough to attract the killer. I made a mental note to ask Simone about it the next time I saw her.

It had been less than four hours since I'd left her apartment, and already I was trying to find excuses to go back there. With an effort, I pushed thoughts of her from my mind and focused on the case. Our day was just beginning. And we were no closer to finding our elusive killer.

****

Cantrell absorbed the idea of the religious angle without much reaction one way or the other. During all his years with the department, he'd seen many bizarre crimes. The motivating factors were as complex as quantum physics. He gave me a nod, then wagged a finger over my shoulder. I reached back and swung his door closed.

"Y'all know the governor's on my ass now."

"We expected as much. But we haven't even had the case for forty-eight hours. How are Barksdale and Jarrett doing with the latest victim?"

He shrugged and pulled a fresh cigarette from his pack. "Jarrett might just surprise us. She's sharp. Ah expect she's giving Barksdale fits. The boy thinks he's in charge, but she's workin' him just the same."

"We're going to interview family and friends today. Maybe we'll catch a break."

Cantrell stood and with a practiced motion flipped his cigarette into the air. It floated toward the ceiling, turned over once and arrowed toward him. He leaned out slightly and caught it in his mouth by the filter. A cocky smile crossed his wrinkled face as he winked at me.

"How many hours it take you to master that trick?"

"Hell, Chene, that one's easy. My daddy learned me that when I wasn't but six. He said it would help me charm the ladies."

"Does it work?"

"Every time." He raised his lighter, then had a change of heart and walked toward the exit. "Git out of here, Chene. Go find me a killer."

****

We cruised quickly to the home of Artie's parents. Edgar and Evelyn Grange lived in a modest house in St. Clair Shores, not far from the lake. The house was a small ranch, probably built in the early fifties with the onslaught of residential construction after the war. There were two cars in the driveway, an old beat-to-shit Ford and a brand new Toyota. We parked out front and studied the house for a minute. I could see someone pacing back and forth through the living room windows as we climbed out of the car. Were they nervous or impatient?

"You ready for this?"

"The girl's been dead for over a month. In a way, we could be pulling the scabs off the wound if they've started to get on with their lives." Megan swept her blonde hair back. "But there was something weird when I called to schedule this."

I leaned my forearms on the roof and looked at her. "What do you mean?"

"I talked to the husband. He started giving me some bull about it not being convenient to meet with them at this time. I reminded him we're investigating the murder of his daughter. He still pushed back."

We started up the sidewalk. "So I'm sure you were

understanding and diplomatic with your response."

Megan flashed me a wicked grin. "Said we could do it here, or I'd personally bring them in to the post for interrogations. And we'd do it around midnight."

"You can be so intimidating."

"I learned it from the penguins."

Edgar Grange greeted us at the door. They had witnessed our arrival, and he kept impatiently glancing at his watch. Megan introduced us. He grunted a surly hello and pushed the door open.

He was an average guy. Average height, average looks, with coarse black hair that was shot through with gray. Grange was in desperate need of a shave and a haircut. He was wearing a tattered sweatshirt, torn blue jeans, and sneakers. I noticed dirt under his fingernails, which were long and jagged. It took him a minute, but he eventually made eye contact. It was brief.

Megan and I sat on the sofa that faced the window. We knew their background from the Warren police files. Edgar was a handyman's helper, mostly doing landscaping jobs. This time of year, he wouldn't be working yet. Evelyn Grange was the breadwinner of the family. While Megan pulled out her recorder, I took a good look at Mrs. Grange. At first glance, she reminded me of a witch. Thin, straw-colored hair had been fashioned into a perm, but it looked like it needed constant attention. Traces of gray were evident at the temples. She was rail thin, possibly anorexic. She was dressed in a tan business suit, with high-heeled pumps. It had been her pacing back and forth. Now she leaned against the wall, anxiously flicking the fingers of her right hand out and checking the manicure. Her nails were at least two inches long and coated with bright red polish. Edgar dropped into an upholstered chair across from the sofa. Megan took that as her cue.

"As I explained, the state police is now assisting in the investigation. We know you've both talked at length with the Warren detectives, but we believe it will be beneficial to the investigation if we interview you as well."

"Can we hurry this up?" Evelyn asked. "I'm supposed to be at a meeting with clients at eleven."

I ignored the question. "How often did you see your daughter after she moved out?"

Edgar snorted. "She was here all the time. She'd come by to do her laundry and to have dinner a couple of times a week. She just didn't sleep here anymore."

I shifted my gaze to Evelyn for confirmation. Suddenly, she found the carpeting very interesting. I waited until she looked up. "I often work late in the day, so it was nice for her to be able to come home and have dinner with her father."

"Did your daughter tell you about her dates, about her relationships?" Megan asked.

Edgar shrugged. "She didn't talk much about that. Usually it was about whatever was going on at work. Maybe some plans with her girlfriends. Maybe a new class she was thinking of taking. She couldn't stick with any one subject for very long."

"Why do you think that was?" I asked.

"Beats the hell out of me," Edgar said roughly. "I always wanted her to go to school, but not just to waste the money. I was getting tired of paying for classes where she only went half the time. And nothing would ever amount to her getting a degree."

"So you were paying for her college education?" I

asked.

Evelyn stepped in. "We both wanted to help her with school. But she just couldn't decide what she wanted to study."

In my peripheral vision, I could see Megan's fingers moving. Years ago, she learned sign language. She had taught me a few basic signs. I caught this one. There was something more going on here. I hooked two fingers at her. Megan rose from the couch.

"I could use a drink of water. Mrs. Grange, would you show me to the kitchen," Megan said with calm politeness.

Evelyn Grange had a sour look on her face, but she reluctantly led Megan down the hall. We needed to talk to these two separately.

"When Stephanie was young, did you use a daycare facility?" I asked.

Edgar was puzzled for a moment by the question but shook his head. "No, I stayed home with her. The old lady makes the most money, so I took care of the house and stuff. Stephanie and I were always together."

"So as she got older, it was you who took her on field trips and helped her with homework, school projects, and the like?"

"Yeah, she never woulda passed half her classes if it wasn't for me. Course during the summer when I'm busy, she'd stay with friends or her grandparents during the day."

"You usually start early in the summer, before the heat gets intense?"

"Sure, it's a bitch when the humidity is up. We do the commercial properties early, like five or six, then hit the residential stuff as the sun's coming up. Most days I'm done by two." Grange gave me a look as if I could never begin to understand how difficult his line of work was.

"So even during the summer time, you were able to spend the better part of the day with your daughter."

He nodded. "That's right. By the time she was twelve, she'd just stay home until I got back. Damn teenagers want to sleep all morning and stay up all night long."

"That's normal."

"What's all this got to do with her getting killed?" Grange was fidgeting in his chair. Obviously, something was unnerving him. I didn't think it was recalling the life with his daughter. I studied him closely for a minute before responding.

"I don't know. We just ask the questions. You never know what's important, what can have an impact on the investigation."

Edgar's face showed his discomfort with the conversation. I gave him a moment, thinking I was done. But I was just getting warmed up.

"Was your daughter athletic?"

He coughed out a sound that could have been a laugh. "Hell no, she was more of a klutz than her mother is. She could ride a bike, but she couldn't catch a cold."

"So she wasn't into swimming, maybe going to the beach, or hanging out with friends."

"She never had many friends." Edgar was beyond fidgeting now, as if his body could not find a comfortable position in his chair.

"So most of her free time, she spent with you?"

"Yeah, we were good buddies."

I looked up as Megan came back into the room. "Stephanie still has a bedroom here. Warren PD didn't check it out. What do you think?"

I got to my feet. "I think we better take a look."

Edgar's face got very pale, and I noticed a line of sweat across his brow.

"Why you gotta do that?"

"Like I said, you never know what information may help the case." I turned to Megan. "Let's go."

Chapter Eleven

Evelyn stated the room was the same as when Stephanie lived there. I asked the parents to stay out in the hall as we donned latex gloves. Megan slowly started going through the dresser. I went to the closet. For a girl who moved out months ago, there were still a lot of clothes. Megan and I were going to do a thorough search. At length, Evelyn and Edgar drifted back to the living room.

Megan checked to make sure they were gone before showing me the contents of one drawer. It was filled with skimpy underwear, thongs and bikinis, some so small that I couldn't imagine what they actually covered. There were several push up bras as well, and a couple that had padded inserts.

"Something feels very wrong about this place," Megan said quietly.

"Yeah, I'm getting bad vibes too. Better pull the drawers out of the dresser."

Megan removed each drawer carefully, looking beneath it and at the back, to see if anything was hidden there. I returned to the closet. In addition to numerous blouses, skirts, and sweaters, there were at least thirty shoeboxes, either on the shelf or stacked on the floor. I noticed a picture on the outside of each one. This was a photo of the shoes that were supposed to be inside. I lifted the top box, which was a pair of open-toed black shoes with stiletto heels. The picture matched the contents. I showed the box to Megan.

"Can you really walk in a pair of these?"

Megan shook her head. "Chene, those are FMN shoes."

"FMN?"

"Fuck Me Now. And to answer your next question, yes, but mine are red."

I set the box aside and continued to examine the rest of the stack. I finished the boxes on the floor and was about to start on the shelf. Megan moved to the bedside table. She dropped to her knees and peered under the bed. I took the box from the back of the shelf and opened it. What I saw made my stomach turn.

The room had a student's desk with a small wooden chair. I set the box carefully on the desk and motioned Megan to join me. Inside was a pair of ballet slippers, small enough to fit a nine-year-old girl. The rest of the box was jammed with Polaroid pictures. But these were not of shoes or any other fashion statement. Handling them carefully by the corners, I pulled out a stack and spread them on desktop. Megan was at my shoulder, her eyes locked on the first six pictures.

They were all nudes. Stephanie was perhaps ten or eleven, with just the hint of development taking place. In some, she was standing. Others, she was sprawled on the bed. In a couple, she was on her hands and knees, looking over her shoulder at the camera. Methodically, we went through the entire box. Midway through the pictures, she began to fill out. You could see the small curves of her body and the shadow of pubic hair. Interspersed with these were pictures of Edgar. He was also nude and fully erect. In one, he was sprawled on her bed, arms wide, reaching for her.

Megan laid a hand on my arm, and I felt the fingers dig through my jacket. "This could have a whole lot to do with Stephanie's self-esteem."

"Yeah, but is it motive for murder?"

"I could kill him," she snapped.

"I have no doubt about that. But he wasn't the one who was killed. Maybe someone found out about her relationship with her father."

We agreed to keep searching. I stacked all the pictures back in the box, then returned my attention to the closet. I didn't find anything else. But Megan found something stashed between the covers of a book. There was a digital picture here, from a color printer. The angle was higher, not like the pictures we found in the shoe box. It showed Stephanie on her back, wearing a short nightgown that ended at her hips. She appeared to be pleasing herself. Megan looked at the picture closely, then peered over her shoulder.

"Bastard must have put a camera in the air duct."

"Maybe she cut him off, and this was his way of reminding her who was in charge." I looked at the grate. I could have climbed up and unscrewed the cover, but there really was no point to it.

"Think Mama knows what was going on?"

"Only one way to find out," I said.

I took the shoebox. Megan brought the book as well. Edgar was back in his chair, one leg crossed at the knee. It was jumping up and down with nervous energy. Evelyn was standing by the windows, her back to the room, staring out at the gray light of day.

"What you got there?" Edgar shifted anxiously in the chair.

"Oh, I think you already know what we found," Megan said. "The question is did your wife know about it as well?"

"What are you talking about?" Evelyn spun quickly from the window as if afraid she was being accused of something.

Megan glanced at me. I simply nodded. This might carry even more weight coming from a woman. The way we were standing, I could watch both parents' reaction.

"We found evidence that your husband had an incestuous affair with your daughter that apparently lasted for several years."

"You lie." Edgar jumped to his feet. "You lie!"

"Proof's in the pictures, Eddie." Megan held up two of the shots we had taken from the box. These were some of the more damning ones from the group, with Stephanie as an early teen and Edgar in full bloom.

Edgar shriveled under Megan's glare. But Evelyn crossed to her and stared with wide eyes at the pictures. She whirled and attacked Edgar, digging her claws into his face, shredding the skin. Blood raced from the tracks along his cheeks. Then she began kicking him, striking his shins, his knees, and ankles. I wrapped my arms around Evelyn's waist and yanked her free, holding her off the ground. As I pulled her back, she lashed out with one foot and tried to kick him in the crotch. Edgar just stood there, glaring at her. From the reflection in the window, I could see the rage flowing from Evelyn's face.

"You promised me! You swore you didn't touch her! She was your own daughter! How could you have sex with her?"

There was a defiant look as he stared at her. "I had to get it somewhere."

****

It was after two when we left the Grange residence. Things had degenerated quickly once the initial confrontation had taken place.

While I kept Evelyn occupied, Megan called it in to Cantrell. He immediately dispatched a crime-scene team and two uniformed troopers. Edgar was taken into custody. There would be a whole shopping list of charges filed against him, including statutory rape. The technicians would be busy for several hours, checking out the entire house for evidence. After Edgar was placed in the cruiser to be taken to the post, I realized I hadn't seen Evelyn for several minutes. Megan found her in the bedroom, changing into another business suit. Apparently, she had torn the jacket on the tan one and gotten a few bloodstains on it as well. We watched in amazement as she left the house, supposedly on her way to work.

"That is one frosty bitch," Megan said as we drove away.

"Hungry?"

"I'm starving. And I need some time to process this before we keep going. How about stopping at Sharkey's?"

Ted was in his office, going over the weekly invoices. We took our usual table. Megan ordered shrimp scampi, and I opted for the Cobb salad. We were both quiet. I was thinking about the interview with Edgar Grange in his kitchen while we were waiting for the crime-scene team. The two uniformed officers stayed with Evelyn in the living room.

Grange had been informed of his rights but opted to answer our questions without an attorney. We had the conversation on tape, using the small recorder Megan dug out of her pocket. Grange had been preening in his chair, despite the handcuffs.

"She was always daddy's girl. It was like I was a single parent. I'm the one who raised her, who bandaged her skinned knees, who took her to the park and the beach and the movies and the games. The Ice Queen was hardly ever in the picture after the baby was born.

"It got to the point where I think Evelyn was jealous of what Stephanie had with me. So she started holding back. If I was lucky and maybe she was a little bit drunk, I might get laid once a month. That ain't normal. So when Stephanie started to grow, it just sort of happened." Grange turned his head, wiping some of the blood from his face on the shoulder of his sweatshirt. "She was supposed to be getting ready to go swimming. But she was taking forever. I walked in on her. She couldn't decide which bathing suit to wear. She looked so innocent, so good, that I just couldn't help but kiss her."

He had gone on in great detail, describing their physical activities from that point. Apparently, his daughter never denied him. The way he told it, she was anxious to try whatever he wanted. It made her feel special. It made me disgusted.

Megan stirred her coffee and nudged my leg with her toe. "It's a by-product of our investigation, but I'm not sure what it does to our efforts."

"Maybe it will help us get a better sense of our victim. It could be that there's something all three had in common."

Her eyes went wide. "You think all three were the victims of incest?"

"No. But there could be a common thread there. I keep coming back to the low self-esteem. We learned that Stephanie had an eating disorder and a long sexual relationship with her father. Maybe some of her recent actions were a result of that."

Megan nodded. "Her mother told us about the bouts of anorexia where she would take food for lunch at school, then pitch it instead of eating it. I'm wondering if all the recent changes weren't a sign of her rebelling against her parents."

"Elaborate on that."

Our food arrived, and Megan dug into her lunch. "Think of it this way. You saw her mother. Stephanie was built almost exactly the same. Maybe she was afraid of turning into something just like her. Not just physically, but in her marriage, the way she treated her husband. It's obvious that Evelyn's career is more important to her than whatever she has or could have with Edgar. So Stephanie wanted to make her body distinctive. First, she goes anorexic, trying to get even skinnier than her mother. Then she starts to mark her body. She had multiple piercings in her ears and gets her navel done. Add to that the tattoos, the tanning salon, and the breast and butt enhancements. It's like she was trying to physically distance herself from her mother."

"Hard to believe the mother was clueless to the whole incest thing." I poked at my salad.

Megan nodded. "She's pretty absorbed in her career. I'd bet she had suspicions but chose to ignore them. Her hubby was a piece of work."

"He probably resisted his daughter moving out. With her gone, he had no chance to exert his manliness."

We were quiet for a moment, working on our food. We have seen enough carnage with this job that it rarely impacted our appetites. Food was a necessity. The lack of fuel for the body could result in a delayed physical reaction or a lack of mental acuity. Cantrell drilled that into us for years. No matter what you're confronted with, you needed to keep the body fueled. Megan pushed her plate away, leaving a thin smear of sauce on the perimeter. My salad was history. I ripped off the heel of a loaf of crusty Greek bread from a local bakery Ted favors. I ran the bread across my plate, capturing the last dregs of the vinaigrette dressing. If only I could capture the killer as easily.

"She certainly thought she emasculated him. She was the big-shot executive, making all the money in the house, supporting the whole family. It left her husband alone with a very gullible, vulnerable girl."

"Makes you wonder what secrets Momma Grange is hiding."

Megan thought about that a moment. "I don't know if it would have anything to do with our case, but as Cantrell would say, 'Y'all better check it out. Don't leave no rolling stones unturned.' So that should be our next step."

I had no argument with that.

Chapter Twelve

Evelyn Grange was employed with a well-known marketing firm in downtown Birmingham, one of the upscale communities in Oakland County. We didn't bother to call first. Nothing keeps people on edge more than an unexpected visit from the police. And neither one of us wanted to give Evelyn an opportunity to prepare for this impromptu follow up visit.

The receptionist was a high-maintenance blonde perched behind a half-circle desk that looked like the spaceship command post out of a bad science fiction movie. She wore enough makeup for three women and spoke in a breathy voice, as if she had just run up three flights of stairs wearing stilettos. Megan took one look at her, let her eyes glaze over in frustration, and stepped back to let me announce our intentions. The blonde's eyes grew to the size of hubcaps when I explained why we were there.

"Ms. Grange is meeting with a client right now," she gasped in that breathy voice as if that would change our minds.

I kept my voice low and stern. "I'm going to have to insist on interrupting. We're in the middle of a homicide investigation, and it's imperative that we talk with Evelyn right now."

She started to respond but hesitated as Megan stepped up beside me and placed her palms down on the desk and leaned forward.

"Get her now, or we'll tear this place apart until we find her." Megan's voice was a low growl. I don't know whether it was her tone or her demeanor, but the combination worked. The blonde vaulted out of her command center and hurried down the hall. Megan angled her head to look up at me while she still leaned on the counter.

"I've got twenty bucks that says Evelyn has been sleeping her way to a better pay grade."

"You giving odds?"

"Even up."

"You're on." It was a sucker's bet. After seeing Evelyn a few hours earlier, I wondered the same thing. She wasn't physically attractive to me, but that didn't mean anything. Different strokes for different folks. Maybe she was a contortionist.

The receptionist was hurrying back down the hall. I noticed that she was in fact wearing stilettos and a pencil skirt, which made moving quickly nearly impossible. She didn't bother going behind the command center but slid to a stop beside us.

"Ms. Grange asked that you wait in the Aquarius Conference Room. It is right this way."

Megan tilted her head. "And I'm sure she will be joining us in that room before my ass has enough time to warm a chair."

The blonde gulped and nodded vigorously. Then she turned on her heel and led us to the conference room. We could see Evelyn Grange striding down the hall from the opposite direction. Her expression was pure indignation. We arrived at the door to the conference room simultaneously.

"Thank you, Gretchen," she snapped. Without further comment, Evelyn pushed the door open and marched inside. Megan followed. I glanced over my shoulder to make sure the blonde was headed back to her desk. She was wiggling away on her stilettos, giving us no further consideration. I entered and closed the door tightly behind me.

"I certainly do not appreciate being interrupted at work like this," Evelyn snapped again. She was standing on the opposite side of the conference table, her fingers digging into the leather back of one of the chairs.

Megan turned her head slightly in my direction. The look on her face was a mixture of disgust and humor. I nodded. Megan reached for her hip beneath her jacket and removed the handcuffs from the pouch on her belt. She tossed them on the table and they slid to a stop before Evelyn. Her eyes went wide with surprise.

"Listen up, lady, and listen well. We can either have a civil conversation right here, right now, or we will take you into custody. That means I snap those cuffs on you, and we make a big show out of walking your skinny bitch ass out of this building, stuffing you into a car, and taking you to the post for a thorough interrogation. The choice…is yours." Megan made a show out of pulling back the sleeve of her jacket to check her watch. "You've got twenty seconds. I'm a bit low on patience today."

Evelyn stared at the silver cuffs for about three seconds before she pulled out the chair and collapsed into it. Megan reached across the table and retrieved the hardware, deftly sliding them back into the clip.

"I can't believe you would talk to me this way, knowing my daughter was killed," Evelyn said softly, as if all of her defiance had leaked out of her like an ancient helium balloon, "considering what I learned today."

Megan and I took seats across from her. "There are so many questions we need answers to, Evelyn, that we don't have time to be polite. Your daughter was killed a month ago. We need all the information we can possibly gather in order to figure out who killed her," Megan said. "You do want her killer caught, don't you?"

"Of course I do." There was just enough indignation to make it sound real.

I joined the conversation. "Sometimes a daughter will confide things to her mother that she won't share with anyone else."

"I can't believe that was happening right beneath my nose."

"Edgar said you were rarely home, often working late," Megan said. "But there still must have been some time you spent with your daughter."

"It's obvious that Stephanie and I were never that close. She never asked me for advice. She never asked me for help."

Evelyn Grange had been nervously twisting her fingers, as if she were trying to unknot a puzzling piece of yarn or thread. Her head was bowed. Since she had collapsed into the chair, she hadn't been able to look either one of us in the eye. Megan's impatience was rubbing off on me. From my jacket pocket, I withdrew the picture of Stephanie that I'd been carrying since we began the investigation. It was the same photo the

Warren detectives got from the family when she was identified. I also had the one from the autopsy, but that was something no mother should ever see of their child. I extended my arm and placed the photo on the table right in front of Evelyn's downcast eyes.

"She's asking now."

Evelyn clutched the picture as if it were a lifeline. Megan and I exchanged a glance. She leaned back in her chair and waited. Now it was my turn.

"Tell us about your daughter. Whatever you can think of, no matter how insignificant it might be."

Evelyn sniffed back tears. "I don't know where to start."

"When did she move out?" I asked quietly.

"It was about four months ago now. I remember her saying it was her Christmas present to both herself and to us. It was a chance for her to spread her wings, to experience life on her own. She'd found a little apartment that she could afford."

"How was she behaving back then?"

Evelyn thought for a moment. "She was happier than I had seen her in a long time. This was going to be her place. She could decorate it any way she liked. Have some friends over whenever she wanted."

"We're going to need a list of her friends, anyone who was close to Stephanie, as far back as you can recall. We'll need names and phone numbers and any other information you can give us."

She bobbed her head in agreement. "Of course."

"Tell us more about the relationship between the two of you," Megan asked.

"We sort of drifted apart. When she was younger, we would spend a lot of time together. Weekends were special. Some nights, I'd come home from work and take her out to dinner. Or to the movies, or we'd go shopping."

"When did it change?"

Evelyn shook her head, her eyes locked on the photo.

"Was it when she learned about your infidelity?"

Her head snapped back as if Megan had grabbed a handful of that straw-colored hair. "How do you know about that? Who told you I was having an affair?"

"You did," I said.

Once she realized her mistake, Evelyn admitted everything. Not that either one of us was surprised. It had started about ten years ago. The owner of the company had selected her to work on a bid for a large contract. It resulted in many late hours, constantly refining the strategy, coming up with artwork and samples and slogans by the truckload. One night while working late, they had stepped out to a nearby restaurant for dinner. A few drinks helped to chase away the stress of the day. Once back in the office, the owner had little trouble coaxing her out of her pantyhose. He plied her with compliments, dangled promises of promotions in front of her, and introduced her to a fringe benefit she never anticipated.

Whenever she worked late, Evelyn made it a point to always stop in and give her daughter a good night kiss, no matter how late it was when she got home. It was within two months of the affair that Stephanie noticed her mother was acting differently. But she didn't say anything until one night when Edgar was out with the boys from work for a few beers. Evelyn came home and was getting changed when Stephanie walked into her room without knocking. She noticed her mother's stockings were torn and there were scratches on her legs. Stephanie was old enough to understand, but she couldn't come right out and ask her mother. Evelyn had quickly covered herself with a robe. Although she never discussed it, she assumed her daughter suspected the truth.

"So the affair has continued all this time?" Megan asked.

"Yes. I can't end it." She hesitated for a moment. "I don't want to end it. We both get what we need, what we can't get anywhere else. I've got too many years with the firm to leave, even if I wanted to. I helped make this company successful."

"Yeah," I said, "but at what cost?"

****

It was our third day on the case. We all arrived at the post in time for the six o'clock meeting. Each team was due to present the results of their efforts from that day. Cantrell was in his usual spot, a mug of cold coffee on the table before him. He picked at a scab on his left thumb absentmindedly while we settled into our seats.

"Y'all git cozy so we can git on with it. Oakland County wants answers. Barksdale, let's start with you. Whatcha got?"

Barksdale jerked his head toward Tess Jarrett. "I'll let her tell it."

"We met first thing with her parents. Janet was an only child. An average student, she kept in the background. Didn't do anything to distinguish herself in school, either high school or college, got mostly B's. No extracurricular activities, just focused on her studies. They gave us the details for her doctor and her dentist. They also gave us a list of people she was friends with, going back to high school."

"Did she have any religious affiliation?" Megan asked.

Tess checked her notes. "Minimal. Her family went to church on the high holy days, you know, Christmas and Easter. That was it."

Cantrell grunted and reached for his coffee. Tess picked up the narrative.

"The roommate gave us a list of the places she liked to shop, where she hung out. From what she described, the girl didn't have many close friends. I did get a list from the roommate, and we compared it with what the family gave us. There were only a few additions, but they might be people she met through work. Janet was an office manager at an insurance agency. Well-liked by everyone there. She was shy but a hard worker. Seems like the agency focused on small businesses, lots of personal accounts, with the usual mixture of plans."

"Did she interact much with the clients?" Koz asked.

"Rarely. She'd been working with them for almost a year. They were gradually giving her more responsibilities, letting her get familiar with the operation."

"Are there any possible candidates on the client list or staff?" Laura chimed in. "Maybe someone she met through the agency?"

Tess gave her head a negative shake. "The agency is owned by a husband and wife. From the looks of it, she's got the bucks and the brains of the operation."

"And the body too," Barksdale added quickly. "She

could stop traffic on Woodward and Maple in the middle of rush hour."

Tess ignored the comment. "There are a couple of other people who work there, but we haven't checked them out yet. I'll do some digging into their backgrounds after the meeting."

"What else ya got?" Pappy was growing impatient.

Tess detailed the rest of their efforts. They had paid a visit to both the doctor and the dentist. The doctor had been reluctant to share much information at first, but Tess credited Barksdale with gaining the lady doctor's cooperation. While at the apartment, Tess checked both the bedroom and the bath. She'd found a few prescriptions, but nothing unusual. There were pills for allergies, birth control, and an antibiotic. All prescriptions were written by the same doctor. There had been evidence of alcohol and GHB in her system, but no recreational drugs.

"We've hit the wall on her personal contacts. There was no address book or diary in the apartment," Tess said.

Megan was sitting beside me, her right leg bouncing in rhythm to an unheard tune. I knew her well enough to recognize this as a sign that she'd made a discovery. She didn't disappoint.

"What about her personal computer? Was that recovered from the apartment?" Megan asked quietly.

Tess and Barksdale exchanged a glance and both shook their heads. "No, we didn't think about that."

"Whatcha got, girlie?" Pappy growled.

"Most people nowadays have their cell phones synched with their personal email accounts. So this would have a list of their contacts and maybe an appointment calendar. That way you get reminders on your phone when you're supposed to be somewhere."

While Megan was talking, I quickly checked the inventory list on the two previous homicides. Personal computers had been collected as part of the property. We would need to get those from the local cops and turn them over to our own cyber unit. They would crack any passwords and gain access to the details. I said as much when Megan finished.

"Good work, girlie." Pappy hooked a thumb at Laura. "Whatcha got on your case?"

Laura calmly outlined the steps she and Kozlowski had taken that day. They conducted interviews with the victim's coworkers and supervisors, then tracked down classmates from high school and college to see if anyone had been in recent contact. They were trying to get appointments with her doctor and her minister. There was one surprise in the mix. Her parents indicated that she recently started seeing a therapist.

"We need to get a fix on this therapist," Kozlowski said. "Maybe the computer will give us a lead."

"Makes me wonder if the others might have been seeing a therapist or a counselor too," Laura said.

Cantrell let his gaze float around the table slowly. "Check it out."

Megan reported the events of our day. The others absorbed the information about Edgar Grange's incestuous relationship and the family dynamic. Kozlowski slowly shook his head in disgust.

"Situation like that would definitely have an impact on a girl's self-confidence," he said. "From what we've seen, all three of these victims had very little self-esteem."

"Which is exactly what appeals to our killer," Megan said.

We all grew silent for a moment. There was no magic bullet pointing us to our killer. If there was, we weren't able to see it yet. Cantrell gave a slow nod. "Keep at it."

No one left the post yet. We had hours of reports to review and updates to enter. There was still a long way to go before the day would end.

Chapter Thirteen

Using the contacts we had gotten from the Warren detectives and the Grange family, Megan and I started to track down and interview the people Stephanie was close to. Since her most recent job was at a family restaurant called the Flame, we started there Tuesday morning. We arrived at the restaurant after the breakfast rush.

The manager was a large Italian woman named Rose who gave Megan a brief look, then turned her attention on me. She pointed us to a table in the corner. On her way to join us, she grabbed three worn earthenware mugs in one hand and a pot of coffee in the other. Rose filled our mugs and settled into a chair.

"So you want to talk about that poor girl that got killed," Rose said quietly. "I don't know what more I can tell you. It's been a while since she worked here."

"Wasn't she working here before she died?" Megan pulled out her recorder and flicked it on.

Rose took a healthy sip from her mug. I watched her eyes go vacant as she stared off into the distance. We waited a moment before she came back to us.

"I checked the books when you called. For a while, she was working full time, grabbing as many shifts as she could. But about three weeks before it happened, she started cutting back. Her last week, she was only here three days."

"Any idea why she reduced her hours?" I noticed that Rose was staring at the recorder.

"Nah, she was getting pretty good money. We do a solid business at lunch and dinner. We've got a beer and wine license, so that adds up on the tab. The smart girls learn quickly how to offer a beer or two and swing their butts a bit to get a bigger tip. She wasn't an early riser, so she never pulled a breakfast shift."

"Did Stephanie get along with the customers and the other staff?" Megan asked.

Rose thought about it. "She usually worked when I was on the floor. I don't remember any problems. But I think she was looking for a change."

"What makes you say that?"

"One of the other girls quit a couple of weeks before Stephanie died. She was trying to recruit girls to work at another place." A disgusted look crossed her face. "Only trailer trash would want to work like that."

"What's the place?"

"Bronson's. It's over on Van Dyke, by the freeway. They call it a sports bar, but there's nothing sporty about it."

"What do you mean?" Megan's curiosity was evident.

"Cheryl, the girl who used to work here, said they get to wear club clothes, no uniforms or such. But I saw some pictures she took on her phone, and the girls working there were wearing bikinis."

Megan and I exchanged a look. "Do you think Stephanie was going to work there?"

Rose let out a coarse laugh. "That girl didn't have enough to fill a thimble. And she wasn't very outgoing. I can't picture her in a place like that, where everyone can see what you've got."

It seemed obvious to me. "Money can be a powerful motivator."

"I'd be surprised. She might have gone out with a couple of the girls after work, but she pretty much just stuck to herself." Rose shook her head in dismay. "I have a difficult time picturing her like that or being comfortable waiting tables that way. Any tips she made were probably out of sympathy."

"We're going to need the names of the others that she worked with."

Rose lifted her mug. "I'll get you a list. A couple of the girls are working now. Since it's before the lunch rush, I'll send them over."

"We appreciate it," Megan said.

We watched Rose move back toward the kitchen. "You think she might have gotten up the nerve to work at a bikini bar?"

"You're the one who said she was trying to distance herself from her mother. Maybe she wanted to give it a try. I doubt she'd tell her parents that she was working in a place like that."

"And maybe that's where she caught the attention of our killer."

We interviewed two of the waitresses and got the list from Rose. It was methodical work, but it was necessary. By now I knew everything that was in the murder book from the Warren PD. There was no mention of Stephanie going to work at the bikini bar. But that didn't mean she hadn't. Bronson's was situated on Van Dyke, just north of the freeway. A couple of miles further north the gigantic tech center for General Motors, where thousands of people worked every day. Other industrial complexes cropped up along the highway, with office buildings sprinkled in for good measure. Tucked back from the main roads were subdivisions filled with family homes of a variety of shapes and size. This was only a few miles from the Warren Police Department. It would be ironic if Stephanie worked here, and this had any bearing on the case.

From the parking lot, it looked like any other saloon. The building was solid, with a long, low canopy over the front doors. At the far end, I could see a delivery truck from a brewery. We watched the driver haul in several stacks of beer cases and two kegs. He was in a hurry to get out of there before the lunch rush hit. I scanned the parking lot. More than twenty cars and pickup trucks were already in attendance.

The noise level was high as we walked inside. Several large screens were showing a spring-training baseball game. Another screen offered highlights from yesterday's basketball and hockey competitions. There were large tables filling every available space and a long bar in the center of the room. I spotted four girls running with food and drink orders, each one wearing a skimpy bikini and tennis shoes. Two women were behind the bar, dressed the same way. Megan and I headed for a corner of the bar.

The bartender at that end was named Josie. She was probably in her forties, a peroxide blonde with very dark roots. Tattoos of roses adorned her shoulders. She raised an eyebrow at us as we settled on stools. Megan flashed her badge.

"I'm McDonald. This is Chene. We're investigating a homicide. We're wondering if this girl ever worked here." She slid the picture of Stephanie Grange across the counter.

Josie lifted the photo and turned it toward the light. I thought a flicker of recognition danced across her features. Before I could say anything, she motioned to the other bartender. They met in the center of the bar and whispered for a moment. Then Josie returned and set the picture gently on the counter in front of Megan.

"She was here, more than a month ago. She came in to try the place out. She was a real wallflower. I didn't think she was going to work out. She only lasted about three days. I don't remember her name."

"Did she work days or nights?"

A smirk crossed Josie's face. "Days. We save the real hustlers for the after-work crowd. It takes a good attitude to banter with the guys, the right mixture of flirt and schoolgirl to survive. You know, part virgin, part hooker." She gave me an exaggerated wink. "I'm sure you know the type."

Megan waved the picture in front of Josie. "Never mind him. Let's focus on this girl. Is it uncommon to have someone come in and work for a couple of days like that?"

Josie shrugged her tattooed shoulders. "No, it happens a lot. Some of the girls here will recruit friends. It's steady work, no matter what the economy is doing. And most of our customers get pretty generous with their tips and extras. Hey, you guys gotta order something. My boss sees me just yakking with you and not pouring something, I'll catch hell."

Megan started to protest, but I waved her off. "What's on draft?"

Josie grinned and gestured at a row of taps adorned

with corporate logos from various brands. "What ain't?"

Halfway down the counter were two guys working on burgers with the dregs of a beer in the mugs before them. I jerked a thumb in their direction. "Buy those two a round of Labatt's on me."

Josie grinned, revealing two crooked front teeth. She moved quickly down the bar, topped off the mugs and returned. The guys raised the drinks in salute and returned to their lunch. "That's six bucks."

I threw a ten on the counter. "Keep talking."

"You said something about extras," Megan said. "Are we talking sex?"

"Relax, this ain't no strip club. The extras are things the customers ask for. It's nothing illegal. Like the weekend of Valentine's Day, we had oysters. We do get a lot of couples coming in here in the evening, especially when there's a game on. Anyway, a guy offers his waitress twenty bucks to down an oyster. She tells him nothing that slimy is going in her mouth. He ups it to fifty. They're each holding one end of the bill, and she slurps it down." Josie shrugged. "That's an extra."

Megan raised her eyebrows at the barmaid. "Some guy paid fifty bucks to watch her eat an oyster?"

"Hey, don't knock it," Josie said with a shrug. "But that goes back to what I was saying. The girls who do well here are the ones who know how to mix with the guys. Chances are she's had oysters before but made a show of it with this guy and walked away with an easy fifty. On a good night, most girls can tip out with over two hundred bucks. That's one night."

Megan gave her head a long, slow shake.

"Unbelievable."

"You want to give it a try, let me know," Josie said. "Something tells me you could handle anyone in this crowd without a problem."

In my peripheral vision, I could see Megan's face flush red. It was an effort to keep my focus on Josie and not comment. Instead, I brought the conversation back to our investigation.

"We'd like to talk to a girl named Cheryl. I believe she was the one who referred Stephanie here."

Josie nodded. "She's not working now. Let me go check the schedule."

We watched her move toward the far end of the bar. Megan slugged my shoulder to get my attention. "Those hips don't normally swing that much, Chene. And you know that body has had some major work."

"I was merely being observant. It's part of the job."

"My ass," Megan snapped. Before I could respond, the color flared on her cheeks again. "And if you make one comment about my ass working in a bikini bar, I will shoot you right now."

****

We left Bronson's saloon and headed out to Madison Heights to interview Cheryl Jacobson. She wasn't scheduled to work until Thursday. Josie provided her address and phone number. Cheryl was expecting us.

She lived in an older apartment building, part of a large complex set back from the traffic on Twelve Mile Road. I made the mistake of following Megan up the narrow staircase toward Cheryl's apartment. Her denim-covered ass was right before my eyes most of the way. It was a challenge not to imagine it in the wardrobe of Bronson's staff. I slowed my pace to let her get a few more steps ahead of me. There was no way I was willing to test her earlier comment.

Cheryl Jacobson quickly answered our knock. Her apartment was warm and brightly lit. A stack of textbooks covered the kitchen table. I saw history, communications, statistics, and English books in the pile. She offered us coffee, but we both declined. We sat at the kitchen table.

Cheryl looked like the average girl next door. She wasn't wearing any makeup, and her blonde hair was pulled back in a ponytail. Her figure was hidden under a bulky sweater and loose jeans. Her feet were in worn tennis shoes. I noticed her nails were clipped short. There was no polish on them. She had been talking with Megan while I made these observations. Her tone was calm and serious. Her demeanor was polite. Then she shifted her attention to me. I saw no nonsense in those deep blue eyes.

"What's your major?"

There was a brief hint of a smile. "I'm going for marketing, with a minor in mass communications. It's a challenge to go full time, but I'm determined to make it work."

"How many credits are you carrying?"

"Sixteen this semester. I managed to get all my classes scheduled on Monday, Wednesday, and Thursday. Tuesday and Wednesdays are my days off from the bar. I study during the day." She thumped the stack of books with her knuckles. "This is my junior year. I'm not always going to be waiting tables."

"Tell us about that," Megan joined in. "What made you switch from the Flame to a place like Bronson's?"

Cheryl folded her hands on the table. "I liked the Flame. I really did. But it's a matter of economics. Tuition is expensive, and the textbooks and other fees add up fast. Like I said, I'm determined to make it work with school. But with rent, groceries, and all my other expenses, I just wasn't making enough money at the family restaurant to cover everything. I'm on my own."

"When did you start working at Bronson's?" I asked.

"I picked up a few shifts during the Christmas break. I cleared more money in tips in two nights than I did for a week at the Flame. When I found out they would work with my school schedule, it was a no-brainer. The work is the same. The guys are mostly well behaved. My bottom might get pinched, but that happened at the Flame too!"

It was obvious she was defensive about her job. I held both hands up, palms toward her. "Relax. We are not here to judge you. What you're describing makes perfect sense to me. But we really want to talk about Stephanie Grange."

Cheryl took a deep breath and let it out slowly. "Sorry. I guess I'm afraid what people will think of me when they find out how I pay the bills."

"There are worse ways."

We were quiet for a moment while Cheryl gathered her thoughts.

"It's a shame what happened to Stephanie. She was really a nice person, but she had a hard time getting comfortable with people."

Megan took the lead with the questions. "Did you know her long?"

"We met at the Flame. She started working there

just before Thanksgiving. Stephanie wasn't very outgoing. She kept her head down, worked her shifts, and didn't complain. Sometimes when there was a lull in business or during our breaks, we'd talk a bit." Cheryl folded her arms across her chest and leaned back in her chair. "She reminded me of a lost kitten. Not sure where she wanted to go or what she wanted to do with her life."

"Did you two ever go out socially?"

A smirk crossed her lips. "I can't afford a social life. If I'm not working, I'm studying. On a rare night when I'm not working and don't have homework, I have dinner with my sister and her family out in Mount Clemens."

"You recruited Stephanie to work at Bronson's?"

"Sure. If you recommend someone and they get hired, Bronson's gives you fifty bucks as a bonus. So I stopped by the Flame and talked to the girls I worked with." Cheryl paused, recalling the event. "You can't imagine my surprise when Stephanie wanted to learn more about it."

Cheryl pushed away from the table and walked over to the sofa. She came back with a photo in an ornate silver frame. It was a picture of her and Stephanie Grange, dressed in bikinis in front of the bar at Bronson's. The curves and physical attributes Cheryl possessed were proudly on display. Stephanie looked anorexic. Cheryl was beaming at the camera, a bright smile and eyes sparkling. Stephanie appeared uncomfortable. I passed the photo to Megan.

"Since I brought her to Bronson's, I worked with her for the first couple of shifts. Some girls just take to the atmosphere. Others warm up after an hour or two.

Stephanie gave it a good try, but I could tell it wasn't going to last. She was too unsure of herself."

"How many days did she work?" Megan handed back the photo.

"Three or four, and then she didn't show up. I thought she went back to work at the Flame. I tried calling her a couple of times but never heard from her. It was a week before I found out what had happened."

"Do you know if she was seeing anybody?"

Cheryl gave her head a brief shake. "It's funny. Just before she started, Stephanie mentioned that she'd made a new friend. But it didn't sound to me like someone she was dating."

"Any chance someone from the bar took an interest in her?"

"Anything is possible. But Stephanie didn't really try and make friends with any of the customers. She didn't put it out there. Do you really think the killer saw her at Bronson's?"

It was my turn to shake my head. "We can't take anything for granted, but since she was only there such a short time, I doubt it."

Megan placed one of her business cards on the table. "If you think of anything else that might help us, please call me. No matter how insignificant you might think it is."

"I hope you find the guy who did this," Cheryl said with a flash of anger. "Stephanie never hurt anybody. She wasn't the type. Why would somebody kill her?"

"That's what we're trying to figure out."

Cheryl walked us to the door. "Will you let me know when you catch this guy?"

Megan nodded. "Good luck with your studies."

"Thanks, but I don't need luck. I'm acing every class."

Chapter Fourteen

We spent the rest of Tuesday chasing down people who knew Stephanie Grange. It was slow, frustrating work, but it needed to be done. I could only hope that one of the other teams was having more success with their investigations. Our last conversation took place in Roseville, with the landlord where Stephanie lived. It was an upper flat in a house that had been converted into apartments. There was a row of similar units down the block. There had been some lapse in communication between the landlord and the Warren Police Department. The landlord, who was a roly-poly older woman with slate gray hair, was under the impression the apartment was supposed to be sealed off. There had been no effort to empty it out or to put it back on the market. This gave us a chance to see it as Stephanie had left it.

"I hope we don't find any more evidence of her incestuous relationship," Megan said as we entered the room, pulling on latex gloves.

"With any luck, we'll find something that will give us an idea who she was spending her time with."

The upper flat was surprisingly roomy. The largest room was a living area, with two bay windows that looked out over the street. A small kitchen was off to the right, with linoleum flooring that dated back to the 1950s. The cupboards and counters were from the same era. There was a narrow stove and refrigerator tucked in next to the sink. A small wrought-iron table and two chairs took up most of the floor space. Megan started in the living room. I took the kitchen.

There was not much in the cupboards, mostly crackers and cereal and several packages of ramen noodles. There was a matching set of dishes that looked new, possibly a gift from Evelyn for the first apartment. In a cupboard next to the stove, I found a new set of pans and lids. It didn't look like they had been used. The refrigerator held a six-pack of Canadian beer, a pint of sour milk, and two apples that were starting to shrivel. The freezer compartment held several frozen meals, an ice cube tray, and a package of waffles that was opened. I checked the seals on the packages. All the others were intact. Inside the waffles, I found a stash of marijuana. I slid it into an evidence bag.

Megan methodically checked the living room. There was a small table stacked with fashion magazines and a couple of paperback books. No notes or messages were inside. The sofa cushions had been pulled out, revealing a tube of lipstick. Nothing was hidden under the sofa or behind the table. I noticed power cords were dangling there. Probably from her laptop computer which had been removed by the Warren detectives. We moved together into the other part of the flat.

The bathroom was small and narrow. There was an old tub with claw feet. The sink was a pedestal job, with no storage beneath it. There was a mirror above that opened into a medicine cabinet. Megan checked the tub. There were several bottles of body wash and shampoo. A woman's razor was perched behind the water handles. Dolphins and seahorses were depicted on the heavy plastic shower curtain. I looked behind the toilet and in the tank. No surprises. Megan nodded toward the medicine cabinet.

"Think the Warren guys pulled everything?"

"Let's take a look."

She tugged the door open. Inside were several bottles of scented lotion, a box of tampons, blades for the razor, and deodorant. What caught my eye were the six pill bottles lined up in a neat row. Megan slowly went through them.

"Two of these are antibiotics; one is for muscle pain. There are two more for codeine." She lifted the last one and gave it a shake. "And the winner is for anxiety. Looks like it was filled a week before she died."

Before I could respond, Megan pulled a clamshell off the shelf. "And what woman past the age of consent doesn't have birth control pills."

"Don't you find it odd that a girl without a steady boyfriend, who isn't having even occasional sex, would be on the pill?"

Megan checked the contents as she had with each of the other scripts. "There are some other medical reasons for women to be on the pill. Besides, we don't know when she stopped having sex with Edgar. My guess is she wanted to make sure he wouldn't get her pregnant."

That was a grim reality I hadn't wanted to consider. Megan placed all the prescriptions in an evidence bag and shrugged.

We moved into the bedroom.

After being in Stephanie's bedroom at the Grange house, I wasn't sure what to expect. There was an old double bed in the center of the room, with an ancient pine headboard against the wall. A matching pine night table stood on either side of the bed. Frayed lace curtains hung on the narrow window that faced north. There was an old-fashioned window shade that was drawn halfway down the window. A chest of drawers was at the foot of the bed. This didn't match the pine, looking like an afterthought.

We moved to the bed. Together, we lifted the mattress from the frame and propped it against the wall. The box spring followed. There was a layer of dust on the floor but no surprises taped to the frame or hidden beneath the bed. Quickly, we replaced everything. Megan paused to smooth out the spread, then turned her attention to the closet. I went to check out the chest.

There were five drawers in all. I pulled the top one out of the dresser and set it on the bed. This was filled with socks, everything from little ones that would barely cover the toes and heel, to knee-high sweat socks. I removed everything, lifted the paper that lined the drawer, and checked beneath it. There was nothing hidden there or taped to the back or bottom of the drawer. I returned the clothes and repeated the process with the second drawer on the left. This next one held lingerie, bras, panties, and camisoles in a variety of fabrics and colors. Apparently Stephanie had no qualms about spending a significant part of each paycheck on this kind of clothing. There was nothing beneath the silk, satin, and cotton mixtures in this drawer.

The third drawer held lightweight sweaters and T-shirts, with no surprises. Drawer four was packed with jeans in various shades of blue and black. I noticed that several pairs had tatters across the knees and the seat.

Megan pointed out that stores sold them this way. She made a derogatory comment about my lack of knowledge of current fashions. I ignored her and returned to the last drawer.

There was no clothing in this one. I found it crammed with papers. Sitting beside the drawer on the bed, I started to look through them.

"Did you find anything worthwhile?" Megan called from the closet doorway.

"Maybe. Take a look at this."

Wrapped together by a piece of gold ribbon was a haphazard stack of papers. I pulled the ribbon slowly apart. This was a collection of cocktail napkins and bar coasters, some with imprints from bars, but most of them were plain white. There were brief cryptic notes with numbers in the corners. Each had a word or two written across it, such as "at last" or "wow" or "yes." The last was in capital letters and underscored several times.

"Keepsakes?" Megan turned the stack over slowly. "There are a couple of bars here I recognize, but many of them are blank. What do you make of the numbers?"

I considered it for a moment. "Maybe those are the dates when she was there."

"We need to find Stephanie's calendar. If we know where she went, we can go back to those places and see if anyone remembers her."

"Let's start with the ones you recognize. It's worth a shot."

"Right now, Chene, it's the only shot we've got.
****

We wrapped up the day back at the post. The briefings helped us all brainstorm ideas after sharing whatever activity each team had undertaken that day. Cantrell rarely spoke, preferring to just absorb the information as it was passed around the room. He did offer one glimmer of good news. Since the judge approved our requests for the phone records, each provider had complied. With no idea what may have been pertinent, I had asked for the last six months of call activity. Cantrell passed the records on to the cyber squad, instructing them to look for any patterns or heavy call volume, particularly in the last two months of each victim's life. He expected to get reports back by the end of the day Wednesday. It was his next comment that caught me by surprise.

"Y'all look like hell."

Kozlowski spoke up first. "We're pushing it, Pappy. Every one of us knows what's at stake. We want to nail this bastard soon."

"But y'all might miss somethin' since you ain't as sharp as you should be." He let his gaze drift around the room, letting his eyes come to rest on me. "Git outta here. Leave your reports until morning. Go have a beer an' a burger an' git some sleep. If you got somebody you like gettin' horizontal with, go do it."

I tilted my head back to respond, but he snapped a hand at me. "That ain't a suggestion. It's a damn order. Y'all git."

Megan looked at me and shrugged. Slowly, everyone gathered their notebooks and filed out of the conference room. Cantrell wagged a finger at me. I waited until the rest of the team left. It was already past six, and we were four days into this complex investigation. Pappy watched me silently for a bit. I waited. In the distance, we could hear the muffled conversations of the squad as they headed for the exit.

"We gotta break it up a little, Chene."

"You'll get no argument from me, Pappy. But Koz is right. We all want this bastard. And we want him now."

"Have faith, Chene. Y'all gotta have faith."

Everyone was gone when I reached the bullpen. For a moment, I seriously thought about taking the files with me to review at home. But Cantrell's message rang in my head. I locked everything in my desk. Before reaching for my jacket, I saw the light blinking on my desk phone. I had two messages. One was from Tim Kiley, the attorney prosecuting a case I worked on six months ago that was coming to trial next week. The other was from one of the lab techs working with Rudy Fen, with a question about the toxicology report on Janet Calder.

The mention of Janet made me think of Simone. Was it really only yesterday morning when I saw her? I used my cell phone to call. She answered on the second ring.

"I was hoping I'd hear from you," she said. Her voice sounded good, much stronger and more natural than when we'd talked on Sunday night.

"I meant to call you yesterday. Things have been busy." I really didn't want to talk about the investigation. "Look, I know this is short notice, but I was wondering if you wanted to get some dinner."

"Really?" There was genuine surprise in her voice.

Her reaction made me laugh. "Yes, really. What restaurants do you like in Royal Oak?"

She hesitated for only a moment. "There's a really good Japanese place right on Main by Eleven Mile. It's called Little Tree."

"Can you meet me there in twenty minutes?"

"Make it thirty, and you've got a deal."

I was grinning at the phone. "See you there."

****

It took me half an hour to get to the restaurant. Parking was always a challenge in Royal Oak. I had just been shown to a table when Simone came through the door. As she was chatting with the hostess, I took a long look at her. She was wearing a gray leather jacket, with a pale yellow blouse beneath it and a knee-length gray wool skirt. This was my first glimpse of her legs. Her calves were shapely and well-toned. I wondered if she did a lot of running or jogging or if this was a result of genetics. A pair of pumps with a modest heel completed her ensemble. Simone's hair was swept back from her face. There was something playful about her expression as she approached.

There was an awkward moment. I was standing next to the table, uncertain how to greet her. Simone hesitated for a moment, then leaned in and brushed her cheek lightly against mine.

"Hello, Jeff," she whispered. She pulled away before I could respond. Simone did that girl thing, sweeping her skirt against her thighs as she settled into her chair.

"You look good, Simone."

She gave me a little nod. "Not great, but I'm definitely doing better. And I owe a lot of that to you."

I wasn't sure how to respond to that so I picked up the menu. Simone sensed my discomfort and did the same. The waitress was hovering. We each ordered a sushi platter and a glass of wine. We were quiet until

135

the wine was served.

"I know you probably can't talk about work." Simone kept her voice low and soft.

"You're right. Let's talk about something else. Anything else."

She was slowly turning the stem of her wine glass. "Okay. Will you answer questions honestly?"

"Sure."

"No matter how personal my questions are?" There was a playfulness to her eyes now. It looked natural.

"Okay, but I get to ask my questions too."

"That's fair. What kind of name is Jefferson Chene? I did a search on the internet and the only thing that came up was restaurants and shops at some intersection. What's up with that?"

"It's a long story."

Simone nodded. "Those are often the best kind. Start talking."

Normally I ignore questions about my name or my heritage. But I sensed Simone had a genuine interest and that made me willing to share. So I told her the whole thing. I had been abandoned at birth and left in a box next to a bus stop on the corner of Jefferson Avenue and Chene Street near downtown Detroit. Two Dominican nuns, out for an evening stroll from the nearby convent had discovered me. Somehow, the cops who were called to the scene inadvertently put down the intersection as my name. After a brief stay with Children's Services, the nuns had been awarded custody. I was placed in the orphanage at their parish. We finished our soup and were waiting for the main course by the time I completed my tale.

"So you never knew your parents." Her voice

remained low and soft. "That's so sad."

I shrugged it off. "I had plenty of attention from the nuns and the priests at the parish. And there were always a few other kids hanging around, although they often were there for a short while and got placed for adoption."

"Jefferson Chene does have a nice ring to it."

"It's memorable. Now it's my turn. I want to know more about you. Where did you grow up?"

"My family is from Ann Arbor. My mom works at the children's hospital, in the administration wing. My dad taught engineering at U of M. He's originally from France. They met there when she was on vacation. They had a fling. She came home, and two weeks later he appeared at her door. He proposed on the spot."

"That's pretty impressive. Do you have any siblings?"

Simone nodded. "I've got three brothers, all a lot older than me. I was a late baby."

Our sushi platters arrived. I watched Simone take a chunk of wasabi and dissolve it into a small saucer of soy sauce. With her chopstick, she deftly picked up a piece of California roll, dipped it into the sauce mixture and popped it into her mouth. She closed her eyes and savored it. I did the same thing with a piece of yellowtail. It was delicious.

"Wait a minute, I thought you and Janet were friends in high school. But her parents live in Farmington Hills."

Simone raised her wine glass in a salute. "That's very good, Sergeant. My mom and I moved to Farmington Hills just before I started high school. That's where I met Janet."

I tried some salmon. Simone watched me, the glimmer in her eyes still there. After a few minutes, she put her glass down and toyed with her chopsticks.

"Aren't you going to ask why we moved from Ann Arbor?"

"Okay, why did you and your mom move?"

"My parents divorced." Her expression darkened for a moment. "But you already knew that. How is that possible?"

I shrugged. "I didn't know. You just told me. When you said it was you and your mom, I figured one of two things happened, either death or divorce."

"But you didn't ask."

"I figured if you wanted to tell me you would. Sometimes staying quiet is the best way to let the conversation find its own pace."

Simone relaxed and worked on her dinner. "I suppose they teach you that at cop school, how to make people tell you everything."

"Actually, I learned it when I was tending bar."

We talked quietly through the rest of dinner. Cantrell was right. I needed a break from the investigation, a chance to clear my mind of murder and incest and a manipulative serial killer. I imagined the rest of the crew felt the same way. Simone and I lingered over another round of drinks. She had the green tea ice cream for dessert. After a while, the conversation seemed to wind down. I caught her smothering a yawn.

"It's getting late." I paid the bill.

Simone had shed her jacket earlier. She gave me a demure smile while I helped her slip it on.

"Are you the last chivalrous man?" she teased.

"We're a dying breed."

"That's too bad."

I walked her to her car. There was that moment's hesitation when we stood beside it. Then before I could think about it, she leaned up and kissed me. I held her close, enjoying the warmth of her lips on mine. After a while, Simone slipped out of my grasp, ducked into her car, and drove away. I smiled all the way home.

Chapter Fifteen

The riddle was annoying. "Why 319?" What was the significance of that number or group of numbers? What was the connection with the motel rooms? There was no link that we had been able to find yet. We pulled a listing of all employees, including former employees going back five years. Nothing added up. I had even gone so far as to call the library to see if there were any books on numerology. It turns out there was more than I ever thought about numbers. Megan suggested having one of the civilian staff do some internet research to see if there was any significance to the numbers. Cantrell wasted no time assigning it to a cadet. Unfortunately, all of this research had yet to give us any kind of a lead. I could tell the others were frustrated as well.

It was Wednesday morning. By seven thirty, we were all in the bullpen. Updates were done. There was a sense of determination to the squad. The night off had obviously done everyone some good. I was picking up on a pretty strong vibe from both Kozlowski and Megan. Koz and Laura stopped by my desk as they were heading out.

"Reports are all in from yesterday. We're heading over to Plymouth to take another run at the motel. I want to check the surrounding area, see if we can figure out where our victim went before the motel."

Kozlowski shrugged his massive shoulders, adjusting his jacket so it hung properly.

"Good luck with that," I said.

"Thanks, boss."

In my opinion, Cantrell is the boss. I was about to respond sarcastically when I caught the look on his face. Koz was serious. I silently watched him and Laura head for the door. Barksdale and Tess were getting to their feet as well. Barksdale didn't check in, but he did give me a minuscule nod. That was the most I'd ever get from him. Megan and I finished our own updates for yesterday and were about to leave when Pappy appeared.

"So whatcha think it means, Chene?" Cantrell perched a hip on my desk. "Them damn numbers must be a link."

"Yeah, but to what? Is it this guy's lucky number combination, the digits he plays on the daily lottery? Is it some kind of code, or a part of his phone number or address?"

"Thought y'all was trying phone numbers?"

"Yeah, Laura came up with that on Monday. She ran all the variations, but we came up empty."

Laura's idea was that maybe the WHY was taken from the keypad on a telephone, which would be 949. Perhaps the killer was leaving the first six digits of their phone number. So she did the research, trying those six numbers and then one through zero for the seventh, with all of the various area codes available in the tri-county area. After determining who the active lines were registered to, Laura called each one. It had been a good idea, but it fizzled out.

"Maybe it's some mathematic equation," Megan

said. "You know, like the answer to some algebraic formula."

Although I knew there was a connection to the numbers, it continued to elude me. And it was pissing me off.

"What about that priest y'all went to see? Did he have anythin' that might be worthwhile?"

Megan shrugged. "We haven't heard back from Father Dovensky yet. He did say he'd do some research."

Cantrell waved a couple of gnarled fingers in her direction. "Make the call, girlie. Ah don't wanna be sittin' around waitin' for a holy man to make a discovery."

Megan reached for her phone. Pappy inclined his head toward the door and pushed off my desk. I followed him back to his office. He paused long enough to light a smoke before kicking the door shut behind me.

"Y'all putting any faith in this preacher?"

"I'm not holding my breath that he turns something up, but like you've taught us all, every angle is worth considering."

Cantrell was leaning against the wall, slowly letting the smoke roll from his nostrils and out the window. "Donna Spears been doing any good on her end?"

"She has reviewed each of the three homicide files and has been building a spreadsheet, trying to find some similarities. I've been getting daily updates from her. If there is a connection…"

"…and y'all know there is," Cantrell interjected.

"…then I think she's got a good chance of finding

it. But there's still so much that isn't in the files."

"Like what?"

"None of the three victims' personal items have been recovered. No purses, wallets, cell phones, jewelry, or the clothes they were wearing that day were found at the scenes or in their cars. We've pulled the activity from their cell phone providers, and the cyber units are checking that out today, but so far, we haven't seen anything."

Cantrell gave me a slow, sagely nod. "We'll find it. Y'all can count on it."

"Yeah, but when?"

"Better be soon. I'm fixin' to shake things up, but I ain't got it worked out yet."

I had a sense where Cantrell might go. If he shuffled the teams around, we might notice something, some small insignificant detail that had been overlooked. A fresh set of eyes. I was reluctant to voice the idea, because I definitely didn't agree with it. Sensing he was waiting for me, I told him as much.

"Wouldn't do no good, Chene. Breakin' up the teams would be a whatchacallit, a counter somethin'."

"Counterproductive."

"Exactly." He let a stream of smoke out and wagged a finger at me. "Y'all can work with anyone, even Barksdale, but you get best results with Megan."

There was no argument for that, so I kept my mouth shut.

"And Kozlowski, that giant has taken Laura under his wing. They gotta pretty good rap going."

He meant rapport, but it was pointless to correct him. And he was right. Laura played well off Koz. They were working out to be good partners.

"Maybe Barksdale and Tess are making progress. That's the best chance we've got, that the killer slipped up with the latest homicide."

"Y'all know better than to hol' yer breath on that one. Unless our boy got rushed, chances are he's getting' better. Ah doubt he'll be makin' mistakes."

It was obvious that I wasn't the only one frustrated by the case. "So what are we missing, Pappy?"

"Beats the hell outta me." Cantrell exhaled a final cloud of smoke. For a moment, it left his face shrouded in shadows before it slowly leaked out the window. "It beats the hell outta me."

****

We were back in Dovensky's office in the rectory. No sooner had we taken our seats than one of the staff appeared with a tray laden with steaming mugs of coffee and a heaped platter of baked goods. She was a jolly woman in her fifties, with a full head of bright red hair. A playful smirk crossed her lips as she placed the tray squarely on the center of the priest's desk. She winked at Megan and me before ducking back into the main part of the building. Dovensky gave his head a slow, solemn turn.

"Temptation knows no limits," he said softly.

"Looks like this time it's coming in the form of chocolate-frosted brownies." Megan grabbed one and took a quick bite. She made it disappear in three more bites.

"Did you even taste that?" I was surprised at the way she attacked the food.

"No, so I'd better get another one to make sure it was good."

I leaned back to watch. Dovensky smiled and took

a sip of his coffee. Then he pulled an orange from a basket on his desk and began to peel it with his fingers. He hesitated for a second before flipping another one to me. I caught it in midair and began to peel it as well.

"These are navel oranges from Florida, sent to me by a former member of the parish. They are exceptionally good this time of year."

"It's nice to see that your relationship with the household staff still has some humor to it." Megan licked chocolate frosting from her fingertips.

"Yes, some things never change. Agnes is notorious for her wit." Dovensky had his orange peeled and in sections on his desk blotter. With his foot, he nudged a garbage can around the edge of the desk as he deftly swept the peels into it. He nodded, encouraging me to do the same. I popped a section of orange into my mouth and tossed the peels in the can. He was right. The fruit was delicious. I set my sections on the plate beside my coffee. Megan snagged one as I reached for the cup.

"How does your investigation go?"

"I'd like to say we're making progress, but that may be wishful thinking."

Megan gave him an abbreviated update, merely stating that we had three teams working the cases individually and had yet to determine a common denominator that could lead us to our killer. Dovensky leaned back, slowly rocking in his chair. His coffee and the orange were forgotten.

"So the number has some significance, but you're uncertain as to what," he said slowly. Shifting his weight, he leaned forward until his arms were on the desk. Once again, I had the feeling of déjà vu as he propped that left elbow on the desk and rested his chin on his thumb. "I reviewed the Bible as you requested."

This wasn't my area of expertise, not by a long shot. I still have a Bible, resting on the bottom row of the bookshelf in my place. But an archeologist could probably tell the last time it was opened by the amount of dust it gathered. Dovensky would have guessed as much. I shifted my gaze to Megan.

"Tell me what you learned," she said respectfully.

"I looked at each passage, trying to determine if there was a message that someone might inadvertently take as a direction from the Lord to do harm. While that's not to mean that someone couldn't misinterpret God's words, I was looking for a more direct correlation. There was a good possibility I would find something in the Old Testament. But as I considered each verse, I was unable to find anything that would fit.

"However, I did see two passages that gave me pause. John and Philippians both made me wonder if these weren't directions, but perhaps a confirmation of someone's actions."

Dovensky reached to the credenza behind him and picked up a Bible. He had already tagged the two sections. He cleared his throat and began reading in that strong, authoritative voice I remembered so well.

"Here it is. 'This is the verdict: Light has come into the world, but men loved darkness instead of light because their deeds were evil.' That's from John. This is the verse from Philippians. 'Their destiny is destruction, their god is their stomach, and their glory is in their shame. Their mind is on earthly things.' "

"We know that's not the only references to evil in the Bible," Megan said. "I remember that much."

Dovensky gave a quick smile. "Yes, and I'm sure Jefferson remembers those passages just as well."

"I seem to remember another verse by John that gets a lot of reference." I ignored the jab from the priest.

"You're probably referring to John 3:16. 'For God so loved the world that he gave his one and only Son, that whoever believes in him shall not perish but have eternal life.' That shows up frequently in the crowds at sporting events. Usually, it is just a reference to the chapter and verse."

"That's the one."

We talked about other interpretations of the numbers for a while, but it was apparent that Dovensky had come up empty. Still, it was one of those things that go with any investigation of this magnitude. You just never know when an idea might turn into a solid lead. As we stood to leave, Dovensky handed Megan the platter of brownies. She kissed his cheek and turned for the door. The priest caught my arm.

"Spare me a moment, Jefferson." There was no mischief in his eyes as he spoke.

"Sure thing, Father D." I looked over my shoulder at Megan and handed her my keys. "I'll meet you outside."

The priest leaned back on his desk once she was gone. I hesitated, uncertain whether to reclaim my chair or remain standing. He chuckled and folded his arms across his chest. I stayed on my feet.

"I worry about both of you in such dangerous roles."

"There is danger in many jobs, Father. But we don't take unnecessary risks."

"It's Megan who causes me the most concern. She projects a tough veneer, but I sense that recently she's been having some doubts about her role."

I thought about that for a moment. Were there comments she was making that I hadn't been picking up on? Was the combination of long hours, violence, and desperate criminals taking its toll on her? I asked him directly if she had said anything.

"No, nothing so obvious." He gave his head a negative shake. "But I've seen her interact a few times with some of the parishioners here after Mass. I sense a longing in her presence, something that she may be missing."

"I'll keep an eye on her."

"Do that. And perhaps if you came to Mass with her, you might see what I'm referring to first hand." The fact that he was able to say this while maintaining a straight face convinced me that I would never play poker with Dovensky.

"I'll keep it in mind."

He extended his hand. "Go with God, Jefferson."

"I'll do my best."

Chapter Sixteen

We were both quiet on the way out to the doctor's office in St. Clair Shores. In addition to the case, I was now thinking about Dovensky's comments. Was there something going on with Megan? Were there some personal issues I was oblivious to? If I came right out and asked her, she'd deny any problems or shut me down without comment. I'd have to pay attention. See if I spotted anything in particular. There was always the chance Dovensky was messing with me.

The doctor's office was part of a large modern complex. Megan called yesterday and made an appointment. Despite the crowded waiting room, we were escorted immediately into an office down the hall from the examination rooms. There was the usual amount of office clutter, with a stack of medical journals perched precariously on the desk. But unlike some sterile conference rooms and offices I've seen, this one was crammed with photographs. I thought these were family photos. Megan corrected me.

"It looks like Dr. Harwood works at a lot of clinics."

I took a closer look. Dr. Harwood was in the center of each shot, wearing some form of brightly colored surgical scrubs. Alongside him was a pretty woman with dark hair in a similar outfit. Grouped around them were clusters of kids. There was a banner in each photo, showing the name of the clinic, the location, and the date. As I was moving along the wall, the door swung open, and Harwood stepped quickly into the room. He was about five foot six with a solid build. His hair was receding and moving from black to gray in the process. He wore a trim goatee that was showing more gray than black.

"I'm Jim Harwood. Sorry to keep you waiting." He shook hands with a firm grip and pointed us to a pair of visitor chairs.

"Not a problem, Dr. Harwood. We appreciate you taking the time to meet with us," Megan said with a charming lilt to her voice.

"We were admiring your photo gallery." I hooked a thumb over my shoulder.

He flashed a genuine smile. "That's my wife, Valerie. She's a registered nurse. We started out working at a free clinic one day a week about twenty years ago. Then we got into the Doctors Without Borders program. Usually two weeks a year, we'll go somewhere on assignment. Some locations can be exhausting, but it's rewarding work."

"You know why we're here."

Harwood rested his forearms on the desk and lightly tapped his fingertips together. "Stephanie Grange. It's such a terrible situation. I did speak with a couple of other detectives shortly after her demise."

Megan explained our involvement with the case. "But we've learned more about Stephanie's health during our investigation. We have some other questions we're hoping you'd answer."

"I'm sure you're both well versed in doctor-patient confidentiality. But her mother did call and asked me to give you my full cooperation. Stephanie was my patient for many years. It's a little uncomfortable discussing her medical history with you."

Megan threw me a wink. She'd contacted Evelyn Grange before making this appointment and persuaded her to call Harwood.

"Whatever information you can share may be vital to helping us find her killer," I said. "Do you need to review her file?"

Harwood gave his head a brief shake. "I did that last night, after her mother called. There wasn't a great deal of information there."

"How often did you see her?" Megan had her recorder going. She was taking the lead on the interview.

"She got a physical exam every two years. Otherwise, it was a couple of sprains and some sinus infections. She did go through a bout of urinary tract problems for a few years, but those were always cleaned up with antibiotics. The same held true with the sinus infections." He tapped his fingertips together, keeping a quiet rhythm.

"Do you know when she became sexually active?"

Now he reached for the file. A quick glance and he snapped it shut. "It looks like she was sixteen when I became aware of it. I noticed some bruising on her hips when she came in for the urinary problems. Apparently, she had been experimenting with a boyfriend. But by then she was going to an OB-GYN. I remember her mother asking for a recommendation. She wanted to get her on birth control pills."

"When was the last time you saw her?"

"It was about a year ago. She had an upper

respiratory infection. It was a very routine appointment."

"Do you remember anything unusual about Stephanie?"

Harwood laced his fingers together and leaned forward. "What's unusual?"

"You tell us."

"This is a busy office. We've grown over the years. There are six doctors on staff and a full complement of nurses, physician assistants, and support people. Of the six doctors, only two are men." He hesitated. "Stephanie had an issue with women."

"What kind of issue?" I realized Harwood was looking at me.

"She was…uncomfortable around other women. If one of the nurses or female doctors came in to examine her, she'd get upset. She always wanted a male doctor to be the one to treat her. She wouldn't undress for an examination with just a woman in the room. Although when I came in, there was always a nurse present."

"What did you make of that?" Megan redirected his attention.

He shrugged. "I chalked it up to her family situation. Her father was always the one who brought her in for appointments. And until she was eighteen, he was the one in the room with her."

"Was there anything unusual about her physically?" I caught Megan's eye. "Beyond the bouts of infections you mentioned."

There was a quick glance at the file. "Stephanie was like many young women we treat. I thought she was a victim of the stereotyping you see with body types. She was terrified that people would think she was fat, so she struggled with her weight. Not that it was really an issue, but the perception of it bothered her. I expressed my concerns to her father on several occasions."

"What was his reaction?" Megan leaned forward.

"He said he would keep an eye on her. He reminded me that her mother was a very similar body type and that chances were she had the same genes."

"Did you ever mention this to Mrs. Grange?"

"No, I can't recall the last time I saw her. As I said, her father brought Stephanie in until she was an adult. Then she made her own appointments."

Megan asked for the name of the OB-GYN that Harwood had referred Stephanie to. Her mother did not have that information. When we had searched Stephanie's apartment, the only prescriptions we had found were from Harwood. There had been no details on the birth control pills. We thanked Harwood for his time. Megan gave him a card and asked him to call if he remembered anything else. As we were about to leave, there was a knock at the door and a nurse poked her head in. I recognized Valerie Harwood from the photos. He quickly introduced us.

Valerie moved to stand beside her husband. She was a petite woman with a ready smile and lively green eyes. I watched her smoothly place a hand on Harwood's arm. "Did you remember to tell them about the call?"

"What call?"

Harwood was shaking his head. "I forgot all about it. There was no office visit, so there was nothing on her chart or in her files."

"It was late one day," Valerie explained. "We had

just closed the office, and most of the staff was gone. Jim and I were updating files. It's so much easier to do here than to haul everything home." She hesitated, looking to her husband for guidance. He gave her an encouraging nod.

"Stephanie called. I answered, and she asked to speak with Jim. She sounded very nervous. Excited. It was as if she was having a hard time catching her breath. I put her on hold and told Jim who it was."

"I had my hands full with files and dictations, so I punched up the call on the speaker phone. There was just the two of us here. Stephanie wanted to know if people who suffered from anorexia had difficulty getting pregnant. I explained that many women with anorexia have more trouble eating enough food to sustain a baby. She then asked what I thought was a very bizarre question."

"What was that?" I asked.

"If she stopped having sex with men, could she still be able to become pregnant someday with a female lover."

****

My head was spinning. We were in the parking lot of Dr. Harwood's office. Megan was calling the OB-GYN to get an appointment. The office was in Mt. Clemens, another suburb further north. From her side of the conversation, I could tell Megan was getting the runaround. Disgusted, she disconnected the call and smashed her fist on the dashboard. I could easily relate to those feelings.

"The doctor doesn't have time to see us today."

"Want to bet?"

"This is a lead we can't ignore. As Pappy would

say, 'fuck me hard.' "

"Let's see if the gynecologist has the same reaction."

It was almost noon by the time we got there. This was another modern commercial building with lots of medical offices. Megan wasted no time marching into the building and finding the right suite. I followed. We don't normally do the good cop, bad cop routine, but something told me I was about to witness bad cop. Maybe we could do bad cop, worse cop.

The waiting room had a half dozen women sprawled in uncomfortable chairs. Three of them were obviously pregnant. They were gazing vacantly at a talk show. Several other women were impatiently flipping through magazines. No one paid much attention to Megan as she approached the receptionist. But I got several confused stares. Guess they don't get many men in this office. I leaned against the reception counter.

"State police, detectives Chene and McDonald. We need to see Doctor Walker right away." Megan showed her badge to the woman behind the counter. On the way in, she had unzipped her coat. Now she put her left hand on her hip so that the coat flapped open, revealing the handle of her gun in the shoulder holster. It rarely fails to get someone's attention.

"Doctor Walker is with a patient, and there are several people waiting." The receptionist was short and stocky with the demeanor that she considered herself to be the guardian of the gate, a job she took seriously.

Megan shifted her gaze to me for a moment, then gave the receptionist her full attention. She leaned across the counter and curled a finger at the woman as if they were about to conspire on a big secret. The receptionist inched forward.

"Here's the deal. You get us in to see Dr. Walker right now, and I won't have to file charges against you and the good doctor for obstruction of justice, interfering with an ongoing police investigation, and accessory to murder. And the good sergeant here won't make that phone call to his close personal friend who is an investigative reporter at Channel Four. I don't think that kind of publicity would be good for business, do you?"

The woman's mouth dropped open. I pulled my phone from my pocket and started scrolling through my contacts. From the corner of my eye, I saw the receptionist bolt from her chair and waddle quickly down the hall. She was back in less than a minute.

"Dr. Walker will spare you five minutes in his conference room. He has a very busy schedule today."

"We can appreciate that." Megan's response was filled with sweetness.

The receptionist escorted us quickly into the conference room. Neither one of us took a chair. Megan was studying the various degrees displayed on the wall. In less than two minutes, the door swung open, and the doctor walked in. He was close to six feet tall, with wavy black hair and chiseled features. I imagined his bedside manner was that of a calm, kindly doctor. But there was anger in his dark eyes as he clicked the door shut behind him. He was wearing a lab coat over a heavily starched white shirt with a blue and red rep tie. He made no effort to shake hands.

"I'm Matthias Walker. What's the meaning of this?"

Megan kicked a chair in his direction. "Have a seat,

Doc."

"I prefer to stand. I have patients waiting."

"Suit yourself. We're investigating the murder of Stephanie Grange. It has come to our attention that you were her gynecologist."

"Stephanie was murdered?" The surprise was evident on his face.

"Yes, over a month ago. You didn't know?"

He shook his head. "I rarely watch the news. And I can't tell you the last time I read a paper. This office handles a large number of patients. Unless there was a problem that required frequent attention, I wouldn't have been aware of Stephanie's absence."

"Can you look at her records?"

He kept his eyes on Megan. "I'm not at liberty to discuss my patients."

"Not even if you have information that might help us track down her killer?"

"I am restricted by law. Unless you have a court order, I can't reveal those confidential records." Walker's voice had taken on an authoritative edge, as if he were instructing a group of underlings.

I could sense Megan was about to lay into this guy, so I took a step forward. "Let's try a different tack. Why don't you review her records and tell us if there was anything unusual?"

He took a moment to consider it. Then he walked to a phone in the center of the conference table, dialed an internal extension, and asked for her chart. We waited silently until the receptionist brought it to the door. Walker examined it quickly. I watched him slide a finger down the center of each page, making small checks as he studied her information. At length, he set the file on the table, taking care to turn it upside down in case the cover bore any confidential information.

"There's really nothing I can tell you," he said, although his tone was quieter now, more subdued than before.

Megan jumped back in. "Let's try it this way, Doctor. There are some facts that we have. If we share those with you and we're correct, you just nod once. If we're wrong, you shake your head. That way, you're not violating anything."

"I suppose there's no harm in just confirming what you already know."

She glanced at me quickly. I nodded in agreement. "Stephanie was sexually active early, like maybe twelve or thirteen."

His eyes widened in surprise, but he held still. Megan watched him closely, but he gave no other clue.

"She wasn't a virgin when she first became a patient of yours."

Walker confirmed this with a nod.

"You treated her for urinary tract infections, and you saw evidence of rough sex."

He gave her another nod.

"Recently, she began to ask some unusual questions about different methods of pregnancy."

Walker didn't respond. But he pulled out a chair and collapsed into it. Slowly, he began to run his fingertips across the edge of her file. Megan sat down across from him. I perched a hip on the table. It was a time when silence was the best approach. When he was ready, Matthias Walker started talking.

"Stephanie Grange was a very confused young woman. She was about sixteen years old when she became a patient here. The first visit, her father brought her for the appointment, but Stephanie did not want him in the examination room. It's unusual that a man would be present anyway, so I really didn't think much about it at the time. During the examination, it was evident that she had been experiencing frequent sexual activity. She expressed her concerns about pregnancy. She wanted to know the options. We talked about different methods of contraception, including birth control pills, using an IUD, and condoms. Stephanie gave me the impression that abstinence was not a possibility.

"I was concerned about her attitude, but otherwise she was perfectly healthy. At one point, I thought it might do her good to talk with a therapist. When I suggested it, she became very defensive. I gave her the card of a psychologist. She took it, but I don't know if she ever made contact."

"When was her last appointment?" Megan's tone was cordial now.

"Six months ago. But she called once in late January or early February. She had questions about artificial insemination. Which I thought was very odd. Since most of her conversations with me in the past focused on methods of birth control."

"Anything else you can share with us?"

Walker slowly shook his head. "She was a troubled young woman, but I never expected her to die so young."

"Nobody does," Megan said.

Chapter Seventeen

Megan and I were on the way back from interviewing Dr. Walker. From all the indications both doctors had, she should have lived a long and healthy life. That was until the killer stepped in.

Megan was driving. She'd been pestering me for weeks now to ride in the Mustang. I am a lousy passenger. I admit it. She knows it. Koz knows it. Cantrell knows it. Hell, everybody knows it. I prefer to drive. It's just that simple. Megan insists it's a control issue. I think she's full of crap. So today after we had talked with Dovensky at the rectory, I relented and let her drive. We had to go right past the post anyway for our meeting with Harwood. Now she was zipping through traffic, swerving between cars like some NASCAR wannabe.

"You almost hit that van." I pressed myself away from the dash and adjusted the seat belt.

"I saw him. And I had inches to spare."

"I notice you don't cut it so close with your side of the car."

"Chene, you are such an old woman. I have never had a ticket."

I grunted in mock disgust. "That is probably the result of professional courtesy. Most cops let fellow cops slide."

The light up ahead on Metropolitan Parkway

flashed yellow. Just to shut me up, Megan tapped the brake, rolling to a stop.

"Happy now?"

"I'll be happy when I make it back to the post in one piece. The way you drive, this car should come with passenger warning labels and a crash helmet. I'm surprised your attorney doesn't make anyone crazy enough to ride with you sign a waiver." I tried to keep my expression serious, but it was a struggle.

In a show of her maturity, Megan waited until I turned to face her before sticking her tongue out at me. As the light changed, she nailed it, goosing the Mustang to sixty in a flash. We didn't talk the rest of the way back, each turning our thoughts back to the investigation. She managed not to squeal the tires as she pulled into the lot. As we got out of the car, she pointed to a purple Corvette that was being towed into the impound lot next door.

"That will be my next baby. Then I'll have to get some personalized plates to go with it."

I stopped in mid-stride and swung around in front of her, blocking her path.

"What?" Megan's eyes went wide.

"Say that again."

She leaned back and thought for a moment. "That will be my next baby. Then I'll have to get some personalized plates to go with it."

I couldn't stop the grin from spreading across my face.

"Chene, you're acting crazy. What are you thinking?"

"He's telling us who he is. It's the license plate."

For years now, Michigan has a number of options

when it comes to license plates. In addition to the standard white with blue numbers and letters, there are scenic ones, plates that support a number of charities and universities, vanity plates, commemorative plates, and more. The standard plates are comprised of six characters, usually three letters and three numbers.

Megan made it to the dispatcher's desk first and had the duty officer run the message WHY 319. I remained in the parking lot for a moment, watching the Corvette disappear into the impound yard before joining her.

"Chene, you may be onto something." She flashed an excited grin.

"Let's hope so."

We waited impatiently for the response from the duty officer. He rattled off the details from the computer screen about whom the license plate was registered to. I pointed at the printer, and he nodded. Seconds later, the copy was extended over the counter. I grabbed it before Megan could even get close.

"Do you want to call the squad together right away?" We were back in ahead of schedule, planning on reviewing the autopsy reports.

"Let's dig a little deeper first. I'll brief Cantrell."

Without waiting for any instructions, Megan went to work, pulling the background information from the computer. She started with the name the plate was registered to and went forward from there. Then she would check criminal background for prior convictions or pending cases, employment history, credit history, and motor vehicle records. And that was just the tip of the iceberg.

I poked my head in Cantrell's office. He was on the

phone. I could only hear his side of the conversation, but his answers were terse. Pappy rarely elaborated. He motioned toward his visitor's chair. I closed my eyes and tried to put the pieces together. I guessed Cantrell was on the line with someone high up, maybe from the governor's office. It took him another five minutes to complete his conversation. At last, he racked the phone, firmly snapping it back in the cradle. I recalled seeing him hammer the receiver into plastic fragments when he'd been dealing with a difficult judge three years ago. Either he was calmer today, or he did a better job managing his anger.

"Whatcha got?"

"I think we finally caught a break."

I showed Cantrell the copy of the printout from the motor vehicle records and explained what Megan was working on. He waited until I was done, then pulled a pad from a stack of files on his desk.

"Y'all remember the date of the Wayne County homicide?"

"January eighteenth."

"And Macomb County was?"

"February seventeenth."

"And the last one was when?"

"March sixteenth. At least, those were the dates based on the coroner's report as to the time of death. What are you getting at, Pappy?"

"All three was a month apart. All adds up to nineteen. Found in the same room number in different cities, different counties, within our territory. Y'all shoulda been playin' those numbers on the lottery, Chene."

"We've been over this, time and again. Even to the

extent of doing research on numerology to see if that would give us any clue." I slumped lower in the chair and propped my feet on the edge of his desk. Only Kozlowski and I were able to get away with it.

"So where y'all go from here?"

"I want to keep the other two investigations going. Let Barksdale and Kozlowski continue digging. Megan and I will pull every detail we can find on this guy and see if we can make any connections."

Cantrell waved a crooked finger at me. "Y'all gonna tell the others about this lead. Bring them up to speed at the caucus session."

"Sure. But I don't want to jump the gun. I want to make sure this adds up before we go running."

He glanced down at the legal pad he'd been doodling on. With a flick of his wrist, he tossed it to me. "All adds up to nineteen, Chene, one of them prime numbers. This boy's in his prime. And he's countin' 'em down. If you don't catch him, he's gonna strike again, on April 15. And the tax man ain't the only one gonna be wantin' his due."

We had this case less than a week. In three weeks, the killer would act again, unless we stopped him first. But we had no guarantee that he would stick to his timetable. If he sensed we were onto him, was there anything stopping him from killing another girl?

****

Cantrell had the uncanny ability of cutting through the details and getting right to the heart of the matter. Megan and I spent our time compiling everything we could find on our suspect. When the others arrived for the briefing, Cantrell settled into his usual seat and thumped a fist on the table.

"Before y'all give the updates, Chene and McDonald may have come up with sumthin' worthwhile." He jerked his head at Megan and she handed out copies of what we were able to accumulate in the last couple of hours.

"Here's what we think. We've all believed the message on the mirror was his signature, or something to identify him by. Chene and I think it's his license number. Plate number WHY 319 is registered to Charles Alan Myers. He lives in Eastpointe. He has a record for criminal sexual conduct. Myers did eighteen months in a minimum security facility. He was also brought up on charges for date rape about a year ago, but he was acquitted. You can read the rest."

There was silence as the group scanned the contents of the folders. We had found a few details, but there remained mountains of information that we didn't know. Barksdale closed his folder and slapped his hand on top of it. Then he began anxiously drumming his fingers on the edge of the table while the others finished reading. It was obvious that he had merely skimmed the pages. Cantrell waited until everyone else had read the file.

"What's your plan, Chene?"

"I'd like to put Myers under surveillance, while Megan and I check him out more thoroughly. We need to know everything we can. Where he works, what his connections with the victims were, what his motive is."

Barksdale jumped right in. "Guy's a pervert. He already did time. Maybe he took his kinks to a new level, has to snuff them before he really gets off. I say we go pick his degenerate ass up right now and see if we can rattle him."

"No." Cantrell didn't offer anything else, just the one word. But the look on his face was enough to prove he was serious.

"If we act rashly, we may not have an opportunity to prove our case," Megan said. "If we have to cut him loose, we could lose him for good."

"Y'all stick with your assignments." Cantrell waved his hands at Kozlowski, Laura, Tess, and Barksdale. "Chene and McDonald will see what they can dig up. If we git enough to go for a warrant, then y'all be brought in. Meanwhile, keep diggin'. We still need to find a connector between Myers and these poor girls."

"I still think we should go bust his ass," Barksdale retorted.

I started to respond, but Pappy cut me off.

"When you're in charge of the unit, Barksdale, y'all can make that call. Until then, it's up to me. And ah already told ya how we're gonna handle it."

A trace of red was visible on Barksdale's cheeks. Twice, he started to respond but thought better of it. Cantrell may give the impression of an easygoing country boy, but he was no one to mess with. Barksdale knew it, but that didn't mean he liked it.

Cantrell approved the use of two troopers for surveillance. He would call the post near Eastpointe and have them cover Myers's residence. They were to observe only and not make contact. They would notify Cantrell when he was in sight and report any movements that occurred. They would also follow him but not approach him. Pappy listened to the other teams give their daily summaries on the individual cases, then reminded them to update the log. The meeting broke up without any further comment on Myers.

He gestured for the others to leave. Megan shifted in her chair, anxious to get back to researching whatever she could find on Myers.

"Before y'all go runnin' off like John Wayne, let's get sumthin straight," Cantrell said when the door closed. "This may be the break we've been looking for, but I don't wanna forget the basics. Y'all better hogtie this up nice and neat afore I go for a warrant."

There's an old quote from a famous author. I think it was Burns who said something like "the best laid plans of mice and men often go awry," or words to that effect. No matter how much planning goes into something, we often overlook a detail, or a player. Or a contingency that is one of those million-to-one shots. Like picking exactly the right numbers in the lottery and having the only winning ticket. Of course, there's the old Yiddish expression: "Man plans and God laughs." The irony that Cantrell was the one who'd shared it with me didn't escape me at the moment.

We began to dig deep on Myers. Megan had everything we could hope for. Criminal records, including the court files on both his conviction and the acquittal for the date-rape charge. We had his employment history, tax returns, and credit information. We had plenty of background.

"The date-rape charge could be a clincher," Megan offered. "If he stepped up the game by using GHB, to get them where they couldn't resist him, there would be nothing that could keep him from having his way with our victims."

"But we still don't know how he connects to the girls. We haven't been able to identify any type of common denominator yet."

Megan gave her head a shake, which caused her shoulder-length hair to dance back and forth. She did that often when she was tired or confused. This time it was a combination of the two.

"And that bothers me, Chene. It would be helpful if we could find something where their paths all interconnected. But we've got absolutely nothing there."

We were sitting in the bullpen. Everyone else was gone for the night, focusing on their own investigations. I turned to look at the three photos pinned to the wall. Megan had downloaded sections of area maps and put them beneath the pictures. We had pinpointed where each victim lived, where they worked, where their families were and anything else we could think of. Each one was in their own little orbit. And absolutely nothing intersected.

"Chene, I'm hitting the wall here. What do you say we call it a night?"

"Has there been any movement on Myers?"

She gave her head a slow shake. "The guys on his place are checking in every hour. He came home from work and hasn't left since. Lights are on, and he's visible from the street."

"Go home, or wherever you were going. We'll start again in the morning."

Megan made a show of locking up her desk, pulling her coat on, and fluttering her lashes at me. "Don't stay here all night, Chene. Maybe you need to visit whoever you saw last night and pick up where you left off."

"Good night, McDonald."

She headed out the door. While the idea of another evening with Simone was appealing, I was reluctant to rush into anything. Instead, I checked the address we had on Myers and drove by, just to get a closer look at our suspect.

Chapter Eighteen

Thursday morning, Megan and I got right back to the files. With the other teams still pursuing their investigations, I wanted to gather as much information as possible for the briefing today. But before I got too deep, I made it a point to log all of our details from yesterday's conversations into the system. While Megan began her research, I reviewed the notes from the others and checked on the progress from Donna Spears.

"Don't forget to read the autopsy report on Artie," Megan mumbled.

"I thought you were going to do that."

"That was before we tripped to Myers. I don't want to lose my train of thought here. And I'm having a hell of a time finding any kind of connection."

"It's got to be there. We need to find out where he spends his free time."

She raised her eyes from the computer screen and shot me a steely gaze. "Free time? That sounds vaguely familiar. So did you go get horizontal last night?"

"Focus on your research."

"I'll tell you mine if you tell me yours."

I knew she would persist until I gave her something. "I drove by Myers house, just to get a look at him. Then I went to Sharkey's for some pasta and scintillating conversation with Ted. That was it. And you don't have to share your evening's activities. I'll use my imagination."

Megan threw a pen at me. I saw it coming and snagged it in midair. "For your information, I stopped by Kathy's house for a quick visit."

I remembered Kathy. She was her cousin, a year younger than Megan, married a couple of years ago, and with a new baby. Megan confirmed everyone was well. It made me wonder if the newborn had triggered some longings in Megan at her own chances for motherhood and a family. I pushed that aside and focused on work.

Unearthing the autopsy report, I slowly read through it. I noticed there were no bruises that would indicate a struggle. There had been no trace elements on the body, such as saliva or oils you might normally find with fingerprints. Had her killer been wearing gloves? There was nothing that stood out. The coroner determined that she had been smothered with one of the hotel pillows. The pillowcase had smears of Stephanie's lipstick and some saliva that was matched to her. I looked up the toxicology report and punched in the number for Rudy Fen.

"Hello, Chene. Do you have another victim?"

"No, I just have some questions for you. I'm reviewing the toxicology report on the Grange girl. Do you have a copy?"

In the background, I could hear his keyboard clicking. "Here you go. What are you looking for?"

"Was there anything in her system that you wouldn't expect?"

Fen was silent for a moment. "There were some antibiotics, but it looks like a very low dose. Then the amount of alcohol in her system was quite high. For a woman of her build, unless she was a very heavy drinker, it would have been enough to disorient her. The GHB or date-rape drug was evident as well. She would have no control over her own actions during that time."

"So she had no chance to fight back."

"I doubt she could have pushed the pillow off her face even if someone wasn't holding it down." Fen was thoughtful for a moment. "What are you suggesting, Chene?"

"I'm wondering why she wasn't on birth control pills. Do you see any other forms of contraception?"

I waited while he checked the reports again. Since he knew exactly what he was looking for, it didn't take him long.

"There is no indication of any type of birth control being used. No pills, no long-term patch, no intrauterine device. She could have used a diaphragm, and the killer may have taken that when cleansing her body."

"You know a lot of twenty-something girls who use that method?"

"Hey, if the sex is infrequent, it's a possibility. How does this fit in with your case? She wasn't a virgin. Are you thinking she wasn't promiscuous?"

"I don't know what to think. I'm just trying to get as much information as I can."

"She could have used a spermicidal foam. Maybe that and a sponge were her methods of choice. But again, there are no traces of that in the report."

I considered everything for a moment. "Is it possible the coroner missed something during the exam?"

"Anything is possible, Chene. But I know Tyler Adams, the guy who did this work, and he's good. He does a thorough job. You'll have to accept what you've got."

"Yeah, there isn't enough here to make me want to exhume the body."

Fen quietly cleared his throat. "The body's gone, Chene. Her parents had her cremated when she was released."

****

We spent the day digging. It still amazed me how much information you can get on someone from the internet. Cantrell called in a favor or two and even got us a credit report on Myers that included copies of his credit card purchases for the last six months. Megan analyzed everything. When she was done, I read it over as well.

Myers had left his home about 7:45 this morning and driven directly to work. He was employed at one of those quick-oil-change places. When he got there, he grabbed coffee and donuts from the place next door and had not left work since. Cantrell had kept one trooper stationed across the street to observe. There was nothing suspicious to report.

I pushed away from my desk and walked outside. The weather was gray and overcast, with a strong wind whipping from the northwest. Not even the hardiest of smokers were out in this weather. After a minute to clear my head, I went back inside.

Rather than return to my computer, I sat on the edge of the desk and stared at the pictures of our three victims and the map segments beneath each one. They were so far apart, the only commonality I could find was that they all resided in Michigan. Megan appeared at my side with two fresh cups of coffee.

"This is driving me crazy. There should be something obvious these girls had in common with our suspect," she said quietly. "But I'll be damned if I can find it."

"I know. It's not like they knew each other. They didn't go to the same school, use the same doctors, were members of a sorority, or lived in the same neighborhood. They were all homebodies. Not your typical party girls."

"So what are we missing, Chene?"

"If we knew what it was, it wouldn't be missing."

When I had spoken earlier with Donna Spears, I'd learned that she had finished with her second pass on the Grange file and was starting on the Janet Calder case. Donna had not been able to spot any connections either. As requested, she was taking her time, slowly reviewing each report. She assured me that she was making thorough notes. I relayed that information to Megan now.

"Does any of our victims have a bestie?"

"A what?"

"A bestie. A best friend. They are the kind of friends who have each other's backs. They look out for each other and spend a great deal of time together."

I shook my head. "I don't see where any of them were that close to one particular person. Are you thinking they all had a common friend?"

"I'm not sure. All I know is Cantrell won't let us spend too much time on Myers before we approach him. I just wish we could find that connection."

****

Pappy Cantrell decided Friday it was time to move. Myers lived in a small house in Eastpointe, just north of Nine Mile Road. Two miles south and we would have been dealing with the city of Detroit and all the complications that went with it. We had enough information accumulated to get a search warrant from a judge in Mt. Clemens who was tight with Cantrell. That he was even civil with a judge was a rarity, but Pappy is always full of surprises. We pulled the team together and reviewed the details.

Myers's house was on a small lot in the middle of the block. There was a detached garage, big enough for one vehicle, on a street with a lot of old bungalows and ranch houses that had flourished right after World War II. Myers lived alone. We requested the warrant to cover the house, garage, and his place of employment. I made sure his Jeep was included.

It was almost five o'clock in the afternoon. We were gathered around the conference table, anxiously waiting for Cantrell. It wasn't a long wait. He came in five minutes after we'd gotten settled and sailed a thick envelope to Megan, who occupied her usual chair beside him.

"Y'all got yer warrants." He jerked his head in my direction. "Call it, Chene."

"He's at work but due to leave anytime. We've got the two plainclothes troopers on him now. Let's head for his house."

Earlier, Cantrell and I had discussed options. At one point, I thought about sending one team to the shop where he worked, to search the premises and his locker. If I chose Barksdale, I'd never hear the end of the bitching that would follow. I wanted Kozlowski with

175

me at the scene. Koz has great instincts and even greater powers of observation. Chances are the house was where we'd find something to tie Myers to the killings. Cantrell talked about sending Tess and Laura to the shop, but decided to keep the teams intact.

We took three cars. From the post, it was a twenty-minute ride to Myers's place in Eastpointe. I could still feel the thrum of rush-hour traffic as we pulled off Gratiot onto one of the many side streets. Megan's phone buzzed five minutes before. Myers had left work on schedule. We cruised by slowly and got our first good look at his house in the fading afternoon light. As I drove by, I saw Myers closing the garage door and turn for the house.

It was a small brick ranch. The front door was on the left side, with a large picture window taking up most of the front wall. There was about a four-foot square of cement that made up the stoop, with three steps rising up from the walk. A narrow cement driveway ran from the street past the house to a small wooden garage at the back of the lot. There were a few shrubs in the front, little evergreen bushes that were getting ready for spring. The yard was several shades of brown, with patches of old grass and mud puddles. The wood trim on the house was in dire need of scraping and painting.

We parked two doors down the block. The group circled around for instructions. There was no disguising who we were. Each person was wearing a bullet-proof vest and a dark blue nylon jacket emblazoned with the word police in bright yellow foot-high letters. There was no mistaking us for the welcome wagon or the Avon lady.

"Koz, you and Laura take the garage. Barksdale and Tess, take the rear entrance. Megan and I will go in the front door. Keep it quiet, and let's hope we get some good luck."

"Christ knows we're overdue," Barksdale muttered.

Megan and I stayed back for a minute, letting the other two teams move up the driveway. Kozlowski stepped onto the grass beside the garage and was peering through a cloudy window. Barksdale was standing at the back door. Megan took the three steps from the walk up to the stoop in an easy stride. I was right behind her as she rapped on the door. My eyes flicked to the window at the front of the house. I saw movement seconds before the glass exploded in every direction.

It was reflex, plain and simple. My mind must have registered the movement an instant before the window disintegrated. I don't remember doing it, but I wrapped an arm around Megan's waist and dove to the left, pulling her off the stoop. My shoulders hit the driveway. Her head snapped back, catching me on the chin. The back of my head kissed the pavement, and I saw stars. She slid off me and banged her head on the driveway.

She rolled left, aiming her weapon and rising to her feet in one smooth motion. Movement in the street caught my attention. One of the troopers who had been on the surveillance assignment had moved to the sidewalk, directly in front of the picture window, to back us up. I saw his legs go out from under him, and he clutched at his thigh. His partner rushed over, used a parked car as a shield, and dragged him back. In the distance, I could hear sirens. Somebody must have called it in. This whole thing made no sense. We had a warrant to search the place, and we were going to bring him in for questioning. What triggered this attack? I swung my gaze back from the street.

"What the fuck?" Megan's face was filled with rage.

Before I could respond, we heard gunfire coming from the rear of the house. Myers must have company, or he'd been waiting for us.

"Front door?" Megan hooked a thumb at the stoop.

"Damn right."

We jumped back to the porch. I glanced through what remained of the window and didn't see any movement. Rearing back, I slammed my foot beside the cheap doorknob. The door burst open. Megan hesitated, making sure the door wouldn't swing back into her, and that no one was standing in wait. She went through the opening fast. I was right behind her.

We checked the front room and moved down the hall. The other two teams were covering the rear of the house. There was no way Myers could escape. We stopped in the hallway beside the kitchen. Myers was swinging back and forth, firing shots from a big automatic out the rear window toward the garage, alternating with shots at the rear door.

"Police! Drop your weapon!" Megan pressed her back against the wall, anticipating gunfire.

Myers turned slightly. "Kiss my ass! I'm not going back to prison. There's no way I'll survive."

Myers looked like a wild man. His lank brown hair was in his face, but his eyes penetrated. I didn't have time to debate right or wrong. He brought his gun around and aimed it at the spot on the wall where Megan was. Maybe whatever ammo he had could punch through plaster. I didn't wait to find out. His chest was in my sights. I squeezed the trigger and pumped two rounds at him. Yet as I was firing, he was hit from behind in the back of the head. Blood erupted from his body like a geyser as Myers dropped to the kitchen floor.

Chapter Nineteen

The sirens grew closer. With my heart still hammering in my chest, I glanced at Megan. She had a nasty cut above one eyebrow that looked pretty deep. It was bleeding steadily. When I reached for her, she slapped my hand away. I called the others from the wireless communications device clipped to my right ear.

"He's down. Hold your fire."

"Chene, you'd better get out here," Koz called back.

I moved into the kitchen, kicking the gun away from Myers's outstretched hand. Reaching down, I pressed two fingers against the carotid artery. There was no pulse. Megan stepped up beside me, carefully avoiding the pools of blood around Myers. There was glass everywhere, crunching under my feet as I moved toward the back wall. Where there used to be a door was now a gaping hole. Bits of brick, wood, and glass covered the narrow driveway. Kozlowski was squatting down on his haunches, his gun dangling from his fingertips. Laura had her arm around Tess Jarrett. Tess sat on the pavement, her left arm at a peculiar angle. Barksdale was on his back. He wasn't moving.

Megan and I picked our way through the debris. We stopped in front of the others.

"Guy must have freaked when he saw us. He had

the rear door wired, maybe with a grenade or some homemade bomb. Barksdale took a chunk right in the throat. He's dead." Koz stared up at me. "Blast drove him all the way back here. He knocked Tess back. She was tossed around like a rag doll."

"You make that head shot?" I asked.

"Nuh-uh. I was trying to save Barksdale. Laura took him out."

"That was a hell of a shot."

Kozlowski straightened up to his full height. "That's why she's on my team."

****

I called Pappy Cantrell and took charge of the crime scene. Megan contacted Rudy Fen and requested the full services of his forensic team. We secured the perimeter quickly. Several squad cars from Eastpointe arrived and rapidly barricaded the street. Two ambulances were there in a heartbeat. The paramedics taped up Megan's forehead, telling her she needed stitches. She gruffly suggested where they could put their needles. Tess had a dislocated shoulder and a broken arm. They gingerly put her in the ambulance and took her to St. John's Hospital. Laura went with her.

Cantrell arrived as the ambulance was pulling away. Koz was wiping the blood off his hands as we stood over Barksdale's body.

"Fuck me hard. This here looks like a goddamn war zone."

"This makes no sense at all," Megan said.

We moved aside so the forensic team could do their work. The four of us were standing on the muddy patch of lawn between the rear of the house and the garage.

"There is something very strange about this whole place," Koz stated. "I went to the side door of the garage and looked through the window. I could see his Jeep inside. There's a hasp and a padlock on both the pedestrian door and the overhead garage door. There's no power door opener. We'd need keys or a pry bar to get inside here."

We told Pappy about the exploding rear door and the way the front window disintegrated before Myers started shooting. He listened quietly, his eyes flicking across each of us.

"When does a serial sex killer start usin' bombs?"

Megan shook her head once, then winced in pain. "Like I said, it doesn't make any sense."

"Whaddya think, Chene?" Cantrell was solemnly staring at me.

"Call in Squad Five. Let the bomb freaks run through this place. If he had the front and back wired, he could have the whole place booby-trapped. And we'll want our guys to do it before the ATF crew shows up."

Cantrell nodded. "Who's got the warrant for his job? I want them bomber guys to check that out. Sumbitch might have rigged sumthin there too."

Megan had the warrants. She stuck out her hand for my keys. "I'll meet them there. Make it ten minutes."

"Done," Pappy agreed. Then he reached over and caught her by the arm. "I'm glad y'all right, girlie. But after the bombers check it out, y'all get to the hospital and let them patch you up."

"I'm fine, Pappy."

His hand slid up her arm, and he cupped her chin in

his gnarled hand. "Y'all still bleeding, darlin', and I don't like the look of yer eyes. Do the search, and get yer ass to the hospital. That's an order."

She hesitated, then let out a slow sigh. "Okay, Pappy. I'll go to St. John's. That's where they took Tess."

We watched her walk to the car and drive away. Cantrell turned back to survey the crime scene once more.

"Fuck me hard," he muttered again.

****

Cantrell wasted no time getting Squad Five on the road. A guy named Naughton led the team of four weapons freaks. Naughton learned his craft in the military and swore he could make a bomb out of five items found in most bathrooms. One of these days, I was going to have him prove it, but not today.

Naughton arrived with two of his crew. Ten years out of the military and he still favored the brush-cut hairstyle. The odd part was that nowadays, it was almost in fashion. He was built like a bowling ball, short stout legs and arms that didn't seem to match the rotund body. He wasted no time getting ready.

"I sent the other two to check out where this guy worked. From what you described, we need to go slowly through this place. He may well have it wired beyond the points you already witnessed." Naughton's eyes turned up the driveway to where Kozlowski was standing. Three feet beyond him, Rudy Fen was crouched over Barksdale's body. Squatting besides Fen was one of his team, snapping photos and quietly making observations into a wire-thin microphone that fed a tape recorder. Naughton took in the scene, then blew out a ragged breath and turned back to Cantrell.

"Where's your machine?" Pappy was back to business.

"It's in the truck. My guys are unloading it now. We'll use the robot to check the house first, before we tackle the garage. From what you've described, we will take every precaution to secure this location safely." Naughton glanced at me. "You'd never know it by looking at this place from the outside. This nut job must have been one paranoid son of a bitch."

"That's what worries me." I turned away and walked down to the street.

"We'll make sure it's safe," Naughton claimed. "The robot is also equipped with a sniffer, so if it matches any chemical signatures normally found in explosives, it will alert us. We don't want any more casualties."

"Damn straight," Cantrell muttered.

Eastpointe police cars blocked both ends of the street. Together with uniformed state troopers, they had successfully evacuated all the homes nearby. Cantrell had instructed the troopers to talk to all the neighbors, gathering background information on Myers. There was a good chance we'd learn more about him from the people who lived nearby. Two ambulances and a fire truck stood at the end of the street, precautions in case the house or the garage went up. The trooper who had been injured earlier had been patched up and remained on the scene. Apparently, shards of glass had blown out all the way to the sidewalk and several of them had gashed his leg. But he refused to leave until he knew the place was safe. I felt the same way.

I sensed movement beside me. Glancing to my left,

I saw Kozlowski draw to a halt. His jacket and shirt and the bulletproof vest were covered in bloodstains from his attempts to help Barksdale. He still had blood on his hands. An evidence tech appeared at his side and handed him a cloth treated in alcohol. Koz began to scrub his hands as we walked to his car. The tech followed. Kozlowski popped the trunk and handed the cloth to the tech. It was bagged for evidence. We watched as Koz pulled a thick sweatshirt from the trunk and proceeded to remove his jacket, the vest, and his shirt. The tech took each one, bagged it, and wrote on the attached label. As he walked away, Koz pulled the sweatshirt over his muscular frame. Only then did he turn to me.

"It could have been me. Or Laura." His voice was so low and quiet, I almost didn't hear it.

"Myers had the front of the house rigged as well. He could have gotten Megan or me with that blast too."

Koz nodded slowly. "Barksdale saved the Bloomfield cop. In that split second when the blast was going off, he knocked her out of the way. The guy was a cop for almost thirty years. He was a pain in the ass, but deep down, he was all right."

I leaned against Kozlowski's trunk, thinking about the fallen cop. Although we never saw eye to eye on most things, I realized Koz was right. Cantrell had recruited Barksdale, just as he had the rest of us. It wasn't in Pappy's nature to take someone who wasn't a good detective. Barksdale worked with Cantrell for years before I came along. I remembered stories about some of the more difficult cases that had been solved by the squad. During that time, Barksdale was the lead. He was arrogant, bullheaded, opinionated, and antiquated in his methods. But he still got results. When Cantrell started naming me the lead in our cases, I knew it irked Barksdale. But truth was he was going to retire at the end of the year.

"Yeah, I guess he was at that."

****

The bomb squad did their job well. As Kozlowski expected, the garage was rigged with a couple of homemade devices, ones that were easy enough to deactivate by Myers as he entered the building. Naughton and his team disarmed them and cautiously checked the rest of the property. Inside the house, they found two small devices in the bedrooms, taped in a corner of the window where they would do the most damage to any intruder. Naughton also found a stash of weapons. There were two shotguns, several handguns, and an extensive collection of knives. Everything was meticulously recorded, tagged, and bagged by the team.

Cantrell watched as Fen worked without comment, moving with precision over the bodies of Barksdale and Myers. It was one of the few times I could remember Pappy going longer than five minutes without a cigarette. Eventually, he walked down to the street and fired one up. He took a call, then motioned me to join him.

"That was McDonald. They found nothin' at the shop. Guy didn't leave his tools there, just brought his gear with him. She's going to the hospital. Ah told her to go home after that. Ain't no need for her here."

I nodded in agreement. Pappy seemed to be waiting for me, but I didn't know what to say.

"Y'all had no way of knowing this would happen, Chene. Don't beat yourself up over it."

186

"We came to question him and to search the property. But Barksdale died because of me, Pappy. I must have missed something."

He fixed me with a stare that shut me up. "Y'all can't miss what ain't there. Barksdale died saving that Bloomfield girlie. He knew what this job was about. Y'all do."

"So what do we do now?"

"Y'all keep digging. Find sumthin that will make sense of this mess. Ah need to talk to the damn media."

At the end of the street, I could see several of the local news vans, their antenna towers jutting out into the darkening sky. There were enough harsh lights from the camera crews to guide an aircraft in for a landing. As Cantrell trudged up the street, I turned back to the house.

The building had been declared safe by Squad Five. Kozlowski and I began a slow, methodical search. We worked together without conversation. Myers had converted the smaller bedroom into a workroom. There was a set of barbells in the corner along with some battered free weights. This was where he kept the majority of his weapons. He had a small cabinet mounted to the wall, where each piece had a special shelf inset with memory foam. There had been boxes of ammunition for the various weapons here as well. Naughton and his crew had confiscated it all.

We moved into the other bedroom. On top of the dresser was a laptop computer. It was on, and the screen was split into four sections. As we entered the room, I heard a muted ping. My eyes had been sweeping the room. Turning, I saw movement on the monitor.

"Son of a bitch," Kozlowski grumbled behind me.

"This bastard had the exterior wired with cameras and a motion detector."

"No wonder he freaked out. He saw us on camera."

Koz faced me. "We never had a chance to take him down."

"No, we didn't. This guy was paranoid to the max. That just doesn't sound like our serial killer to me."

We worked slowly through the room, opening drawers, looking under the furniture, behind it, and through the closet. We checked everything, never sure exactly what we were looking for. But we had to keep looking.

Squad Five had set up portable lights in each room to combat the growing darkness outside. The bedroom was brightly lit now, but something was bothering me. We checked every possible place. Or so I thought. We started to walk out, but I stopped in my tracks. Kozlowski saw me hesitating in the doorway and turned back.

"What have you got?"

"Turn off those spotlights." I pointed at the stand by the door. Koz found the switch and clicked it. Darkness enveloped the room. Before he'd turned off the spotlights, I found the wall switch for the bedroom. I waited a moment for our eyes to adjust and then flipped up the lever with the back of my knuckle.

Koz was beside me in the doorway. Our eyes swept the room once again. Almost as an afterthought, I glanced up at the light fixture in the ceiling. Both bulbs were lit. But something else was visible in the frosted globe of the fixture, something that blocked a portion of the light.

"Gotcha!"

Chapter Twenty

Koz got one of the techs to come in and photograph the room, paying particular attention to the ceiling. Then he brought in a small stepladder. We stood against the wall, impatiently watching him climb up and remove the globe over the light bulbs. With the care of a surgeon, the tech climbed down and set the globe on the dresser. He took a series of pictures of where the globe was now and the light fixture without it. Then he climbed back up the ladder, removed the package, and brought it back down.

While this had been going on, I'd called Naughton and had him come back inside. Someone as paranoid as Myers might have rigged a booby trap on this as well. I wasn't inclined to take any chances. Naughton laid it gently on the dresser. In the mirror behind it, I could see his actions as he checked it carefully, his stubby fingers dancing across the plain brown paper.

"I don't feel any wires or anything that makes me concerned. Nothing at all like those little surprises we found on the windows or in the garage," Naughton said quietly.

He turned the paper over and an edge flipped up. This was the same type of paper you'd see in a butcher shop or perhaps a florist. It was thicker than copy paper, probably off some kind of a long roll. With the tip of a knife blade, Naughton carefully unwound it. Satisfied that there was no explosive device hidden inside, he stepped back and slowly exhaled.

"It's all yours."

Together, Kozlowski and I moved forward to examine it.

****

We went to Sharkey's. I couldn't remember the last time I'd eaten, but right now it didn't matter. What I wanted was a drink: something cold and strong and sizeable. Ted took one look at the two of us coming in the door and stopped in mid-stride. He sent one of the waitresses, a pretty young girl named Emma, to the booth we commandeered.

"Double Jack Daniels, on the rocks, water back," I requested.

Koz held up two fingers. Emma scurried away and returned a moment later with our drinks. Koz raised the thick glass with the amber liquid and looked right through me. "To Barksdale."

I repeated the toast. We clinked glasses and sipped. Kozlowski sat there silently for a moment, then slowly began to wag his head back and forth. I could see the anger pulsating from his body like a series of ocean waves crashing on the beach.

"It's bullshit, Chene. It is pure unadulterated bullshit." He dragged out the last word, as if it consisted of a dozen syllables.

"You don't think Myers was our killer." It was a statement, not a question.

"No, I think he was just a punk. Some poor dumb punk that got caught up in the game. He was a patsy."

"That's a pretty convenient patsy. You're saying someone went to all kinds of trouble to set him up?"

I watched him mash his mammoth hands together, cracking the knuckles so loudly the shock waves nearly made our water glasses vibrate.

"Yeah, he was set up. I don't think he had the bones or the stones to pull off these crimes." He paused to drain the whiskey, then precisely set the glass on a coaster. "Myers was an uneducated punk. He did a year and a half for CSC, behaved for a while, then was picked up on a date-rape charge. He beat that one. Supposedly, he's been clean ever since. My guess is somewhere along the line he got wrapped up with a different way to get his rocks off."

"So what bothers you?"

"The same things that bother you. You could see through this guy in a New York minute. So how is it he was able to outfox the detectives from three different cities, plus you and me and still run free?" Kozlowski slammed his palm on the table in disgust, making the water slosh in the glasses. Good thing the whiskey was already gone. "This guy was into weapons and booby traps. There's nothing subtle about that. So how did he get up the nerve to make the jump to serial killer and taunt the cops in the process?"

I thought about the little bundle we'd found. At first glance, we thought we could make a tentative match of the contents to pictures of two of the victims.

"Maybe he had help." I couldn't say this with much conviction. "He kept the earrings and the jewelry close at hand but out of sight. Nobody would think to look at that light fixture. He saved them as a souvenir of his kills."

Koz growled in disgust. "You don't believe that any more than I do. So what does it mean?"

I gave it a long moment's consideration. "That we only found what we were supposed to find."

"And what exactly is that?"

"What the real killer left behind."

"Yeah, so where are the other goodies?" He hunched forward, eyes glaring at me. "What about the clothes, Chene? What about the cell phones? A lightweight like Myers would probably get his thrills playing with the pushup bras or lacy thongs from the victims. He would keep those very close to hand. We tore that place apart and didn't turn up a thing! So where are they?"

"Not in the house, the Jeep, the garage, or in his locker at work. Forensics went over everything with the proverbial fine-tooth comb."

Koz just glared at me. The whiskey was burning a hole in my empty stomach, and I was quickly feeling the effects. As if by telepathy, Emma reappeared. She placed two bowls of clam chowder, a platter of various appetizers, and a small loaf of rye bread on the table. I looked past her at Ted who was leaning against the bar, watching us. He flicked his hand at me, the type of wave I've seen him use a million times over the years. It was his way of saying, "shut up and eat your food." So we did.

"We agree that this whole thing with Myers was just too neat. Too convenient." The bowls were empty. We were picking at the appetizers. I could feel the fire in my stomach going out and the impact of the alcohol diminishing.

"Yeah, the prime suspect dies in a hail of bullets, taking out a cop with him. The cop dies a hero, having captured and killed the creep everyone thought was a serial killer. And meanwhile…"

"The real killer is still walking around. If he's slick, he packs it up and moves to another part of the state or country. And he gets away clean," I said. Emma returned and cleared the table. Ted stepped up and placed two more whiskeys before us and walked away without a word. It was apparent to everyone we weren't there to socialize.

"You're assuming this guy can stop, Chene. What if he can't?"

"Then he kills again. Which puts us right back at square one."

Koz downed most of the whiskey as if it were iced tea. "That's not a place I want to be."

"So what are we gonna do about it?" But I already knew the answer.

"You're the boss, Chene. Just say the word."

Cantrell wouldn't want it any other way. "We go back to work. First thing in the morning, we do our job."

Kozlowski's eyes were fierce as he stared across the table. "And we don't stop until we nail this bastard."

****

Cantrell entered the conference room with as much finesse as a hurricane slamming into a bamboo shack. When he kicked the door open, the window rattled in its frame. With his head shrouded in smoke, he looked like a demon awakened from its hibernation in hell.

"Start talkin', Sergeant Chene. Y'all got three minutes."

If his entrance wasn't a clue, his statement was. Usually the only time he called me by rank was with superiors present or when he was pissed. "Have a seat, Pappy. This may take a while."

He grunted, taking his usual chair beside Megan. She slid him a mug of coffee, just the way he liked it strong and black. He tested it, nodded, and swung his attention on me. "Go."

I started with the conversation Kozlowski and I had last night. Then Laura jumped in with her observations.

"We've been unable to put a link between Myers and any of the victims. How did he meet them? Why the three different counties? How did he get them to the motel rooms?" She held Cantrell's gaze while he blew smoke rings at the ceiling.

Megan took her turn. "Nothing in his history indicates violence. The criminal sexual conduct charge refers back to his having sex with a fifteen-year-old girl. He was seventeen when convicted. She was a neighbor. He always claimed it was consensual and that he thought she was older." She checked the file before her. "So how does he go from a hormonal teenage indiscretion to successfully committing three homicides?"

Cantrell lit a fresh smoke from the stub of the last one. He turned to Kozlowski. "Suppose y'all agree with this crew?"

"Yeah. Chene and I tore it apart last night. Pinning these homicides on Myers makes as much sense as saying the freaking butler did it."

"So whatcha want from me? Barksdale is dead. The suspect is dead. Jarrett is busted up and back to her base." He ground his old cigarette out on the sole of his shoe and flicked the butt into the garbage can. Turning a blank stare in my direction, he repeated, "So whatcha want from me?"

All eyes were on me. "Don't close the case. Give us time to solve it. Don't assign us to anything else."

"Y'all think you can find the real killer?" He looked from one face to another. Each time he got a brief nod. He came back to me at the end. "Y'all get no one else. It's just you four."

"We'll do it."

"Don't know how long I can keep this quiet," Cantrell muttered. "Suppose you want the press to think the real killer's dead?"

"Yeah, Pappy, no one else should know that we're still working on it. We're close. So close I can practically taste it. I can almost touch this guy."

He looked around the room again, checking faces once more. There was no uncertainty, no hesitation. Each one was a reflection of the determination I felt. The real killer was still out there, and we were going to find him. At length, he brought his gaze back to mine.

"Don't waste no time talkin' to me. Go do what the good citizens pay y'all for. Find this sumbitch and bring him in."

We pushed back from the table and started to rise. But Cantrell wasn't finished. "Or bring him down."

The others filed out of the room. I gathered my notes, but Cantrell held up one gnarled finger. Megan closed the door behind her as she left. I didn't have long to wait.

"Y'all better find this guy soon, Chene."

"We will. This squad doesn't back down. You know that, Pappy. You put us together. Hell, you trained most of us. Always ask the questions. Always keep digging. Always…"

His eyes were on the conference table, where he had been making geometric patterns with the sweat from his coffee mug. Slowly, he looked up from beneath his bushy eyebrows. "Yeah?"

"You're pretty slick. It didn't take a whole lot of convincing to keep this case open."

He gave his shoulders a quick shrug but didn't say a word.

"You expected us to argue about Myers being the killer."

"Said it yourself, Chene. Ah brought y'all in. Ah trained y'all. The evidence against Myers was flimsy at best. If y'all didn't think it was planted, Ah was gonna have to recruit a new team."

"So your little outburst this morning?"

"Motivation. Let them others think they convinced me. Now they'll work twice as hard to find the real killer."

"Where did you get your degree in psychology, Pappy?"

He chuckled dryly. "Manipulation U. They don't allow Yankees there. We want y'all to keep thinkin' you actually won the war."

"You are a piece of work."

"Damn straight. Now do me a favor, Chene."

"Name it."

"Go find me that real killer. And find him fast afore he kills another girl."

Chapter Twenty-One

The four of us gathered in the bullpen. Everyone was looking at me for orders. After what happened yesterday, we needed a new approach.

"Okay, let's get to it. Koz, you and Laura are on Myers. Obviously, the background information we had didn't include his paranoia and his interest in weapons. Was he a zealot? Did someone at work turn him onto it? Maybe somebody he met while in prison caught his attention."

I shifted my gaze to Laura. "We have absolutely nothing that shows how Myers ever came into contact with the victims. Find me something. Talk to his coworkers and his boss. Find out who his friends were, who he hung out with. Did he go drinking on Saturday night? Where did he go, and who was he with? Talk to his neighbors, and see if anyone was friendly with the guy."

"We're on it, boss."

Megan tilted her head at me. "What's our plan?"

"We're going back to the house. There's got to be something we overlooked, some other hiding place, something innocuous that will give us a clue. Right now, we need to turn over every rock we can find and see what's underneath it."

Koz and Laura quickly left. I went to my desk and unlocked it. Since I shot Myers yesterday, my regular weapon was taken. That was normal procedure. I had been carrying a backup piece, a .38 revolver that Kozlowski kept locked in his trunk. I'd handed it back just before he split. From my locked desk drawer, I removed a small ornate box. Inside was a gleaming 9 mm Berretta. I checked the clip, loaded it, and secured it in the shoulder holster. I made sure the spare clip was full and tucked that in my pocket. The gun was a gift from Ted when I was promoted to sergeant. Megan rested a hip on her desk, watching without comment. As I was returning the box to my desk, my phone rang. With a distracted expression on her face, she reached over and answered. As she listened, her face tightened, and her eyes became sharp with interest.

"Twenty minutes, we'll be there." Megan racked the phone and jumped to her feet. She pulled her jacket off the back of her chair.

"That was Donna Spears. She may have found something."

****

Donna met us at the door of her condo. She was still using the crutches, but I noticed her movements were a little steadier and there was more energy in her walk. She jerked her head toward the kitchen table, which had become her desk. A fresh pot of coffee was brewing on the counter. She pointed toward it, where a couple of mugs were laid out.

"Help yourself, boss, you too, detective."

I started to remind her not to call me boss, but Megan gave me a warning look. Lately, everyone was referring to me that way. I moved to the counter and poured us each a mug. Donna nodded her thanks as I refilled hers.

"So tell us what you discovered," Megan said calmly.

Donna took a deep breath and let it out slowly. She gestured toward the stacks of binders on the table. Each stack related to one of the victims. There was a preponderance of paper that had been generated by the original detectives investigating the homicide. On top of that was the veritable mountain the squad created while performing our own investigations. I noticed that every stack was neatly arranged.

"I don't know if you've been able to follow my reports," Donna said. "They get kind of mundane."

Both Megan and I nodded. "I've been reading them. You've done a thorough job reviewing all this material."

She brushed away the compliment like it was a cobweb. "Yeah, well, I was beginning to doubt that I'd ever find anything worthwhile. These poor women had so little in common. And after what happened in Eastpointe, maybe what I found doesn't matter at all."

We were all silent for a moment. The events of yesterday were still too fresh for either Megan or I. She touched the stitches above her eyebrow. Donna reached over and dragged the laptop computer close. Her fingers swiftly danced over the keys. I leaned over, watching as a spreadsheet appeared.

Donna explained that she had methodically read through each case file, starting with the first one in Wayne County. After the review, she began to build a spreadsheet with every pertinent detail she could think of: age, height, weight, hair color, occupation, education, religious affiliation, siblings, parents, and more. A lot more. Each victim was color coded.

She described her efforts reviewing each case and trying to cross-reference anything the victims had in common. There were no activities they shared, no clear link. Donna had grown frustrated. Then she tried another approach.

"And that's where I think I found something. It's so obvious I don't know why we didn't pick up on it before."

"So who is the connection?" Megan asked patiently.

Donna held up a hand. "Well, I don't have a who. But I think it's more of a what. We know each one of the victims was single, not in any kind of a relationship. Each one had an apartment, and one had a roommate. All three were meek. None of these women were very outgoing. They were plain girls, who had jobs, or were going to school, whatever it was, living relatively quiet, mundane lives. So how did they become victims of a serial killer?"

I drank some coffee. There was no point in rushing her. Donna would tell us what she found her own way. I caught Megan's eye. She ignored me and looked at Donna.

"So the connection would be…"

"It's social. I'm no psychologist, but I'd bet all of these women were lonely. They were all bored with their lives. They wanted something out of the ordinary. They needed something to remind them that they were alive, something…different."

"And that something different would be what?" I asked.

"Something they may have been curious about, but were unsure of how to explore it. Something that was daring and exotic and adventurous."

Whether it was from yesterday's events, the overindulgence of whiskey, the perpetual lack of sleep or the strain of this investigation, I could never say for sure. But I was getting a headache listening to Donna drag this out. She must have recognized this by my expression, because before I could say anything, she jumped back in.

"I think the killer is a woman."

****

Donna held her hands up like a politician trying to calm an angry crowd. Both Megan and I started talking as soon as she made the statement. Reluctantly, I shut up and leaned back. Megan got to her feet and refilled the coffee mugs. Donna waited until she returned to her seat.

"Before you both think I'm strung out on pain meds, hear me out. The connection I saw was that each of these girls had nobody in their lives. No lover. It's possible there may have been a boyfriend or two in the past, but other than a close female friend or two, there was no one outside of their family. And that's what our killer was looking for."

"Okay, we don't argue the point that each of these girls could have been lonely, but how do you make the leap that the killer is a woman?" Megan asked solemnly.

Donna pulled a set of color photos from a folder. Each was of the victim when she was still alive. The expressions were similar. Shy, reserved with the eyes downcast or looking away. These were not the gazes of someone flirting with the camera or whoever was standing behind it.

"We've always been in agreement that the killer preys on this type of woman. They are all young, early to mid-twenties, without the glamour or physique of a fashion model. They are all plain. Now let me explain why."

Donna calmly described her scenario, keeping her voice steady. "Let's pick the first one. Mary Rosen had no romance in her life. She had no potential suitors on the horizon. The few close friends she had would get together occasionally. She was the only one available even on short notice, because she had no life, no other commitments that would get in her way. Detectives who inspected her apartment found a large number of romance novels, with some very erotic stories mixed in. I've skimmed some of those titles. They are the type that feed into the belief that there will always be a Prince Charming riding over the hill to save the day, even when there isn't a hill in sight.

"But what if the girl was so desperate for love, for an adventure that takes her breath away, for a romance that would shake her to her core that she doesn't care what Prince Charming really looked like, or even if he was a prince at all. The thirst for the adventure, the desire was so great, she got to the point where it didn't matter whose arms she ended up in, whether they were masculine or feminine. It's where the journey is the important thing, not who the cruise director is."

We were quiet for a moment, considering Donna's theory. Megan cleared her throat and sat straighter in her chair.

"Okay, I can understand a girl like our victims, lonely, looking for love, wanting to feel some connection with another human being. I mean, that's what life is all about. I can understand how someone who might be feeling this way could be curious and could respond to the attention of another woman. But I'm having difficulty picturing a woman as our killer."

It was obvious Donna had been giving this a great deal of thought. I wanted to see where she was headed.

"Go with me on this. Let's say our girl was out with her friends. Maybe she's at a crowded bar. Everyone else was having a good time. She just sat there quietly, shrinking into the chair. And then someone singles her out, another woman. She could still be nervous, but not as nervous if a guy approaches. The woman could work her slowly, getting her to relax, letting her guard down. The woman would know all the signs, could anticipate how she is going to react."

"Because she's a woman?" I asked.

Donna nodded her head in agreement. "And because she's been there herself."

****

Donna made a very convincing argument. If the victims let their guard down, never considering there could be any danger from another woman, they may have unknowingly played right into the killer's plans. If the killer took the time to gain their trust, to develop what they considered to be a new friendship, it could easily happen as Donna described.

She turned slightly in her chair now, facing Megan. "Let's say you're a potential victim. You're meek and mild. Once in a while, a little bit of your personality might leak out, but only when you're with a friend. With someone you trust. Then one night, you meet someone new. Someone who doesn't come on strong, someone who is shy and quiet and appears to be just as lonely as you are, a kindred spirit."

"Someone you can trust." Megan slowly nodded in understanding. "Someone you're not threatened by, but someone you can relate to, who may have some similar experiences, who can understand what your life is like."

"Now think about the timeframe. There is a month between each killing. That shows a great deal of restraint on the part of the killer."

"Maybe not," I said, joining the discussion for what seemed like the first time in an hour. "Maybe the killer is so gratified by taking another life that the urge to kill is vanquished. They don't have the need to kill again."

Donna tilted her head as she studied me. "That could be, boss. But what if she's already moving on to her next victim, and she's in the process of making it happen. She could be getting friendly with some poor girl, working her way into a relationship. She could be earning some trust. Going slowly, getting to know the particular weaknesses of the next victim, knowing exactly how to manipulate her to do what she wants."

My gaze flicked to Megan. The look of comprehension on her face said it all.

"You realize that fits in with the killer taunting the cops, leaving that freaking message on the mirror," Megan said.

"Take it a step further. That also fits that the killer cleans the victims and arranges them on the bed the same way. It's almost like a beauty treatment."

Nobody spoke for a few minutes. We all just let this sink in. Donna was idly running a forefinger around the rim of her coffee mug. Slowly, I got to my feet and put my mug in the sink. Megan stood as well.

"Do you think I'm nuts, boss?"

"No, I think you actually have a great theory for us to work with. But we still need to figure out how the killer is selecting their victims. And if we can trace that back, then we can identify the killer. Your argument makes sense. The killer could very well be a woman."

Donna gave me a grateful look. "A woman as a sexual serial killer: who would ever have thought of that?"

Chapter Twenty-Two

The Eastpointe house was still taped off as a crime scene. There was one patrol car parked out front with a reserve cop inside. It was dull duty, but necessary since with all the damage to the house, there was no way we could secure it. The last thing we wanted was for the curious types to start snooping around. After logging in, Megan and I proceeded into the house.

We hadn't spoken on the drive over from Donna Spears's place. I had been trying to wrap my mind around the concept of a female serial killer. It was difficult for me to consider that a woman could be so cold, so calculating in her attacks on another woman. If Donna was right, I could only wonder what motivated a woman to kill in such a way.

Women can be violent. After all these years in police work, I've witnessed a great deal. I've seen women involved in fistfights with both men and women, cases where a woman has shot or stabbed a man for a variety of reasons, everything from forgetting it was Valentine's Day, to failing to pick up his dirty laundry. There was a case a few years ago where a guy was poisoned by his wife because he refused to buy her a new car. And the woman who drowned her husband in their hot tub when she discovered he had been sleeping with her kid sister. Those were usually the result of emotions run wild. But this case was different.

This killer was so methodical, it was unnerving. This killer was unemotional.

"Why are we here again, Chene?"

"Now that the dust has settled, I want to take another look at this place. A long, slow careful look."

Megan flexed her fingers, pulling the latex gloves all the way on. "We still have so many unanswered questions."

"Somewhere in this house may be a lead as to how Myers was chosen. None of us believes he was the killer. But somebody went to a great deal of trouble to plant that evidence here."

We worked silently. Since we had no idea what we were looking for, we could not discount anything. Together, we started in the basement. It was a small damp room, just big enough for a furnace, hot water heater, washer, and dryer. We were being cautious, even after the bomb squad had swept the entire house. Megan turned the washer and dryer on to make sure they were functioning properly. People can hide things in the craziest places. I thumped the vent pipe from the dryer, making sure nothing was out of the ordinary.

Moving to the furnace, I removed the cover for the filter. At first glance, it looked perfectly normal. But when I pulled the filter out, I saw a small brown envelope. Megan took a series of pictures, then leaned back as I withdrew it. It was about five by eight inches in size, with a little brass clasp on one end. We moved to the dryer, and I carefully lifted the wings of the clasp. Dumping the contents gently on the dryer, I spread them around with the blade of my pocket knife.

There were a number of articles and papers related to a militia group. There were announcements encouraging people to bear arms, to resist the efforts of government control, to stop paying their taxes, and more.

"Looks like we found GI Joe," Megan said.

"More like GI Joe wannabes. This is probably where our boy Myers got interested in weapons and explosives."

Megan nudged a paper to the side with the tip of her pinkie. Even with gloves on, we took care not to smudge any fingerprints. "This looks like something out of the Anarchist Cookbook. It's a do-it-yourself guide to make an explosive with household ingredients."

"Amazing what you can find on the internet these days."

"Yeah, but I'm willing to bet Myers didn't trip to this on his own. Someone had to give him a nudge in that direction, or get his attention."

Sliding the documents back into a pile, Megan secured them in an evidence envelope. We left the basement to examine the rest of the house.

During yesterday's investigation, the computer had been seized. I was hoping the tech boys from the cyber squad were going to unearth something significant from the hard drive and the emails on the system. But as I thought about Myers and his paranoia, a glimmer of an idea began to form. Now on the main floor, I turned toward the kitchen.

"Are you looking for a snack, Chene?"

A smile tugged at the corner of my lips. "No, but it seems like all the focus yesterday was on the bedrooms. I'm wondering if we might find anything out here."

The kitchen was a mess. Blood smears covered the

floor where Myers had been gunned down simultaneously by me and Laura. The walls were splattered too. We stood in the doorway and surveyed the room.

Megan clucked her tongue against the roof of her mouth. "Why is it we always end up in a place like this when I'm wearing a new pair of boots?"

I glanced down at her feet. These were bright red ones, with a rounded toe and a short heel. It was difficult to determine how far up her leg the boot went.

"How the hell can you run in something like that?"

"I'm a woman. I can adapt to any situation and do it with style."

With a disgusted smirk, I turned my attention back to the room. There was a cheap table pushed against the wall, an old drop-leaf thing that had seen better days in the 1960s. Two padded vinyl chairs flanked it. There was the usual kitchen clutter, salt and pepper shakers, a sugar bowl, and a small bottle propped against the wall. There was also a stack of magazines and mail scattered across the surface. I pointed those out to Megan. She picked her way across the room, taking great pains in where she placed her feet.

I focused on the cupboards above the sink and counter. There was a jumble of mismatched glasses and plates, along with souvenir coffee mugs from various casinos and restaurants. It was obvious Myers didn't care much about the furnishings of his kitchen. I was about to close the last cupboard when something caught my eye. Up near the very top of the door, close to the hinge, was a small round hole. The hinge was too high up for me to see it clearly.

"Find anything good?" I asked Megan.

"A couple of old newspapers, the kind filled with coupons. His bills for the internet service and cable, along with his cell phone bill. There is a magazine about weapons that looks like he bought it somewhere."

"Hand me one of those chairs."

Her eyes flicked to the open cupboard. Megan grabbed the closest chair, then swung it to where I could take it from her without disrupting the mess on the floor.

"This guy was a slob. He couldn't even put shelf paper in the cupboards," Megan said with disgust.

"Men don't bother with shelf paper."

"Yet another piece of evidence that proves women are superior."

"Can you see anything odd from there?" I stepped onto the chair.

"Just the usual stack of dishes."

I took a good look inside the cabinet. Mounted high up against the back wall was a small video camera. It was aimed so that when the cupboard door was closed, it would be able to film through the hole by the hinge. My guess was that it would easily take in the occupants of the little table. If the camera had a wide angle lens, it might capture everything within the kitchen. Glancing over to Megan, I described what I had found.

"But you knew yesterday he had security cameras on motion detectors." There was a touch of curiosity in her voice. "You told me about those this morning."

Before our summit with Cantrell, I met with Anton Yekovich, the lead technician of the cyber squad. I gave him a set of photos of our three victims, in the hopes that we would see them entering the house. His team had already begun the slow process of analyzing the hundreds of hours of video files.

"Yes, but those were all focused on the exterior of the house and were fed into the laptop computer. But we didn't know about this one. And if there's one…"

"…there have got to be others. The question is where do they feed into?"

I stepped down from the chair, narrowly missing a sticky patch of blood spatter on the floor. Megan followed me into the hallway.

"Give Yekovich a call. See if they have discovered any video footage on that laptop for the inside of the house. We'll check the other rooms for more cameras."

****

Cantrell had many old sayings that he liked to drag out. Often, they were a jumble that didn't make a lot of sense at the moment, but every once in a while, he offered up a real gem. This was one of those times.

"Chene, sumtimes you're lucky, and sumtimes you're good. And sumtimes, it's a li'l bit of both."

I nodded. "You won't get an argument from me."

He was referring to our efforts this afternoon. We were waiting to hear from the lab boys to see if we'd struck gold or tinfoil.

When Megan contacted the cyber squad, she'd learned there were no video files of the interior of the Myers house. That gave us two possibilities. Either the camera we found in the kitchen was just for show, or there was another system in place somewhere to receive the images. Knowing that cameras can be disguised in many ways, we resumed our search.

In the living room, we checked every nook and cranny. Megan found another camera, this one tucked behind a picture frame on a shelf in the corner. The angle would cover most of the room.

"Why was Myers this paranoid to have security cameras inside the house?" Megan tried to trace the wiring from the camera.

I was wondering the same thing, but suddenly something made sense. "Maybe it wasn't paranoia, but protection."

She gave me a confused look. "Chene, your insomnia is obviously affecting your cognitive abilities."

"Think about it. If Myers had recently gotten involved with some militia group, maybe he wired the interior of the house to keep a record of what went on. Maybe there were group meetings here. It could have been a sort of insurance policy in case the crew went too far and did something illegal."

"And when we approached yesterday, he must have thought it was tied to the militia activities, which is why he fought back." Megan carefully sat on the edge of the sofa. "He overreacted."

"Right now it's just a theory. Let's see if we can find proof."

We resumed the search. In the living room, we found another camera inside the smoke detector. A quick look revealed smoke detectors in the ceiling of both bedrooms. Megan went back to the basement and found another one there as well. We didn't remove them. We still needed to figure out what they were linked to.

The last place we could think of was the linen closet. It was directly across from the bathroom, a three-foot-wide space with narrow shelves that went all the way to the ceiling. We pulled all the worn towels and sheets from the cupboard, taking the time to sort them out. Megan had pulled the last stack of towels from the top shelf. As she brought them toward the floor, she rocked back on her heels, her face split with a grin.

"Oh, you were a sneaky little bastard," she said gleefully.

As I looked at the towels in front of her, I saw the clear imprint of a shoe. Glancing up into the closet, I spotted the little trapdoor that led to the attic.

"But how sneaky a bastard was he?"

The attic was more like a crawlspace than a full-sized attic. Squatting on the rafter struts, we moved about cautiously, not wanting to disturb the fiberglass insulation or miss a step and go through the ceiling. That's where we found the DVR. It was perched on a small piece of plywood fastened to the rafters. The placement made perfect sense. Most of the cameras were mounted in or near the ceiling, so running the wires directly to the recorder was easy. While we had been assured that the house was safe from any more explosive devices, I didn't trust our luck with the equipment. Megan called in the cyber squad to pick up the device and analyze the contents.

Now we were waiting for those reports.

And the hope they would give us another lead.

****

"Patience is not one of my virtues," Megan said with disgust. It was almost ten on Sunday morning. We were here to strategize.

"I was beginning to wonder if you had any virtues left."

She shot me a look that would have made a lesser man wince. Or stumble over an apology. Before she could snap back a retort, I tossed her a waxed paper bag and set a cup of coffee on her desk. Megan snagged the bag with one hand. Cautiously, she undid the flap and peered inside.

"Raspberry lemon loaf." The delight evident in her voice. "And I'll bet that's mocha hazelnut coffee. You went to Momma Jo's?"

I shrugged. "That's why I'm late. I swung by the cyber squad to check on their progress. Yekovich and I got to talking about the case. They're a little backlogged. But I persuaded him to make our request his top priority."

"I always liked Yekovich. He just proved he's a wise man." She broke off a piece of pastry and popped it into her mouth. I watched her close her eyes and savor it for a moment. Damn the calories. Sometimes simple pleasures outweighed everything else.

We were going to meet with Koz and Laura shortly. Cantrell was on his way to Grand Rapids for business not related to the case. Pappy had discontinued the evening briefings, since it was down to just the four of us. He knew that if we were able to turn something up, we'd notify him immediately.

We remained in the bullpen. There were few others in our part of the building. Outside, the wind was roaring and bits of snow were twisting around, reminding us all that it was still March. Thoughts of warmer temperatures and sunshine would have to wait. Megan gave Kozlowski and Laura the update from yesterday. Now we all gave Koz our full attention.

"We started at the shop where Myers worked. Most

of the crew lasts a year or two, then moves on to something bigger and better. The guy who manages it, Bobby Burch, is used to it. He stays up top, trying to get the customers to upgrade and spend more money. There are four guys besides Myers who do the actual work. Two are listed as mechanics, so if there's something more elaborate than draining oil, they take care of it. We talked to each guy separately. None of them were close with Myers. He was a loner, didn't get together with them outside of work. Myers did his job, joked around a little when it was slow, but not much beyond that."

Laura picked up the narrative. "There was nothing in his locker other than a few old newspapers and magazines. No militia materials, no correspondence, nothing that would raise any suspicions from the other guys. Myers never complained about the work, either when it was busy or when it was slow. With the store being right on Gratiot, it was pretty steady, with a fair amount of traffic."

"What was his schedule?"

Koz checked his notebook. "He took the broken week. The place is only closed on Sundays. He had Tuesdays off. And Burch said if one of the other guys was out, Myers would come in to cover without a complaint."

"Sounds like Myers was keeping his head down," Megan said. "Any luck with the neighbors or his family?"

From his personnel records, Kozlowski had obtained the emergency contact. Myers listed an aunt who lived up in Auburn Hills. Koz spoke to her briefly yesterday. They had an appointment today at one. Laura described their efforts to interview the neighbors.

"That house in Eastpointe was a rental. He'd been living there since he got out and started working at the oil place. We talked with neighbors across the street, behind his house and on either side. They all said the same thing. Myers was a loner. On rare occasions, someone would stop by. There were no parties, no barbecues in the summer, no hobbies that had him outdoors. He cut the grass, shoveled the snow, and that was it."

I leaned back and propped my boots on the edge of my desk. Kozlowski had been staring at me for the last few minutes of Laura's report. In his massive hands, he had been stretching a rubber band out. Now he looped one end around his ring finger, drew the rest of the band around the heel of his hand, and poked his forefinger into the other loop. Pointing his finger at the ceiling, he released it. The rubber band bounced off the ceiling and landed in my lap.

"Whatcha got, Chene?"

"If Myers was in the militia, how come they haven't been holding press conferences, screaming police brutality?"

"We haven't found any connection with a militia unit yet," Megan said.

I flipped a folder across the desk to her. "Here's a list of the email messages that were on Myers computer. The second page is a list of all the numbers from his cell phone, both inbound and outbound for the last six months. Yekovich had those for me this morning."

"Any of our victims appear on those lists?" Koz asked.

"No. We've got nothing."

We divided up the lists. Somewhere in here was a connection.

Chapter Twenty-Three

The list of emails from the cyber squad included all of the necessary details so we could make contact. Cross referencing with the phone numbers brought up three possible leads for the militia. It was after noon when I got through to one, a guy named John Perryman. After identifying myself and the nature of the call, he agreed to meet. He gave me directions to a place out near Chesterfield, about forty miles north. Megan and I headed out while Koz and Laura went to meet Myers's aunt.

"You think we need backup?"

"It's a conversation. Keep your weapon holstered and visible, and we'll be fine."

She was restless on the drive. Remembering Dovensky's words of caution, I wondered if she had gone to church earlier. I pushed those thoughts out of my head and focused on John Perryman.

A quick search on the internet before we left revealed Perryman was the leader of a militia squad that focused on training and preparations. There was link to a website that showed monthly meetings and training events. This was one of several squads throughout the state. There were larger group meetings in the summer. It wouldn't have surprised me to see some police officers as active members.

I followed Perryman's directions and found a large

parcel of land a few miles from the main roads. A huge maple tree was on the edge of the property, right next to the road. There was a large structure out in the middle of a cleared lot. As we got closer, I realized it was an old Quonset hut. There were half a dozen pickup trucks parked alongside the building. Megan and I stepped out into the weather and hurried toward the door. It opened before we could reach it.

A barrel-chested man wearing heavy boots, jeans, and a thick canvas-covered outdoor coat blocked the way. He was clean shaven, with short blond hair going gray. Pale blue eyes were hidden by a pair of wire-rimmed glasses. His face was expressionless.

"You the cops?"

Megan confirmed it, giving him our names. His eyes flicked over both of us for an instant before waving us inside. The door slammed behind us.

"We've got nothing to hide."

"I didn't say you did. Are you John Perryman?"

"I am. That's the only name you'll get."

I looked around. The hut was on a concrete slab. Tucked in the far corner was an old Franklin stove. I could see the heat radiating off it. Between the door and the stove were two large wooden picnic tables. Four men were sitting there, holding ceramic coffee mugs. There was an open box of donuts on the table.

"We're hoping you'd answer some questions about Charles Myers. There's a lot about him we're still trying to figure out."

Perryman stared at us for a second before indicating the picnic tables. "So are we. That was one confused kid. But he was no serial killer."

As we sat at the vacant table, one of the guys got

up and brought us two mugs of coffee. "We ain't bad guys here."

Megan smiled at him. "I never said you were. Can I take a cup out to the guy in the maple tree?"

Perryman chuckled. "Tell Briggs to come in."

"Not much foliage yet to hide in."

"Good point. So what do you want to know about Charlie?"

"When did he join your outfit?" I asked.

Perryman had taken the bench across from us. With the others listening in and offering the occasional detail, he spelled it out. Myers learned about the militia while in prison. He hadn't met a member but heard the gossip and stories. He liked the idea of being prepared, and the training offered a type of camaraderie he hadn't experienced before. He started attending meetings and trainings as soon as he'd gotten out of prison. Perryman expressed his surprise at hearing about the incident Friday night.

"He had no reason not to cooperate. It's not like what we do here is illegal. We're on private property. We work together as a squad. But we come from all walks of life. I've got construction workers, finance guys, techies, salesmen, and some guys in the reserves. There are a few other guys who had problems in their past, but it's no big deal."

"Do you have any idea why he would be so paranoid about his house?"

Perryman shrugged. "We've always talked about being observant. Not taking chances, paying attention to your surroundings. But nothing like that. On the news they said he had booby traps. Is that true?"

"Yeah, it is. And he initiated the action. We were

there to ask him some questions and search for evidence in a homicide. We only returned fire to defend ourselves."

Megan had been quiet through the conversation. She turned her head to the other table. All five men stared at her without expression. "It was never our intention that anyone would get hurt, let alone die there."

"Could he have taken your training to heart, to prepare his house for a possible invasion like that?" I asked.

Perryman shrugged again. "I guess anything is possible. Charlie must have been feeling extremely threatened. Do you have any idea where he got all those weapons?"

"We're still tracing them."

"Charlie was a gullible kid. If he believed there was a threat to his home, he would have protected it. But we train our guys to cooperate with police. There's no winning in a gunfight like that. It's better to surrender and have your day in court."

"That's a good plan," Megan said.

"Yeah," Perryman agreed, "it is. I'm a defense attorney. I'd rather win that way than in a shootout like Charlie."

"There was no winner in that shootout," I said.

****

It took very little encouragement for me to drive to Simone Bettencourt's apartment. She called as we were getting back to the post and offered to cook dinner. Supposedly, it was to pay me back for the meal I'd prepared last week. But I think we both knew there was more to it.

Not knowing what she was serving, I stopped at a liquor store and bought two bottles of wine. One was a Chardonnay, from a vineyard whose wine I'd had a number of times before. The other was a Cabernet Sauvignon.

Simone must have seen me drive up. She was standing in the doorway, a tentative smile on her lips. Beyond her, I could see the room was dimly lit. A soft, jazzy tune was playing on the stereo. After a moment, I heard Diana Krall's sensuous voice floating from the speakers.

As I approached the door, Simone took a hesitant step forward. She paused, then opened her arms for an embrace. Somehow, I managed to draw her against me without dropping the two bottles of wine. I held her close, inhaling the delicate scent of her. Simone brushed her lips against my cheek as she whispered, "I'm so glad you agreed to come for dinner."

"I couldn't pass up such an invitation."

Reluctantly, I released her and we went inside. Closing the door, I handed her the wine. Quickly, I shed my coat and draped it over a chair. I couldn't stop watching her. That shy smile returned. I followed her into the kitchen. Lowering my eyes, I drew a deep breath. There was a heavenly jumble of aromas. "Whatever you're cooking, it sure smells great."

Simone put the Chardonnay in the refrigerator and left the Cabernet on the counter. "It's basic fare. I didn't have enough time to get fancy. It's just some spaghetti, a loaf of Italian bread, and salads. Give me more notice and a chance to show off, and I'll break out my cookbooks."

"You're on."

She came back and stood before me. Her eyes searched my face. I met her gaze evenly. I was about to say something when she leaned up and kissed me. It was a gentle, tender meeting of our lips. But as all the emotion, all the passion flowed between us, it felt like two live wires making contact. Simone moaned and pressed against me. I pulled her close with one arm around her waist, stroked her hair with my free hand. I had no idea how long we stood there kissing. All I know is that I had never been kissed like that before. And I didn't want it to stop.

Simone pulled back once, her face flushed. Her eyes were damp, and there was a slight tremble in her voice as she spoke. "Would you love me, Jeff? Would you make love with me?"

"Yes," I answered hoarsely.

We moved from the kitchen to her bedroom. Softly in the distance, I could still hear the music from the stereo. Simone was nervous. She didn't turn on the light. Through the curtain, there was just a faint glow of light from outside. She drew me into her room and started to remove her clothes. She was wearing a pair of jeans and a thick turtleneck sweater. Now she reached to pull the sweater off. I stopped her with a shake of my head.

"Let me do that." My voice was soft, almost nonexistent.

What followed was a slow, deliberate exploration. I removed her sweater, inching it up from the waist a little bit at a time. I didn't want to rush this. I wanted this moment to last. My lips found hers, and we resumed kissing. The intensity increased, along with my heart rate. I realized her hands were busy, undoing the buttons on my shirt. She undid the last one about the same time I bunched the sweater up to her shoulders. We separated for a moment as I pulled the sweater over her head. I took a step back and unhooked my shoulder holster. Wrapping it around the gun, I set it on the dresser. Simone shook her hair free, then grabbed the collar of my shirt and yanked it from me. We continued kissing as my fingers slowly slid up her ribs, reveling in the softness of her skin. I pinched the clasp of her bra between my finger and thumb and felt it smoothly come apart. It was a suave move that was totally out of character for me. The straps slid off her shoulders, down her arms and disappeared between us.

I almost jumped out of my skin at the touch of her bare breasts against my chest. Simone would never be mistaken for a Kardashian girl, but that was more than fine with me. I have always been attracted to small-breasted women. Hers were just right. I could easily cup them in my hand or slide my mouth over them. She moaned when I did that.

By now we were both growing impatient. Simultaneously, our hands undid each other's jeans. Anxiously, we stepped back and removed our own. It took me an extra moment to kick off my boots and socks. Simone had been wearing a pair of worn leather moccasins. While I shed my jeans, she slipped under the blankets.

"I'm nervous," she whispered as I joined her, wrapping her in my arms.

"Me too."

"I don't want to disappoint you. I haven't been with anyone in a while."

Tenderly, I kissed her. "Why would I be

disappointed?"

"I'm not really who I pretend to be. I'm supposed to be this wild girl who is the life of the party, always doing crazy things. Others see me as some kind of leader, urging people on. But it's all just an act. Inside I'm just shy and nervous and afraid like everyone else."

"That's not the Simone I've met."

Before I could say more, she kissed me. There was such intensity in that kiss. It was filled with longing and desire and passion. At that moment, everyone else in the world ceased to exist.

****

We were tangled together under the sheets. Somehow, the blankets were too confining, almost suffocating in their warmth. Simone kicked them to the side earlier. Now she rested on top of me, her face tucked into the hollow of my neck.

"For the record, there is no way I could be disappointed. Particularly, if you're talking about your physical attributes."

She giggled softly against my throat. "And what attributes might those be? Once the padded bra is gone, there is really not much to see. I've always been a B-cup girl."

Playfully, I gave her bottom a light slap. "B is just fine with me. And you know perfectly well what I'm talking about."

We both heard her stomach growl. Reluctantly, she slipped off the bed and drew on a thick terry-cloth robe. I grabbed my jeans and slid them on.

We went back to the kitchen. Simone turned on the oven and switched on one of the burners beneath a pot of water. There was a large skillet of pasta sauce already simmering. While she was waiting for the oven to heat, she handed me the bottle of red wine. As I was opening it, she watched with her arms folded over her chest.

"If I ask you a question, will you give me an honest answer?"

"Sure."

"The other night when you stayed and held me, how come you didn't want to have sex then?"

I waited until the cork was out so the wine could breathe. "You were very vulnerable. There's no way I wanted to take advantage of you like that."

"Some guys would have. Hell, most guys would have."

I shrugged. "Guess I'm not like most guys."

That shy smile tugged at her lips. "Are you saying that there was no physical attraction that night, but over the last week, one has developed?"

I reached over and unfolded her arms, pulling her to me. "Physically, there has always been an attraction. That night on the sofa I was supposed to be comforting you. Helping you get through a rough time. Not getting aroused."

"Did you? Get aroused? Or was that something else in your pocket?"

There was a playful twinkle in her eyes. She already knew the answer to the question. She just wanted me to admit it.

"Yes, I was aroused. And that's the main reason why we spent the night on the sofa. If we had gone to bed, sex would have been inevitable."

Simone pushed away from me and dropped some pasta into the pot of boiling water. I busied myself pouring us each a glass of wine. When I looked up, the smile was gone, and a very serious expression filled her face.

"So what's different between that night and tonight?"

I pulled a chair away from the table and sat down. Then I extended a hand to her. Simone hesitated, then moved close enough so I could pull her into my lap. I wanted, no, I needed to be touching her while we talked. "In a week's time, we've gotten to know each other a little better. You're not as vulnerable as you were then. And what we shared was very special. What I hope to be the first of many times together."

Gently, she reached up to touch my face. "So I'm not going to be some one-night stand? Will I end up as just another notch on the handle of your gun?"

I looked in her eyes. "Do you think I'm that kind of a guy?"

"No." She slowly shook her head. "If you were, you would have taken advantage of me last week. You would have taken me up on the offer for sex right then and there. So we could be starting something?"

I kissed her gently. "Yes, we could. I have never been kissed with so much passion, such intensity before. You've awakened feelings inside me that I never knew I was capable of."

She rested her forehead against mine. "It's been a long time since I've felt this way. I guess it's not uncommon to hold back a bit when it comes to a new relationship. It's pretty sad really."

"Why is it sad? I think it makes more sense than just rushing forward with your eyes shut. That seems to me like it would be too easy to get hurt."

Simone nodded. "That's what happened to me in college. There were a couple of guys that I was really attracted to. Guys I thought I was falling for. We dated for a while. I really thought one guy was going to be the one. But before we got to the next step, the physical part, he drifted away."

I didn't know how to respond to that. She slipped out of my arms and went to the stove. Simone wrapped the loaf of bread in foil and placed it in the oven. She stirred the pasta. Then she checked the sauce, giving it a couple of turns with a spatula. Satisfied, she replaced the lid.

Moving from the chair, I came to stand beside her. She pulled a bowl of salad from the refrigerator and tossed it, lightly adding some dressing. Simone kept her gaze averted, focused on her work. Satisfied, she placed the bowl on the table. At last, she looked at me, and I could see the pain in her eyes.

My voice was a whisper. "Nobody wants to get hurt. But there are no guarantees in life."

She nodded in agreement. "I know. And there are times when you want to take the chance. I'm not looking for a commitment. But I want to get to know you. I understand the work you do may interfere at times, but I still want to try."

"I'd like that. I'm glad you understand about the job."

"When it comes to new relationships, I'm not like Janet."

I was leaning against the counter with an arm around Simone's waist. I had just raised my wineglass for a sip when her comment registered. "What do you mean?"

"Janet was an all-or-nothing kind of girl." Simone took my glass and tasted the wine. She nodded once and handed it back. "Janet was the type that, when she started dating someone, she expected to see them or talk to them daily. And if for some reason they didn't connect, she would mope around until she did hear from them."

"That sounds unusual, especially nowadays."

"You have to understand Janet's love life was pretty thin. If a guy paid attention to her, maybe asked her out, she'd be ready to start planning the wedding before the end of the evening. Like I said, she was all-or-nothing."

Simone pushed me toward the table. She moved to the oven and removed the bread, sliding it into a wicker basket. I watched her efficiently drain the pasta, then ladle up a plate for each of us. The sauce was thick, with chunks of tomatoes, peppers, and sausage. She made sure the oven and burners were turned off, then we focused on dinner.

The meal was excellent. I complimented Simone on her cooking. She gave me that shy smile once again. It was a bit distracting, knowing that she was wearing nothing more than her robe. Fortunately, it was warm in the kitchen. Afterwards, we stacked the dishes in the sink and took the rest of the wine out to the sofa. Instrumental jazz was quietly oozing from the speakers. We sat together on one end. Simone drew her bare legs up beneath her and tucked them under her robe.

"I keep wondering if things would have changed for Janet if she was a little different. Not that she had to be really outgoing, but just a bit more comfortable with whom she was." Simone was slowly turning the stem of the wineglass in her hands, watching the dark red liquid swirl around the glass. She paused to take a sip. Then she took another.

"Did she ever behave differently?"

Simone gave her head a slow shake. "Not really. Some people change when they get out of high school, maybe go away to college and open themselves up to new experiences. Janet wasn't like that."

"Maybe she was afraid to try. I haven't met her parents. Are they very outgoing?"

"Her dad is. Her mom is more like Janet, kind of quiet and shy. Mr. Calder was a manufacturer's representative, so he's very personable. He's a salesman. So what are you working on that's got you out on a miserable Sunday?"

"I really can't talk about the case with you. If I'm seeing you socially, we can't discuss any of the cases I'm involved with."

That shy smile flashed for a moment. "So you are seeing me."

"It would appear so."

"Want to see more of me?"

Somehow, I managed to get the belt of her robe undone. The wine was gone. The glasses perched on the table. We shifted, sprawling on the sofa. The stereo played on. All conversation was forgotten. After a while, Simone went to the bathroom. She returned dragging a heavy quilt. Once we were covered, the serious conversation resumed.

"Janet and I had more in common than I let on. She was shy around guys. I was more outgoing, but I always knew when I wanted to draw the line. Going to parties, dancing, sporting events, usually with a group, was the way we were. But even then Janet held back. It's as if she was afraid of having too much fun."

"Do you remember anything recently about her that changed?"

"She was starting to get a little friendlier with some of the people she worked with. And there was an office across the hall. I think it was a mortgage company. There were a few women there who kept inviting her out after work. But I don't know if she ever went with them."

I was about to ask another question when I saw Simone fight off a yawn. The humor that had been evident a few moments ago suddenly vanished. "Will you stay, Jeff? I'd understand if you have to leave. But it would be nice if you stayed."

I hesitated for a moment. Then I managed to get up from the sofa while still holding her in my arms. "I think the bed will be roomier tonight."

"Why, Sergeant, if we end up in the bed, we might have sex."

"I guess that's a risk I'm willing to take."

Simone wrapped her arms around my neck. "What a difference a week makes."

Chapter Twenty-Four

I stood and surveyed the scene. It was perfect. All that time and energy, the hours of meticulous study and planning, would soon be paying off once again. It was as if I were a maestro, conducting a famous symphony orchestra, where every player knew their part. Individually, it may not sound like much, but taken collectively, it was an auditory feast. But only I got to revel in the delight of all five senses with this scene. My eyes absorbed the next victim, drinking in the diminutive figure, the meager curves of the torso, and the long, narrow fingers on the outstretched hands.

My ears tingled in anticipation of hearing Melissa's voice. There was the soft, breathy escape of the words when she spoke. And there was the tantalizing thrill when she spoke my name. It was like an enormous adrenaline boost, knowing that my name would probably be one of the last words Melissa ever uttered.

My eyes closed momentarily. Then I drew a long, slow breath. The next victim's perfume drifted across the narrow space between us. The fragrance danced across the brain's receptors, subtle hints of lilac and honey and some mysterious wildflower. It wasn't heavy and overpowering, like so many perfumes could be. This was tantalizing and added to the overall effect. There was the sudden desire to pull Melissa close, with my nose pressed against the tender flesh of her neck, where inhaling the intoxicating essence would be so easy. The scent would be so rewarding. But it might be enough to disrupt my self-control.

My eyes snapped open. My tongue slid out and brushed the lips. Still present was the taste of the Melissa's kiss, her mouth pressed tentatively there only moments before. The tongue had briefly ventured into my mouth, seeking confirmation and reassurance. It had been the kiss of the timid, a daring preliminary exploration before a life-changing journey. If Melissa only knew how her life was about to change and how that kiss would be remembered.

The sense of touch was not to be outdone. I rolled my right thumb across the fingers. These same fingers remembered the tender skin just encountered, the feel of Melissa's hair, of her breasts under my feathery touch, a touch meant to excite, a hint of hidden delights lurking in the shadows.

Yes, all of the senses were in play. And that was just what I relished. For anything less was unacceptable. After going to such great lengths to design the plan, to implement it, not achieving the ultimate prize would not do.

I could not hold back a smile. "Your time is coming, darling Melissa. But we both must be patient. For the anticipation makes the journey so much more rewarding. The anticipation and the imagination make for such a fitting outcome. But even in the darkest recesses of your imagination, you could not possibly consider what I have in mind for you."

The next victim was returning now, walking on shaky legs back to me. If one looked closely, you could *see the energy jumping off her skin, little sparks of electricity that she was unable to contain. This was a combination of many things. It was as if the next victim was enjoying a forbidden cocktail that only I knew the recipe to. It was one part arousal, two parts fantasy, a touch of the great unknown, sprinkled with a dash of excitement. Yes, the next victim was definitely enjoying this cocktail.*

My smile widened as Melissa reached the table.
Yes, it was only a matter of time and timing.
And timing...is everything.

****

I wasn't expecting to hear from the cyber squad anytime soon. There were over a thousand files on Myers's computer that would need to be examined. And that didn't include the video files or the DVR. It was almost eight o'clock Monday evening. Megan and I had just left the post after another frustrating day of chasing leads. Kozlowski had spent the day in court, testifying on another case. Laura worked the computer, doing research. Cantrell was in Lansing, attending meetings. I didn't recognize the number when my phone rang as I was driving down Gratiot.

"Chene, this is Yekovich."

"What's up?"

"I've got something you might want to see."

Was it possible his team had found video evidence of one of the victims at Myers's house? I threw that question at him while executing a U-turn.

"No, it's not one of the victims. It's more complicated than that."

"Everything about this freaking case is complicated. Give me ten minutes."

"Done." With a click, he was gone.

There was no point in calling Megan or the others yet. This could be nothing of consequence. I drove to the building where the cyber squad was housed. Since they worked with such high-tech equipment, it made sense to have them separated from the regular state police posts. This facility serviced the needs of at least four counties. Yekovich was waiting for me at the doorway. He was about five six, with coarse black hair and a mustache that was so thick it didn't look real. He had a habit of smoothing it out with his thumb when he talked.

"You're working late."

"This serial killer got my interest. I was home watching a hockey game when my guy called, so I came back in. If there's anything my team can do to help nail him, we want a part of it."

"Spoken like a real cop."

Yekovich gave me a light jab on the shoulder. "I am a real cop, asshole. See, they even let me carry a gun." With that, he pointed at the pistol clipped in a holster on his belt.

"Damn, they'll give anyone a weapon these days."

He led me down a corridor into a series of large workstations. There were two technicians working. Computer components were spread across the counters, with large-screen monitors streaming data bytes like a stock exchange ticker gone wild. Yekovich stopped beside the last workstation.

"This here is Jeremy," he said, jerking a thumb at the gangly kid who was perched on a stool, staring intently at a monitor. The kid raised his eyes momentarily to look at me. "Sergeant Chene. He's running that investigation."

"Hey, Sarge."

I nodded to the kid. He didn't look old enough to drive, but he seemed right at home behind the pile of computer equipment. "So, what ya got?"

The kid was about to fill me in when Yekovich cut him off. "Use plain English and get to the point, Jeremy. Chene here chases real killers, not video game demons."

He paused to consider the best way to explain it. "I've been reviewing all the video from the external feed, the cameras that were on the motion detectors."

"What did you find?"

"The majority of the files were pretty mundane. Mostly they were of this dude coming and going in his Jeep. A couple of times he had a few other guys over."

"How far back are we talking?"

Jeremy tapped at his keyboard. "Earliest clips I've seen are date stamped around Thanksgiving."

"Is there any video of women coming into the house?" Yekovich asked.

Jeremy shook his head. "Nothing yet, and I've been watching so I could compare anyone with the pictures you gave me earlier."

"So why did you call me?"

"You need to see this, boss," Jeremy said.

I was facing Yekovich. We worked together a few times over the years, and it wasn't like him to call me without a reason. A sly grin crossed his face.

"The kid's talking to you."

Slowly, I spun my attention back to Jeremy. He jerked his thumb at a plasma screen that filled the back wall of his work area. I watched shadowy figures move across the screen. It was a little surreal as I recognized Myers walking into the living room. The quality of the video was poor and grainy. Apparently, Myers had skimped and bought inexpensive cameras. The audio quality wasn't much better.

Staring at the screen, I realized Myers wasn't alone. The room was dimly lit, but you could make out the image of someone else. The person was smaller than Myers. Together, they moved to the sofa that faced the big picture window.

"Any way you can enhance the quality of this?" I didn't risk taking my eyes off the screen. Jeremy froze the scene.

"Not a chance, boss. This is the best resolution I've been able to get. There is no light in the living room, just a little ambient light from outside and something from the kitchen."

"You mentioned the previous visitors were guys. Could this be one of them?"

"No way," Yekovich said quickly. "Jeremy showed me the other video clips. Both guys were bigger than Myers. And you need to keep watching."

Myers was on the left in the picture. The other person was wearing what looked like jeans, a hooded sweatshirt, and a baseball cap. They were sitting together on the sofa, legs touching. Myers had just started to raise his arm. I stepped closer to the screen. "Keep it going. Let's see why you really called me down here."

Jeremy clicked his keyboard. Yekovich moved up alongside me. Jeremy was watching the action on the monitor, so he had his back to the big screen. The video play resumed, showing Myers turn toward his visitor and put his arm around the person's shoulders. From the body size, I suspected this was a woman. The shape of her face was partially hidden by the hood and the brim of the ball cap. Myers completed his turn and now moved in for a kiss. Her response surprised me. This wasn't a romantic, passionate, tender kiss. It was animalistic, filled with hunger. I saw her hands come up to his face. Even with the elevated angle of the camera, there was not a lot of detail visible. All three of us were silent, watching the action play out. Myers's free hand went to the bottom of the woman's hooded sweatshirt and began pulling it up. It took only a few seconds to confirm my hunch. Her flat stomach soon appeared, followed by the image of a lacy bra. Myers kept kissing her, his hand now lifting the cup above her breast, revealing the small, pale globe.

"Dumb shit didn't even try to unhook it," Yekovich said.

"He's in too much of a hurry," I said. "Might be afraid to break that kiss for fear she'll make him stop." My eyes flicked to the date stamp on the bottom of the screen: February 22 of this year.

Yekovich must have been thinking along the same lines. "It looks to me like she was the one controlling the play. Don't think this guy was getting much action. This is the first female visitor. Unless he was spending time at her place, which I kind of doubt. Most of the footage we've viewed shows him home almost every night at the same time."

We watched the girl slide onto her back and pull Myers on top of her. They were still locked in the kiss. After a minute or so, she pushed him back. There was a muttered conversation before they rose from the sofa and headed down the hall. No lights came on. I could hear the clicks as Jeremy's fingers danced on the keyboard. The scene shifted. This was the camera we'd found in the bedroom smoke detector. Myers and the woman moved quickly into the room. They embraced roughly, hands aggressively groping each other. Simultaneously, they began undoing each other's jeans. As the clothing hit the floor, I saw lacy panties on the woman's hips that probably matched the bra she was wearing. Myers reached for her sweatshirt, but she knocked his hands away. He shrugged, then sprawled on his back across the bed. The woman slipped off her panties. She kept the hood and cap in place as she straddled him. Soon, they were moving in unison.

"Tell me you didn't call me here to watch cheap porn?"

"It gets better," Yekovich said. "And this guy doesn't last long."

We watched the woman set the tempo, taking charge of the situation, moving quickly to satisfy her own needs. The only soundtrack was the grunts and groans from the pair and the squeak of the bed. She arched her back and shuddered, then placed both palms on Myers's chest. As he reached for her, she swatted his hands away. Satisfied, she went prone on the bed beside him. Jeremy's fingers did their dance again, and the images flickered on the screen.

"Here's where it gets even better," Yekovich said.

According to the time stamp in the bottom corner of the screen, about an hour had passed. Myers was still sprawled on his back. At some point, one of them had drawn a blanket across their bodies, covering them from the chest down. Now there was movement. The woman rose from beside him, her head turned to confirm that he was still asleep. During the time lapse, she had removed the ball cap from her head. But the hood of the sweatshirt remained in place. The bed was in the center of the room, which enabled her to climb out on her side without disturbing Myers. We watched as she moved across the foot of the bed and began to step back into her jeans. I could feel my eyes straining, trying to draw in every detail, looking for something to help identify her. But there was nothing beyond the lily white skin. No tattoos, no scars, no birthmarks to help single her out in the crowd.

"Almost there," Jeremy said quietly.

She turned once again making sure Myers was still out. Now she disappeared from the scene. Before I could tell Jeremy to switch to another camera, she was back, holding one of those crappy vinyl kitchen chairs. She placed it on the floor, glanced up and then stepped onto the chair. Working quickly, she removed the globe of the light fixture. Holding it in one hand, she dug a small packet from the pocket of her jeans. As she tilted her head to look at the fixture, the hood fell back to her shoulders.

"Freeze that!"

"Way ahead of you, boss."

****

It was well past midnight when I arrived home. My eyes felt so raw and dry, it was as if I'd been walking across the desert. Staring at computer monitors for most of the night without blinking has a similar effect. After peeling off my clothes, I collapsed on the bed and waited for sleep to arrive. Something told me it could be a long way off. I tried a hot shower, but it didn't help. Maybe it was the Korean food I'd had for dinner a few hours ago.

Yekovich had sent Jeremy out to a nearby restaurant. The kid came back with cartons of bulgogi, a barbecued beef dish, rice, noodles, and spicy kimchi, the pickled cabbage that has varying degrees of heat. We devoured the food while staring at the monitors as Jeremy tried every possible trick in his bag to enhance the image from the video file.

There could be no other explanation. The woman who had sex with Myers waited until he was asleep to hide something in the light fixture, about a month before we discovered it after the shooting. Obviously, it was the jewelry from the first two victims. That discovery now opened the door to so many questions.

When did she obtain the jewelry? How did she get it? Was she working with the killer? What role did Myers play in all of this?

The photos Jeremy printed out were the best we could do. The cyber squad had the latest equipment the budget could buy. I needed some sleep and a chance to look at this from a different perspective. And with any luck, the answers to even a few of these questions might surface in the light of day.

****

It was just after six when I arrived at the post Tuesday morning. It would be months before it was daylight this early. But somewhere off to the east, dawn was breaking. I hoped it brought good fortune with it. I wasn't surprised to see Cantrell already in his office. Pappy liked to come in early, just to get caught up on the various reports, especially since he'd been gone the last two days. Leaning against his doorjamb, I rapped a knuckle on the frame.

"Hope y'all brought coffee, Chene. That damn machine down the hall don't work for shit."

I set a large cardboard cup on his desk. Cantrell popped the lid, eyed it suspiciously, and shifted his gaze to me.

"That's hot, strong coffee, with no fancy flavors, no cream, and no sugar."

"Just like ah want my women," he said, "hot and strong." He lifted the cup and took a sip. Cantrell liked the simple things in life. After working for him all these years, grabbing a coffee was easy. He was a steak and potatoes kind of guy.

"Y'all look like hell."

I collapsed into the chair across from his desk and handed over the folder with the photos. Taking a healthy slug of my own coffee, I spelled it out for him. Cantrell was squinting at the pictures, as if through determination alone he might bring more detail into focus. I hoped he could make it happen.

"Y'all think this woman is workin' with the killer somehow?"

"I don't know, Pappy. Some guys end up with groupies, but I just can't get my head around that idea."

He drummed a finger on the desk a moment, then flicked his eyes to the clock on the wall. It was positioned at the very top, dead center across from his desk. Beneath the clock were rows of pictures of the squad, the different versions he had commanded for over fifteen years. On the right hand side were individual photos of three deceased detectives who had served under Cantrell. Evans and Fleming died shortly after retirement, the former in a car accident, the latter of a heart attack. Barksdale was the other photo. He was the first one who had been killed in the line of duty under Pappy's command.

"Run this by me again," he grumbled.

I floated the same bunch of questions that had been haunting me all night. What was this woman's connection with the killer? How had she gotten the jewelry to leave behind? How did she connect with Myers? Was she a one-night stand or was this an ongoing relationship? Who was she? Where could we find her?

"Them's all good ones. Y'all could be playin' dominoes here."

I couldn't make the connection. "What does dominoes have to do with anything, Pappy?"

"Y'all get one answer, it might just knock down some more of those questions."

We talked about the theory Donna Spears had developed. Pappy was open-minded, but I could tell he was still struggling with the idea of a female serial killer, particularly one who was killing other women. After a while, Cantrell pushed away from his desk.

"Y'all member what today is?"

"I didn't forget. My uniform is in my locker. I just wanted to get a few things done before the service."

Pappy nodded. "Y'all bring the squad. It's that Catholic church near the lake."

Barksdale's funeral was this morning. His ex-wife had requested a closed casket. It was expected there would be officers from across the state in attendance. There was a funeral mass scheduled and then a long drive out to the cemetery. Even Pappy was going to be in uniform. As I was headed for the locker room to change, he caught my arm in his vise-like grip.

"Y'all really think a woman could be our killer?"

"At this stage, Pappy, I'm open to the possibility."

"Y'all get surveillance on?"

"Yeah, and I'm calling in a couple of favors too."

The funeral for a fallen officer would be on the news. Yesterday, I reached out to Lauren Podell, a reporter on Channel 4 who had often cooperated with us in the past. She would be in attendance, along with a camera crew. Probably less than sixty seconds of footage would ever be broadcast to the public. But Lauren would have her team film the mourners, both in the church and at the cemetery. She'd give me a copy later. We would have two cameras going from a surveillance squad, but I wanted more footage.

Cantrell locked his office and headed for the door. By the time I got changed, Kozlowski, Megan, and Laura were all gathered in the bullpen. Each was wearing their pressed uniform. There was no friendly banter this morning. We wouldn't discuss the case or trade updates from yesterday's efforts. There would be plenty of time for that later. Kozlowski checked his watch and nodded.

"It's time to go."

Chapter Twenty-Five

I wanted to see it firsthand. There was no reason to worry. The misdirection had worked perfectly. Hell, it worked better than imagined. Who would have expected Charlie to react as he did? Still, it was surprising when the news was broadcast. The scene looked like something out of a low-budget spy movie, with glass fragments reflected in the spotlights like diamond crystals, doors and windows imploded, and splatters of blood visible in the distance. It was too bad about Charlie. But those were the breaks.

A look in the mirror confirmed it. Here was just another mourner, all dressed in black, going to pay their last respects to a fallen officer. I bit back a smile. The place would be swarming with cops. The newscaster earlier said they expected over five hundred police officers from departments across the state to attend. They would all be there as a tribute to Detective Barksdale, just as they should be. But not one of them would be looking for me. As far as the cops were concerned, Charlie had been the killer, and Charlie was most definitely dead.

I slipped on a pair of dark glasses. The sun was actually shining this morning, which was unusual for a funeral. Every funeral I've previously attended always included rain. The drive to the church was uneventful. I fell into step with the crowd and soon was seated in the middle of the group on the left side of the church. Uniforms were everywhere.

I watched as the casket was brought in. Six cops were pall bearers, all in the dark blue uniforms of the state police. They sat in the second row, behind Detective Barksdale's family. Discreetly, I watched that group while the priest began the service. Hymns were sung. Prayers were read. A few people came up to speak about what a great guy the late detective was. Now the priest was completing the service. The pallbearers moved solemnly up to the casket and began to escort it out. The mourners turned to face the casket as it rolled past. I calmly waited until the church began to empty. There would be a procession to the cemetery. A wonderful sense of calm flowed over me as everyone left the church and walked to their cars.

I joined the flow of traffic. How ironic to be surrounded by so many police officers, all wearing their dress uniforms, all looking so strict and serious. If only they knew who was in their midst! But they had no inkling. And I would not give them a reason to think otherwise.

At the cemetery, people lined up inside a large marble building. There were crypts along the walls in some spots. Since the weather was so unpredictable, there would be no gravesite service. Instead, the priest uttered a few more words. An honor guard of state troopers stood outside, rifles at the ready. At a signal, they fired blanks into the air. In the distance, a police officer, wearing a kilt, began playing a mournful tune on a set of bagpipes. The flag that draped the coffin was ceremoniously folded and handed to Barksdale's ex-wife.

What happened next surprised me. The pallbearers turned and saluted the casket. Then each one leaned forward and knocked once on the shiny wooden box. The service was over. Other cops moved forward and thumped the coffin as well. I slowly drifted toward the exit. The six pallbearers stood at the door, solemnly thanking everyone for their support. These were people Barksdale worked with.

My heart was beating a little faster. The pallbearer on the right was a pale-skinned black man. I hesitated behind an older couple. The pallbearer thanked them all for supporting the family. Staying close behind the older couple, I slipped out the door and into the sunshine.

Yes, it had been a good plan.

"I am so smooth, they don't have a clue."

****

It was late afternoon when we returned from the funeral and luncheon. Only after we were secured in the conference room did Cantrell bring out the photos. We spent the next several hours discussing the pictures, Donna Spears's theory about a woman as a killer, and the results of the meetings with the militia unit. Kozlowski and Laura described their meeting with the only living relative of Charlie Myers.

"The aunt wasn't much help," Kozlowski said. "She hadn't seen him since the trial for the date rape. Parents died when he was twelve in a boating accident. She raised him, but they were never close. We learned a little more about his background, but nothing of consequence."

Laura had one bit to add. "The aunt said that Charlie was very shy around girls. Apparently, the neighbor girl he had sex with that led to him going to prison was promiscuous and a bit of a wild child. Once Charlie served his time, he didn't want anything to do with her. The aunt said he deliberately stayed away from her home so he wouldn't accidentally run into her."

"Sounds like he didn't want to be tempted," Megan said.

We worked on the theories until Cantrell raised a hand.

"Y'all beatin' a dead horse. This day's been long enough. Git."

The others didn't hesitate. The strain of attending the funeral was wearing us all down. They headed for the doors. But I wasn't ready to leave.

I had no idea what time it was, but it was obviously late. The squad room was empty. For the last few hours, I'd read Donna's updates. I'd stared at our victims' pictures, determined to spot the link. Where did the mystery woman from the video fit in? I felt stale. Coffee had no appeal. Food was a distant memory. I leaned back. My eyes felt like sandpaper. I closed them for a second and started hearing voices. Well, one voice.

"Hello, Jeff." It was soft, almost a whisper. I was afraid to open my eyes, thinking that I might be imagining things. Reluctantly, I slid them open. What greeted me was a timid vision in blue jeans, with a pale blue sweater and a denim jacket. Her hands fiddled with the strap on her purse.

"Simone. What are you doing here?"

Nervously, she looked over her shoulder. "The officer at the desk said I could come back. He knew you were still here."

"It's okay." I looked around the room, with the empty desks and piles of paperwork everywhere. This was not the place I wanted to be with her, especially with the victims' pictures pinned to the board. "I was just going to call it a night."

"Do you normally work another assignment right after you solve one? I mean, you did get Janet's killer."

"We often work a number of cases simultaneously." I rose from my chair and pulled my jacket on.

"Could we go for a cup of coffee or maybe a drink?"

"Sure."

"Maybe we could talk a little."

After Barksdale's funeral, I owed it to him to stay focused on the case. A thousand excuses shot through my mind. Mentally, I slapped them away like a swarm of mosquitoes. "I'd like that."

****

"I must look like a mess," Simone said, raking her fingers through her hair.

We were sitting in a booth at the small neighborhood bar called Murphy's, not far from her apartment. There was room for about forty people in the whole place. Right now, there was just the two of us, a bartender, and two young couples at the far end of the room. The lights were dim. The greasy odor of burgers and fries filled the air. It was a simple place that probably jumped on the weekends or when the college kids were home for the summer.

We had dropped her car at the apartment, and she'd ridden the half mile to the bar with me. I planned to have one drink, take her home, and split. As we were pulling into the lot, a cloud erupted, drenching both of us. She'd made the comment after ordering a glass of wine.

"It's all a matter of perspective. Cops learn to look at the details from more than one angle. Sometimes, you can stare at something that's right in front of you and never realize what it is, until you look at it another way."

Now she smiled at my response. "So what is it you're trying to say, Jeff?"

"That I don't think you look like a mess."

The smile filled her face a little more, touching her eyes. "You could have just come out and said that."

I gave her a shrug and felt a smile tugging the corners of my mouth. "That would have been too easy."

The bartender placed two glasses of wine on the table and a bowl of honey-roasted peanuts. We clinked glasses and tasted it, a Chardonnay from a West Michigan vineyard, not bad at all. I could get used to this. Simone set her glass down on a coaster and began to dig in her purse while I sampled the peanuts. I pushed everything else from my mind and focused on her. My eyes flicked to the bar as she opened a compact. I could see her reflection in the mirror behind the bar, checking her own reflection in the compact's little mirror. Something went skittering across the back of my mind, but I couldn't catch it. She fluffed her hair, checked her eyes, then returned the compact to her purse and took another dainty sip of wine.

We nibbled the peanuts, drank the wine, and made small talk. In less time than I realized it, our glasses and the bowl were empty. We were watching each other, the unspoken question hanging in the air between us. I paid the bill and walked her outside. She took my hand as we reached the door.

We didn't talk on the way back to her place. The rain continued, following us down the street and into the parking lot. Switching off the car, I turned toward her and caught a whiff of perfume. Closing my eyes, I drew in a deep breath.

"Breathless," she said, leaning closer.

"What?" We were centimeters apart.

"My perfume, it's called Breathless." She moved against me, pressing her lips to mine. Despite my best intentions, I could feel my arms going around her, drawing her close. The kiss lasted several minutes, with neither one of us pulling away. Then Simone leaned back, her eyes somewhat glassy. "Upstairs?"

"Yes."

We didn't notice that the rain was pounding on the roof as we exited the car. By the time we made it to the shelter of the building, we were soaked. Once inside the apartment, I paused in the doorway, watching the puddle quickly form at my feet. Simone smothered a laugh and ducked into the bathroom. She reappeared, clutching two large towels and pitched them to me.

"You'll catch pneumonia if you don't get out of those clothes. Start drying off. I'll be right back."

I pulled off my jacket and hung it on the door, and levered off my shoes. The shoulder holster followed. I had managed to remove my sweater when she returned. Simone was wrapped in a thick cotton robe that reached the floor, with a towel twirled around her hair. Clucking like a disappointed mother, she pulled the sweater from my fingers and went into the kitchen. Curious, I followed. She draped it over a chair, then turned the oven on low and opened the door.

"It will dry faster that way. How about the jeans?" She was doing her best to suppress a smile.

"Thanks, but I'll keep them."

"Suit yourself."

I don't know who moved first. We were locked in another kiss. Suddenly, the kitchen became very warm. I realized my hands were operating of their own accord, instinctively untying the belt on her robe, sliding it off her shoulders. I felt Simone's hands caressing my back, sliding around my waist. There was a snap and the unmistakable sound of a zipper being undone. My jeans were suddenly pooled around my ankles. No man in the world can look suave with his feet tangled in his pants. I kicked them off. Simone stepped back, her eyes full of anticipation. Without a word, she led me to her bed.

****

An hour later, Simone slipped from my arms. She glided off the bed, reached in the closet, and pulled a different, shorter robe around her. I found her modesty endearing, particularly after what we just shared. She disappeared into the kitchen, returned with two glasses of wine and reported that my jeans were now drying nicely. Simone perched on the edge of the bed beside me. I was sitting up, the blankets around my waist, with my free hand wrapped in hers.

"Damn," she said, pulling away to rub her eye.

"What's wrong?"

"It's probably just an eyelash." She stood, setting her wine on the dresser. Simone withdrew the compact from her purse and held it close to her face, trying to flick whatever it was out of her eye. I looked beyond her, watching her reflection in the mirror behind the dresser. That skittering sensation came back. Only this time, it lingered long enough for me to snare it.

"Fuck me hard."

Simone's head came up quickly, having finally dislodged the troublesome lash. "What did you say?"

I placed the glass on the dresser beside hers. Delicately, I took her face in my hands and kissed her forehead, her eyelids, her nose, her ears, and then her mouth. As she started to react, reaching for me, I backed away.

"Thank you, Simone."

Her voice was a whispery gasp of breath. "Don't stop thanking me now."

"I need a lipstick."

"Why, Sergeant, what do you have in mind?"

"Catching a killer." I extended my hand toward her purse. "Lipstick."

She grabbed the purse, clutching it protectively to her chest. "It's expensive."

"Simone, I will buy you two lipsticks and a bottle of that perfume as soon as the stores open tomorrow. But I need a lipstick."

Reluctantly, she handed it over. Uncapping it, I leaned toward the mirror. There was no logical reason to do this, but I did it anyway. In six-inch letters, I wrote out the message on the mirror. Then I picked up the compact from where she'd left it on the dresser, turned around and looked at the reflection of the reflection.

"Gotcha!"

We had been putting in so many hours I knew everyone was fried. I could have made the call and scrambled them all to the squad room immediately, but it wasn't worth it. I made one call to dispatch, placed my request, then silenced the phone. Simone was sitting on the edge of the bed, watching me with a curious expression as I wiped the lipstick off the mirror.

"Will you please tell me what is going on? If this is your idea of romantic afterglow, it's not doing much for me."

I was so pumped there was little chance I would sleep. But it didn't matter. I eased her under the covers and slid in beside her. "It's complicated. But when you used the compact, you triggered something I've been working on."

She smothered a yawn into my chest. "Is that part of that line you were using at the bar?"

"It wasn't a line. It's the truth. You helped me see something from another perspective. It's something that could be very important."

"But you can't tell me about?"

"Not just yet. I need time to follow up on it, to see where it might lead." I was slowly letting my fingers sift through her hair, letting the strands play out to the end. She had such silky hair that I wanted to bury my face in it for an hour or two. Or maybe I would linger for a month or two, or better yet, a year or two.

"And 'fuck me hard'? Was that some kind of kinky request?"

I shook my head and gently kissed her neck, right behind her ear. "Nah, just a term of endearment our fearless leader has been known to use. It's very appropriate. And he often says it when we finally get a break on something that's been eluding us."

She yawned again and snuggled closer. "Will you

stay with me, Jeff? Or does this mean you're going to leave now?" There was a timid quality to her voice that made me picture her as a young girl.

"I'll stay. But I have to get to the post early."

Simone wrapped her arms around me. She was still wearing the short robe and as she pressed against me, I inhaled another breath of her perfume. Maybe she'd dabbed a little more on when I was on the phone. Would I ever forget that fragrance? I hoped not.

"Will you kiss me good night?"

Tenderly, I brushed my lips against hers. "Good night, Simone."

"Good night, Chene. You know, you aren't as tough as you pretend to be."

There was no more conversation. Anything I could say was unnecessary. My body was already responding to hers as the robe seemed to disappear at my touch. We made love again, taking our time, discovering the excitement that accompanies the pleasure.

As she dozed off in my arms, I wondered about her comment. She may be right. But I'm also a lot more screwed up than I pretend to be.

Chapter Twenty-Six

I was the first one at the squad at six. With a fresh cup of coffee and two bagels inside me, I was energized. The caffeine was churning when Kozlowski walked in twenty minutes behind me. He slumped into his chair and started working on his own coffee. His eyes went to the large brown bag filled with bagels. I'd brought in a dozen for the squad. I hadn't bothered with cream cheese.

"Do me a favor."

"This early on a Wednesday morning, it better be good."

"Call Megan and Laura and tell them to get here right away. Then wake Pappy and tell him we've caught another break." Normally, Cantrell was in early, but yesterday he mentioned a district conference on his calendar for today. He had planned to hoist a few drinks in Barksdale's honor last night.

Without a comment, he called the others. Since he didn't know yet what it was about, he didn't waste time trying to answer their questions. He took great pleasure in rousting Cantrell from his bed.

"Pappy said one hour. It didn't sound like he was alone. He also said it better be worth it, and if you start without him, there would be hell to pay." He extended a hand across the desk. "Give. You ain't gonna make me wait an hour."

"What about Cantrell's warning?"

"Letting me read it does not qualify as starting."

I flipped him the folder. There were copies ready for the others. Inside was the little bit of information I was able to garner this morning. I made a list of which steps we should take next, and how I would break them out among the team. While he was reading it, I went over the notes, rearranging a couple of points here, adding a few things. Koz scanned the list. He made a couple of suggestions and propped his feet on the desk.

"What do you think?"

"I think you're on to something. But this is a twisted piece of work, isn't it?"

"Yes, it is."

"You think this is the one?"

"I think within forty-eight hours we're going to find out."

"Fuck me hard," he said with a wide grin.

"That was my reaction too."

****

We were silently sitting around the conference table, waiting for Cantrell to arrive. Koz and I had kicked it around and decided to hold back the details from Laura and Megan. Instead, we compiled folders for everyone with only the basic crime-scene photos and the message from the mirror. It was a sullen twenty minutes that we kept the girls waiting before Pappy showed up.

Cantrell hadn't bothered to shave. He was wearing jeans, an old faded striped shirt, and a pair of battered loafers that hadn't seen polish in a dozen years. He didn't reach for his coffee, which was not a good sign. Instead, he slipped into his chair, made a steeple with his tobacco-stained fingers, and focused his bloodshot eyes on me. "Go."

"The killer was taunting us, right from the beginning. We just never put it together. The killer was autographing each scene." I pointed to the manila folder that was in front of each person. Cantrell opened his to the crime-scene photo that was on the top.

"We been over this. It was Myers's license plate. We went after him. Got the search warrant. Found the victim's rings. Dug up that stuff from his past." The disgust in his tone was so evident it thickened his accent.

"Myers was the patsy. But the real killer was still waving their identity in our faces," Koz said.

"What the killer wrote was 'WHY 319?'. The killer had us chasing our tails, trying to figure out the connection between the hotel rooms and the victims. We did it all. Even went so far as checking with a numerology expert and a priest, looking for the significance of that number." I moved to the interior window of the conference room where earlier I had drawn the blinds. Before the rest of the team arrived, I had written the message on the window in the hallway with a dry erase marker. Now I pulled the blinds back and stepped aside. "Tell me what you see."

Laura answered first. "913 YHW. It's the mirror image of the message."

"It's his autograph," Megan whispered, "his license plate."

Cantrell glared at the window. "It check out?"

"Yeah, it's starting to come together."

"Fuck me hard." Pappy brought his gaze back to me. From the corner of my eye, I could see

Kozlowski's grin. "Give."

"You ain't gonna like it," Koz said.

"Her name is Victoria Marie Samuels. She's twenty-five, five foot six, brown hair, brown eyes." I pointed at the folders in front of them.

"Y'all tryin' to tell me this is our killer?" Cantrell pulled a cigarette from his pocket, but he didn't light it. "What makes y'all sure it ain't another goose?"

Laura flipped her folder open and checked out the photo, which we had pulled from the driver's license files. "Just look at her," she said in awe, "she looks like our victims. She's another plain Jane."

For a moment, no one said anything at all. Kozlowski and I sat back and waited while the others flipped through the scant background. Cantrell finished reading his file and neatly aligned the corners of the papers. Then he slowly tapped a gnarled finger on the stack, waiting for the others to catch up. It wasn't a long wait.

"Start talking, Chene."

"The little bit of information we've got so far doesn't scratch the surface. We need to do a complete work up on her background. Employment history, education, medical, anything and everything that we can find on her will be just the beginning. Then we need to check out known associates and see where that takes us."

Pappy tapped the stack of papers again. "Y'all got a lot to do to convince me this is your serial killer."

Laura chimed in. "A female serial killer? A woman who is seducing other women and then killing them? I've never heard of a female serial killer, unless you count that one that was bumping off residents in a nursing home years back."

"There's always been the theory that Jack the Ripper was really a woman," Kozlowski said thoughtfully.

"Samuels was busted twice for misdemeanors in the last year. Possession of marijuana and writing a bad check." Megan read aloud from the report. "There's nothing to indicate violence here, or instability of any kind. All you have is the license plate number registered to her."

I nodded in agreement. "But we've built cases with less and everyone knows it. This could be a fluke, nothing more than a coincidence. But I don't think so. Remember the summary that Donna Spears gave us. This could be a predator that lulls her victims into a sense of comfort, a false sense of security, someone who has shared the difficulty of relationships and can relate to how cruel life can be."

"Which proves my argument about Myers," Megan said. "None of these women would have given him a second glance. So if we take Donna's theory seriously, this woman could be coyly leading her victims along."

"There's also the picture Yekovich found on that videotape." I pointed at the copies we had all viewed before. While they were grainy and dim, there was no mistaking the similarities between Victoria Samuels's driver's license photo and the still from the Myers house.

Cantrell tapped the thin file and looked around the table at each of us for a moment before speaking. "What's your plan, Chene?"

"We need to put a body on her, but I don't want to spook her. We need to know everything we can before going in for an arrest. The more details we can put together, the easier it will be for a warrant. She lives in Ferndale. Megan, you and I will go to the house. We'll handle the stakeout and see what she does on a soggy Wednesday morning. Laura, get on the computer and work your magic. I want to know everything you can find about her."

Kozlowski interrupted. "Didn't you tell me that you were tight with a guy from the IRS?"

Laura batted her lashes. "It depends on your definition of 'tight.' But to answer your question, yes, I'll call him and find out the details. Earnings last year, who her employer was, deductions, charities, property, the whole works."

"Check the newspaper morgues. See if there's any mention on her anywhere in the last two years. Find out where she went to high school and college. We may need to look at school papers and yearbooks."

She nodded once. "Right away, boss."

"Koz, you work with Laura. Start digging into where she currently works and her known associates. Check the social networks and anything else you can think of. We still need to find a connection between her and our victims."

"I'm on it."

Megan chimed in. "I'll call Donna and have her send that summary over. There may be something in the profile that fills in the blanks."

"Have her take another look at those cell phone records from the victims. We know they were all recently calling disposable phones. See if there's any way she can trace them back to the point of purchase. Maybe our killer got sloppy and bought them all from the same store."

Cantrell nodded and fluttered his hand in the air. "Git busy. Check in when you've got something solid."

The others headed out, but he stopped me with a look. Pappy waited until the door closed before speaking. "Good work, Chene. Now build me a tight case on this bitch fore she kills again."

****

Just in case she was paranoid and looking for a tail, we took two cars to the Samuels house. It was a small bungalow in the middle of a block, a dozen houses east of Woodward on a quiet residential street. Many of the houses were similar, little places that were built after the end of World War I. This was a part of town where the streets were all uniform in nature, running perfectly east-west or north-south. Megan parked down the block, where she could see the front of the house and the drive. There was an older Dodge sedan in the driveway. The plate matched. I made a detour on the way and pulled up beside Megan, lowering the window to pass her a cup of Starbucks coffee.

"You're in a good mood," she said with a smile. She wiggled her eyebrows. "You must have gotten laid last night."

"Shut up and drink your coffee. Don't use the police radio. She may be paranoid enough to have a scanner inside. Cell phones only." I closed the window and drove around the block, parking on a corner where I could see the edge of the house. Megan called me as I switched off the engine.

"Chene, you forgot the sugar for my coffee."

"I can't remember all the flavorings you put in there and still call it coffee. I know you have a candy

262

bar in the glove box. Break off a chunk and let it melt in the coffee."

"More than twenty years you've known me, and I always sweeten my coffee. You think she still lives with her parents?"

"It's possible. Kozlowski was going to run a title search on the property. With the housing market being on the skids, she may have bought this on a foreclosure."

"When you think about it, this house really is a central location."

Maybe it was the lack of sleep kicking in. "I'm not following that."

While Megan was talking, I dug out a map of the metro area. I drew a circle around each of the three hotels where the victims had been found. Another circle went to the intersection where we were currently sitting. You could draw a line from each site. Megan had nailed it.

"Spokes on a wheel," she said.

"Which begs the question, where would her next target be?"

"She could go back to the beginning, start over in Wayne County again."

It made sense. Ferndale was just across the border from Detroit. Half a mile south, you were in Wayne County. Ferndale was the furthest city south in Oakland County and only minutes west of Macomb County. This really was a central location.

We talked about the possibilities, watching the house, drinking the coffee. Stakeouts can be boring, but neither one of us was impatient. We had done this many times before. Megan asked several prying personal questions, which I ignored. She was just about to start describing her date from last night, when the door to the bungalow opened and a woman stepped out. She was wearing jeans, tennis shoes, and a long woolen coat. But her head was bare, and her face was visible. Using the binoculars I kept in the center console, I was able to verify that she was Victoria Samuels.

"She's on the move," Megan said. She slid low in her seat, so only the top of her head was visible.

Samuels started the Dodge, then backed out of the driveway and headed right at McDonald. Megan slumped across the seat, so it appeared as if the Mustang was empty. I put the Pontiac into gear and rolled behind her.

"Looks like the game is afoot, Chene."

We tailed her right out Woodward Avenue. She stopped at the same Starbucks I visited earlier. Megan went in, keeping a couple of other people between them. Samuels bought a latte and didn't linger in the store. I picked her up from the parking lot and we continued north.

"You buy me a coffee?" I asked Megan when she clicked back on the phone.

"Sure did. I got you one caramel latte with skim milk and two sugars."

"I hope you enjoy it. That sounds like an ice cream sundae, not coffee."

"Chene, you really do need to get out more. Where are you?"

I gave her the location, and she sped up. We would leapfrog the Dodge, making sure to keep her in sight, yet not right on her bumper. Megan pulled alongside her at one point and even rode half a mile in front of her. It's harder to spot a tail when two cars are involved and next to impossible to lose it.

Samuels pulled into an athletic club. She carried her latte inside, a canvas bag draped over her shoulder.

"How's your tennis game?" Megan asked.

"I'm guessing racquetball, or a training session."

"You look like you could use a workout, Chene."

I watched Megan drive into the lot and park next to the Dodge, which Samuels had purposely parked in a remote corner. "Guess it's time to find out what sort of amenities this place has. Think you can find something to occupy your time?"

"You check out the club. I'll take the car."

"Keep your phone with you and on. And keep a low profile."

The sarcasm was thick in her voice. "Yes, Father. I have done this before. Besides, the rain will help shroud me, and I'm doubtful anyone will pay much attention at this end of the parking lot."

"Just don't get cocky. Watch out for the security cameras."

Now her voice was filled with subdued laughter. "I see them. Women have different equipment, Chene. We can be confident, not cocky. Someday, you may figure out the difference."

"The day I figure that out is the same day I figure out women. And who invented flavored coffees."

"Aren't you supposed to be watching our suspect?"

"Be cool. I'm on my way."

Chapter Twenty-Seven

The health club was very plush. You could tell that from the walk leading up to the door. This wasn't a chain or franchise, but one privately owned and operated. There were six outdoor tennis courts that would be busy when the warmer temperatures finally arrived and the rains ceased. Right now, it looked pretty desolate. But inside, things were jumping.

A young blonde woman named Beryl, who was struggling to keep her bountiful chest inside her blouse, greeted me at the reception area. She plied me with a glossy brochure of the place, then asked if I wanted to take the tour. She almost did a cheer when I agreed.

From the reception area, Beryl led me past two glass-enclosed classrooms, where Pilates and yoga lessons were being conducted. Down a hallway was another room with spinning cycles. Around the corner, I saw a traditional weight room, where about a dozen men and women were using the free weights and various exercise machines. Samuels was not among them. We passed through the corridor and went into another section, where there were two indoor tennis courts and several racquetball courts. Beryl led me upstairs to an observation area. At the end of the hall, you could also look out over an Olympic-size swimming pool. Serious aquatic types were diligently swimming laps, complete with racing kicks and turns.

We were just turning back when I spotted Victoria Samuels. She entered the pool area, shaking back her hair before tucking it into a swimming cap. She was wearing a tight one-piece bathing suit. Obviously, this wasn't a place for cutoffs and a torn T-shirt or string bikinis. She walked carefully over to the deep end and took a moment to chat with the lifeguard. He greeted her with a quick smile and jerked his head at the last vacant lane by the outside wall.

"Shall we continue with the tour?" Beryl was growing impatient.

"Would you mind if I just wander around? I'd like to watch a little tennis, check out the locker rooms, that kind of thing."

Her smile faltered. But she nodded in agreement then pointed me in the general direction of the locker rooms. I waited until she was gone before moving closer to the edge of the observation area overlooking the pool. Near the plate glass window were several upholstered chairs and sofas, arranged in cozy conversation areas. An older couple had taken up residence on one sofa, sections of what looked like the New York Times spread out between them.

I took one of the chairs and turned to watch Victoria Samuels knife through the water. She maintained a strong, steady pace. The impression that I had seen her before was unmistakable. Laura was right.

She looked exactly like the victims.

In the window's reflection, I caught a glimpse of Megan approaching. She smiled, but I could tell it was strictly for show as her eyes remained cold. I faced her. She bent close, pressing her cheek near mine. Over her shoulder, I caught a glimpse of Beryl turning around.

"She gone?"

"Yes. I'm surprised she didn't offer to give you the tour."

Megan settled into the chair beside me. I jerked my head toward the pool. "She's in the last lane, by the outside wall."

Megan's eyes tracked the movement. We watched Victoria approach the near wall and execute a precise flip turn. She was all arms and legs, churning the water steadily. Megan confirmed my assessment of Victoria's physical similarity to our victims. We discussed options, while keeping an eye on the pool. I considered having Megan walk through the locker room when Victoria was changing. But the more I thought about it, the more I disliked the idea. There was no reason to tip our hand. We still had a lot of work to do to build our case. It was time to call up some help.

****

Megan and I followed her all day. After the gym, she'd gone shopping for groceries and made a stop at Somerset Mall in Troy. Since Megan followed her into the coffee shop, I went in for groceries. I bought a few things and wandered the aisles while Victoria filled her cart. She didn't buy anything perishable, so she didn't have to rush home. By the time we hit the mall, Megan had switched jackets and followed her at a discreet distance. I entered from a different door. Between us, we kept watch.

Cantrell pulled a couple of members of Squad Five to play babysitter. They were watching over Victoria Samuels when she returned home around five thirty that afternoon. Their orders were to observe, from a safe distance. The team was back at the office, gathered around the conference table. Cantrell was in a positive mood. There was a cloud of cigarette smoke clinging to the ceiling. No one bothered to comment. No one cared.

"Awright, y'all here, so let's get started." He jabbed a bony finger in Laura's direction.

She passed out copies as she began her narration. "This girl is something else. She doesn't come from money, worked her way through college. There was a brief marriage when she was twenty-three. I haven't been able to find pictures, but there was a record of a marriage license, followed by a divorce decree nine months later. Somehow, she ended up with a lot of debt."

"Y'all get the work history?"

Laura nodded. "Page two has that, Pappy. She's had a lot of different jobs since getting out of high school, but none lasted very long."

We took a few minutes to read over the details. From the corner of my eye, I saw Pappy's head come up quickly. He waited until the rest of us had finished.

"Y'all should have more questions."

He was right. I pulled out my notes from earlier. "Here's what I can't figure out yet. How did she find out that Myers had the reverse of her license plate?"

"And how does she identify her victims?" Megan said.

"How does she reserve the exact room she needs for the murder?" Koz asked.

Laura piped up as well. "What's her motivation for the killings?"

"Y'all tell me why she signs her killings?"

Everyone looked at Cantrell for a long moment. Megan started to respond, then waited as we all considered it. If the killer had never written that message, chances are we would have never gotten the case. How likely would it be that anyone could have connected three murders in three different counties without that autograph? So Cantrell had a perfectly logical question. Why would someone sign the crimes?

"Maybe it's an ego thing," I said, trying to piece it together. "Maybe it adds to the excitement that she can thumb her nose at the cops. She's been giving up this nice big clue that anyone can read, but we need to figure it out in order to catch her."

"After that goddamn shootout with Myers, y'all best be damn sure we got evidence to back this up. And ah want it before we go charging in." Cantrell stood up. Before any of us could move, he hunched forward and slammed his palms down on the conference table. Hard.

"Ah will not lose nobody else on my team. Y'all been working hard. Leave now, and git some rest. We'll start fresh in the morning."

****

There was no way I could pass up Simone's invitation for dinner. She called shortly after Pappy chased us out. He was right. We'd made great progress during the day on the case. But we all needed a little time off to recharge. Squad Five would watch Samuels all night. They were instructed to log her movements and call me if anything out of the ordinary happened.

Simone greeted me at the door. There was no hesitation, no awkwardness on either of our parts. This was a good sign. She put her arms around my neck and leaned in for a kiss. My hands circled her waist and drew her closer as our lips met. At least we managed to get the door closed.

After a while, we broke the kiss. There was a flush of heat on her face as Simone stepped back. With a smile, she made a show of fanning herself.

"It's warm in here all of a sudden."

I reached into a deep pocket of my leather jacket and pulled out a small packet wrapped in tissue paper.

"What's this?"

"I'm just delivering on a promise."

Simone opened the bundle and laughed out loud. Inside were a small bottle of the perfume she had been wearing last night and two tubes of lipstick. I had sneaked a peek this morning before I left and discovered where the perfume was from. I'd memorized the color of the lipstick. "I have a difficult time picturing you at a lingerie store."

"I stood just inside the doorway. A salesgirl was very helpful. Next time you'll have to go with me. There are some very interesting pieces of clothing on sale there."

The flush on her cheeks went a shade deeper. "I have no idea what you mean."

I pulled her close. "So there's no chance anything like that might be hiding in your lingerie drawer."

She gave me a chaste kiss on the cheek. "What is it that they say on the cop shows? I refuse to answer on the grounds that it may incriminate me."

We moved to the kitchen. Simone took a bottle of white wine from the refrigerator and handed it to me. I took the corkscrew and began to open it.

"I got home and had enough time, so I prepared a full meal. Are you hungry?"

"I'm starved. It's been a coffee and bagel kind of day."

"That's hardly enough to survive on."

"Some days are better than others." The cork popped out of the bottle for emphasis. "So what did you make?"

"We're having risotto from an old family recipe, fresh strawberries, salad, and a loaf of French bread." Simone lifted the lid from a pot and stirred the contents quickly.

I set the wine on the counter to let it breath. "That smells great. Unless that's your perfume I'm enjoying."

"Here, you need to get another whiff." With that she extended an arm toward me. I held her wrist and drew a deep breath. The fragrance quickly got to me. She pulled away with a smile.

"I have to keep stirring the risotto."

From one aspect, it was good that dinner was soon ready. We separated long enough to enjoy the food she had prepared. I was surprised how quickly Simone drank the wine. She turned off the lights in the apartment, lit candles on the table and in a few strategic places. We moved to the sofa. Outside, the rain continued. Simone switched on the stereo. Instrumental jazz floated around the room. We talked very little. We were too busy with physical things.

Despite the rain steadily beating on the windows, the room was warm. So warm in fact that she didn't resist when I slowly undressed her. At one point, she was sprawled naked on the couch, her breath coming in short gasps as I kissed my way down her body.

"No one else exists, Jeff. Right now, there's just you and me." She urged me closer with her arms and legs.

"There is no one else."

Chapter Twenty-Eight

Early Thursday morning, we reconvened around the conference table. Cantrell was in rare form.

"Y'all should have plenty to do today. Who's doing what, Chene?"

I checked my notes. "Squad Five still has two guys watching her. She left home about half an hour ago and drove straight to work. It's a dental office in Royal Oak."

"That matches with the resume I found on a social media site," Laura said. "She's an office assistant. She's been working there since September."

"Is it a safe bet that she'll be there all day?" Megan asked.

Pappy knew she was thinking about pulling the surveillance. Manpower equals money and budgets still had to be accounted for. "Y'all don't take any bets on this un. Ah want that two-man team on her."

"From the top, we still need to figure out how she's connected to the victims. We also have the questions from yesterday. How did she know Myers had the reverse of her license plate? How does she manage to reserve the exact hotel room and get it in the victim's name?" I said.

"How does she manage to elude the hotel's security systems?" Kozlowski asked.

Megan's face was dark with worry. She hadn't

273

spoken for a few minutes, which was unlike her. Cantrell picked up on it too.

"Whatcha got, girlie?'

"I keep wondering if she's already targeted another victim."

"Count on it," Koz said. "She's been methodical as hell. If Donna is right, I'd say she's already started connecting with the next victim. That's why we need to keep the focus on her."

Cantrell nodded as he got to his feet. "The giant's right. Git to it."

****

Together, we hashed it out. Laura was going to pressure her contact at the IRS to get Victoria Samuels's tax return from last year. Kozlowski was going to start from the very beginning. He was going to find out where Victoria got her education. We wanted to see the yearbooks from high school and college, to help us get a better sense of her background. This might also give us some leads as to who her friends were back then and if she was still in touch with any of them. Between them, they would also check her family to see what her home life was like when she was growing up. Megan and I were going to visit Donna Spears and get an update from her. I was restless. Part of me wanted to confront Victoria Samuels right now. But I remembered that our killer was a cold, calculating individual who had confounded several police departments for weeks and even had the forethought to plant misdirection to cover her trail. So I had to be patient because if we tipped our hand too soon, we might lose her. And like Pappy Cantrell, I don't like to lose. Nobody in the squad did. It was a requirement.

There was fresh coffee brewing when we got to Donna's apartment. We got situated around the kitchen table again. Donna was fidgeting. I couldn't tell if it was nerves or excitement.

"Tell me what you've got, boss."

"We have a suspect, a female suspect. Now we're building a case, looking at all the background we can. But there's still a lot of work to do."

She brightened. "Tell me how I can help."

"Were you ever able to find out anything about those throwaway cell phones the victims were calling?" Megan asked.

"They were bought at different locations of a big box store. Each one was the same model with a plan where they could buy additional minutes every month if they needed it. They were all through the same service provider."

I glanced at Megan. She gave her shoulders a minute shrug. "It's a lead we need to follow. Donna, when we get done here I want you to contact Pappy. Give him the name of the service provider and the list of the phone numbers involved. See if he can get a warrant. If the killer is still using any of those phones, we might be able to track her down. And we'll need the exact locations where each phone was purchased."

"Why do we care where she bought the phones?" Megan asked.

"I just want to be thorough. We can always drift in with a picture of our suspect and see if anyone remembers her there."

"What else can I do, boss?"

"I'll contact the cyber squad. By now, they should have pulled whatever details they could find on the personal computers from our victims. They can send everything over to you. See if there are any appointments listed. Check the contact lists. Look for any recent emails or Word documents that were sent or received from the same person that's on all three computers."

Donna scribbled some notes on the legal pad in front of her. As she wrote, I saw her hesitate and watched her head come up. Her eyes went out of focus for a minute.

"What is it?" Megan asked.

"Has anyone looked at their credit card statements or bank accounts?"

"We checked their financial information when we first got the cases, but I don't remember anything out of the ordinary."

Donna pulled the Grange file to her. I noticed a rainbow of colored tabs sticking out of it. Before I could ask, Donna explained.

"I tabbed things by color, so it would be easier to find when reviewing the three cases. Red was medical, green was financial, yellow was for relationships. But when we were first working the cases, we all thought the killer was a man. If our killer is a woman, there may have been purchases made by our victims for her."

Megan perked up. "You think they were buying something for a new beau. Taking them out to dinner, or buying them a CD or some clothing."

"Yeah, but what if she paid cash for these gifts?" I asked.

"Women this age rarely carry cash, boss. Everything is done electronically, from paychecks being directly deposited into the bank to transferring funds online when they pay bills. Using a debit card will take the money out of the account, but there is still a trail. I'd be surprised if any of our victims carried more than twenty dollars in cash."

Megan quickly agreed. "So we need the bank statements with a list of transactions as well as the credit card statements."

"Stephanie Grange was a pack rat. But she was somewhat of an anal pack rat. She kept all of her receipts and stapled them to her credit card bills when they came in. The girl had two bank cards and a couple for clothing stores." Donna was running a finger down a column now, her eyes racing over the details.

"You lost me," I said. "What's the significance?"

"If we can find purchases they made for their new friend, it might just help make the connection with our killer."

"But if the killer was someone very new to their lives, the purchases might not show up on their statements until after they were killed," Megan said.

"She's right." Donna was checking the transaction dates on the paperwork in front of her.

It may not lead to anything, but at this stage, we wanted every possible link that might tie our victims to the killer. Megan called the families and made the request. We were on our way.

****

I could have requested uniform patrols to pick up the documents from the victims' families, but the idea of unknown troopers showing up didn't sit right with me. Megan contacted Evelyn Grange at work about what we wanted. Her husband was being released from jail today, finally able to make bond. I doubted she was living at the house any longer. Megan was able to reach both the Calder and Rosen families. We made the drive through the suburbs and dropped the documents back at Donna's place for her review. I called Yekovich and had copies of the files from the victims' hard drives sent to both Donna and me. It wasn't that I didn't trust her to thoroughly review the contents. At times, I'm a bit of a control freak. So sue me.

It was late afternoon when we got back to the post. I was curious to see what progress Laura and Kozlowski made. And I wanted some time to review the computer files. Cantrell was gone to a meeting out in Mount Clemens. Megan was on the phone with Yekovich, trying to find out if anything of value had come from the numerous files on Myers's computer. I was studying the files from Mary Rosen's computer when I sensed a presence beside me.

"What's up, Laura?"

She hesitated. "I may have something, boss."

I shifted away from the computer monitor. Megan dropped the phone back in its cradle and focused on Laura.

"Tell me what you've got."

"It would be easier if I showed you."

They had taken over the conference room. Paperwork covered more than half the table. I recognized copies of the case files from each homicide, along with maps and diagrams. Kozlowski was at the far end, his arms folded across his chest, deep in thought.

"What's happening, Koz?"

"School is in, Chene. It's time for a history lesson."

Megan and I took our seats. Laura kept pacing

between her chair and Kozlowski's as she began the narrative.

Between them, they had uncovered a lot of details on Victoria Samuels. Her parents were deceased, having died recently in a fire at the family home in Madison Heights. She was an only child. Her father had worked at a meat processing plant down in the Eastern Market. Her mother was a housewife, occasionally providing day care for one of the neighbors. Victoria attended public schools in Madison Heights. Kozlowski was able to get copies of the high school yearbooks from each year she was there.

"Her childhood was relatively quiet," Laura said calmly as she paced. I caught the occasional tremor of excitement building in her voice, but she did well to keep it in check. "Pictures in the first couple of yearbooks focus mostly on the juniors and seniors, which isn't uncommon. But Samuels shows up in a couple of shots of the theater group and the cheer squad."

Koz slid the yearbooks down the length of the table. The pages where she appeared were tagged. A couple of these were candid shots. Samuels might have been unaware that someone was taking her picture, but her appearance seemed reserved nonetheless. I passed the books to Megan and returned my attention to Laura.

"The last two years of high school she got more involved. Not on the academic side, but social things. She joined the swim team. Victoria was cast in a couple of school productions. Not as a lead, but in roles where she would have a speaking or dancing part. After high school, she went to Oakland Community College for three years, finishing with an associate's degree in business. Her resume indicates she went to Oakland University, but their records only show her attending two semesters. Victoria didn't graduate. She hasn't taken any classes in over a year. Her resume online is on one of the professional networking sites. It's kind of sparse, but that helped us fill in a couple of blanks." Laura glanced at her notes.

"From all appearances, it looks like she was an average student." Megan was flipping through the yearbooks.

"More background information is good," I said, "but I'm guessing you're onto something else."

Koz jerked a thumb at Laura. "She put it together. Let her tell you."

Laura finally stopped pacing and took her seat across from me. She put her palms down on the table as if gathering strength, then began speaking slowly.

"I was able to get copies of her tax returns from the last three years. Using those and her resume, I think it answers some of the questions we've been struggling with."

Attached to copies of Victoria's tax returns were the W-2 forms from various employers. She had not stayed in any one job very long. Whether this was due to her lack of satisfaction with the job or poor performance we didn't know. But it was interesting to see that she jumped from job to job every six months or so. Laura pieced together a timeline of her employment. In the middle of the jobs, I saw a pattern beginning to emerge. Obviously, I wasn't the only one.

"Think about some of our questions," Laura said. "Like how does she manage to elude the security cameras at all of the hotels?"

Koz pointed a thick finger at the file. "She worked as a night auditor for a hotel chain for nine months. Basically, she would enter the day's activity into the system, and be on the front desk for any late night arrivals. This wasn't a five-star hotel, but they did have a security system."

"I called the places where our victims were found," Laura said. "All three used a similar computer-driven system. It's pretty standard practice, right down to where the cameras are positioned and where the recording equipment is kept. So she knew where the disks were."

"Which makes it easy to duck in during the middle of the night and remove the ones that would have captured her coming into the hotel," Megan said.

Laura flipped some papers. "Here it is. About a year ago, she worked for five months at one of the secretary of state offices. She would have had access to the license-plate database. So that is how she learned Myers had the reverse sequence of her own plate."

Cantrell would be pleased. Things were finally starting to come together. While Laura's efforts didn't answer all of our questions, it confirmed we were on the right track. Yet it still didn't answer the most important question of all. How did the killer identify the victims?

We spent a few hours reviewing their research efforts. Donna called with an update. During the month prior to their death, each victim had sent and received a number of calls and text messages to a new phone number. Each number was different. There was also a pattern of recent purchases. There were items such as perfume, makeup, clothing, and lingerie outside of the normal routine for our victims. Donna's theory of our female killer kept growing stronger.

I checked with the surveillance detail. Victoria Samuels worked until five o'clock. She had driven directly home. It was now almost seven, and she was headed out. It was time for the others to get a good look at our suspect.

Chapter Twenty-Nine

Victoria led the surveillance team to a barbecue joint called Smokes in Royal Oak. The place was crowded, and there was an elevated stage in the far corner. I recognized Naughton, the guy who ran the Squad Five crew, perched on a bar stool. He had a beer bottle in his hand with his back to the bar. As our eyes met, he raised the bottle as if to sip it. But I realized that the level in the bottle remained the same. I noticed that his gaze never left the direction where our suspect was.

To mix things up, Kozlowski and Megan entered as if on a date. Somehow, they found a high-top table not far from where Victoria Samuels was sitting with several other women. Laura worked her way down the bar to an empty stool. I flanked Naughton and found a space where I could blend in.

On the stage were a couple of guys with guitars, a drummer, and a keyboard player. Their selection was mostly instrumental blues numbers. The crowd wasn't overwhelming with their applause.

Together, we watched Victoria Samuels. With this many people in the room, she felt comfortable. Her jacket was off and draped over the back of her chair. She was wearing tight blue jeans tucked into black calf high leather boots. A black silk blouse with three quarter sleeves clung to her torso like a second skin. Her hair was swept back from her face, just long enough to dust the collar of her blouse. As I watched, a waitress swooped in with a large platter of food and placed it before her.

We might be here a while.

"Food's pretty good." Naughton spoke out of the corner of his mouth. "Beware of the hot sauce. It will take the paint off your tongue."

A platter sat beside his beer on the counter. I saw the remnants of a burger and fries. As if by magic, a bartender appeared. He was a muscular guy with several earrings in each lobe and a pattern of stars tattooed on his neck. I ordered a grilled chicken sandwich and sweet potato fries. I knew Kozlowski would not hesitate to order food.

With a beer bottle in hand, I turned my attention back to the band and the table where Victoria sat. Upon closer inspection, it was easy to eliminate the others with her as potential victims. None of them fit the profile. Maybe this was just her night out. An hour passed quickly. As the band continued to play, she rocked in her seat, swaying to the music while joking with her friends.

"Who else is on duty?" I asked Naughton.

"I've got one guy name of Giles out in the parking lot. We're on until midnight. I'm going to head out and trade places so he can grab a meal, if your team is going to hang around."

"Two more guys on at midnight?"

Naughton gave me his full attention for a moment. "Yes. Cantrell said we rotate until further notice. He even authorized an extra man, so we can maintain two man teams. This must be important."

"We're anticipating it will be very important."

"Does this have anything to do with that explosion last week?"

"Everything and then some."

Something shifted in his features, and his expression bordered on anger. "You need anything else, you let me know."

"What does Giles look like?"

Now Naughton's face took on a smirk. "He's a pretty boy, thinks of himself as a real ladies' man. Of course, he gets shot down more than he scores. Blond hair, blue eyes, he's wearing a red leather jacket and jeans. I'll send him in."

I hooked a thumb in Laura's direction. "Tell him to get cozy with her. That will keep anyone else away. Make it look like he was supposed to meet her here."

"Good hunting, Chene."

I set Laura a text message so she'd know the plan. We didn't dare use the ear buds and radios like a Secret Service assignment. In my peripheral vision, I saw her check the message. The hint of a smile tugged at the corner of her mouth. She turned to face the bar and checked her reflection in the mirror, making minute adjustments to her hair. A moment later, a guy matching Giles's description entered the bar. He strode confidently to Laura's side and leaned in for a kiss on her cheek. They played it up for anyone who noticed. I turned my attention back to Victoria.

The band finished their set. It was almost nine. I was beginning to wonder how late Victoria would hang out if she had to be at work in the morning. I nursed my beer and watched. When Victoria headed to the ladies' room, Laura fell into step behind her. A few minutes later they returned. I noticed some movement by the stage, and it took a moment to sink in.

The band from the earlier set was gone. In its place was a group of five. There was a drummer, keyboards, a bass guitar, a saxophone, and a lead guitar. The bass player was female. The crowd grew quiet as they ran a few scales and warmed up. Just as they were about to begin playing, Victoria finished her beer, smoothed out her blouse, and got to her feet. She climbed the stage and took a place beside the bass player's mike stand. Without an introduction, the band started to play. Stunned, I watched as they did a pretty good job on a Motown classic. The keyboard player was the lead vocalist. Victoria sang backup and thumped a tambourine.

I sensed Kozlowski's eyes burning into my chest. A look in his direction confirmed it. Megan was fixated on the stage. I noticed a few people get up and move to the minuscule dance floor. The song ended to steady applause. The band jumped right into a Bob Seger classic about old time rock and roll. More dancers crowded the floor. Laura dragged Giles up with her. Victoria was hamming it up with the sax player, belting out her lyrics.

They played four songs in a row. Each one got the crowd a little more pumped. I learned the band's name was Scoundrel. They were a local garage band, having grown over the last couple of years, building a decent following. The sax player also worked in a trumpet on a few numbers and had a good voice for rock and roll. The bartender explained this was their first appearance. A flier appeared on the bar, with a group shot and a list of dates. They had a CD available and a website. I tucked the flier into my pocket, while the bartender pulled two beers from the cooler.

"How long are they supposed to perform tonight?"

"They're booked until eleven. We don't go too late on weeknights. This was a taste, to see how well they do and if they can pack the house. If the manager likes what he sees, he'll book them for a Saturday night. You gotta rock this joint on a Saturday."

"So tonight's an audition?"

The bartender nodded. "Yeah, I guess you could say that. The boss heard them last week at some dive out in Pontiac. Thought we'd give them a try. Thursday night is tryouts for bands. We book two each week. No cover for the customers and a chance to hear some new music. And it helps us bring in people in the middle of the week."

"That makes sense. You think they'll be back?"

He shrugged, beefy biceps cinched in a Smokes T-shirt. "I just pour the drinks. But the two chicks in the band are a nice touch. I kinda like the bass player. That backup singer is trying too hard."

I turned back to the band. They changed the tempo and were playing another Motown favorite. People were slow dancing. I noticed Megan and Kozlowski in a corner of the floor, as far from Victoria's position as possible. Laura and Giles were back at the bar. Maybe I should ask Megan for a dance.

The band continued to play, shifting gears to match the crowd's mood. The time went quickly. As they were playing their last number, I saw Victoria scan the remaining crowd. Koz and Megan had left a few minutes ago. Laura and Giles headed out.

And just like that, the next puzzle piece fell into place.

****

"Y'all go to a bar, and ya don't invite me?"

"We were on duty. It's not like we were out getting hammered," Megan said.

Cantrell shifted his gaze to Kozlowski. "How many beers y'all drink?"

"I had one. And three glasses of water." He flashed a smile filled with shiny white teeth. "They had catfish on the menu, but I went for the pulled pork sandwich."

Following our standard protocol, Laura left a copy of her research on Cantrell's desk. There was no doubt he would be in early this Friday morning. True to form, he read everything before I got in the door at six thirty. I told the others to be here at eight. Pappy and I dashed out for breakfast at a diner. I gave him the summary of last night's activities. He was pleased. Now he was taking a few friendly jabs at the crew.

"Next thing y'all be tellin' me Chene got up and danced."

It was Megan's turn to grin. "No. That's not a sight any of us want to witness."

"Can we talk about what we learned?" I asked.

On the back wall of the conference room was a flat-screen television which was used to watch the news or as a computer monitor. Laura's fingers danced across the keyboard and brought the image up on the screen. It was a throwback to an eighteenth-century highwayman, swooping in to steal a necklace from a fair maiden while dazzling her with a kiss. Pretty tame by today's standards, but it conjured up the idea of a scoundrel. Laura worked her magic, and the home page dissolved into a series of photos of the band.

"For a garage band, these guys have started to

generate a following," I said. Copies of the flier from Smokes were passed out. "This is a pretty professional website. They have one compact disc available, which means they must have spent some time in a studio. Somebody's putting up serious money."

"What's your plan, Chene?"

"Squad Five is keeping her under surveillance. Let's dig into these other band members and see what we can learn. Laura, you and Koz work that angle. If you get something worthwhile, go check it out."

Megan glanced at me. "What about us?"

I jerked a thumb at the screen. The site had been updated recently, so it only showed venues where they were scheduled to appear over the next three months. There was no information about previous performances. But in the bottom right corner of the screen, there was a name and number to contact the band's manager.

"You and I are going to pay him a visit."

"Y'all think ya found the missin' link?"

"If the band played in different spots around the area, maybe they played at a venue where our victims were hanging out. Some of the smaller places may not have a website. But it could help us put Victoria in the right area to meet them."

Cantrell slapped his palms together so loudly it sounded like a gunshot. "Go git that connection. Let's bring this bitch down."

****

Megan placed the call before we left the post. Even though it was early, she was able to connect with someone at the office. They quickly agreed to a meeting. I sensed there wouldn't be a crowd waiting for us. We decided to keep the visit unofficial. Megan knew the drill and rummaged in the glove box for the prop.

Premiere Talent Management was in a converted house smack dab in downtown Farmington, another Oakland County suburb. We parked across the street and checked it out. This was a little colonial right on Grand River Avenue that was more than ninety years old. But the deep blue paint looked new. There was white trim and actual wooden shutters framing each window. A small sign out front listed four businesses. We entered and learned the Premiere office was on the first floor in the back. The space must have been the kitchen and dining room when it was a home.

I pushed open the frosted glass door. Inside were two people, reviewing photos on a computer monitor. There was no traditional desk, just an old maple dining table with four matching chairs. Tucked against the wall were a sofa that had seen better days and a couple of upholstered chairs. Framed concert posters lined the walls.

"I'm Jordan Tate and this is my associate, Esmeralda de la Fuentes. Welcome to the headquarters of Premiere Talent Management."

"I'm Jeff and this is my fiancée, Megan. Thanks for meeting us on such short notice." Megan was gently holding my hand. She made sure the engagement ring we used for such situations was visible.

Tate waved away the comment. He pointed at the chairs beside the table. As if on cue, Esmeralda disappeared, returning a moment later with a pot of coffee and four glass mugs. She assured us it was freshly brewed. While Megan passed the coffee mugs, I took a good look at Tate. He was not what I was expecting.

Jordan Tate was in his mid-fifties, with a short goatee and neatly trimmed hair that ran around the perimeter of his skull. The top of his head was bald. What hair he maintained was gray. He had dark brown eyes that were deep set, and his nose was bent to the right. He was about Megan's height. The blue pinstriped shirt he was wearing was high quality with heavy starch and adorned with black onyx cuff links. The khaki slacks showed a sharp crease. Wrinkles surrounded his mouth and eyes, as if he enjoyed a good laugh. I glanced at his associate. Esmeralda was one of those women of indeterminate age, anywhere from thirty to fifty. She had thick black hair that dangled below her shoulder blades in a braid and smooth, flawless skin. She was dressed for business in a green jacket and skirt, with an ivory blouse. The brief glimpse of her legs that I caught suggested they were shapely.

"So, how can we help you this morning?" Tate asked.

"We are in the early stages of planning for the big event," I said. "And we just can't come to an agreement about a band."

"Well, we represent a number of musical acts, ranging from a full orchestra that plays big band and swing music to a harpist and everything in between. Did you have a particular style of music in mind?"

Megan jumped in. "Well, a friend of mine told me about this group she'd heard recently at a bar. It was called Scoundrel. She said they had a lot of different music. Not too big and not too loud."

"They are one of our more recent additions, within the last four or five months. Most of their engagements to date have been in bars. I do have them scheduled for a 'battle of the bands' next month for a charity event." Tate hesitated, taking a moment to consider us. "I'm not sure they would be right for a wedding."

"We're not looking at a traditional event." Megan made a show of patting me on the arm. "It's not exactly our first time down the aisle."

"Would you like to hear a demo?" Esmeralda asked. Her voice was soft and mysterious.

I nodded in agreement. "That would be helpful."

She moved to a compact stereo system on the counter by the rear window. A moment later, we heard the strains of an old rock and roll favorite. We listened quietly until the tune ended. Esmeralda brought a jewel case with a sample CD in it and handed it to over. Megan turned to me with a quizzical look.

"Darling, maybe we should think about a band with more experience. They've only been together a few months."

I bit my lip on the "darling." Obviously, she was enjoying our charade. Jordan Tate raised a hand before I could reply.

"Actually, the band has been together for some time. We've only been representing them a short while. But we can offer you some other excellent musicians. Do you have a particular date in mind?"

"My sweet squeeze here can't seem to commit to either a summer or fall wedding." I reached over and laced my fingers through Megan's. "Her inability to be decisive is one of her endearing qualities."

"Perhaps you'd like to hear some other samples?" Esmeralda asked, tactfully changing the topic.

Megan turned and smiled at the other woman. "Can

we borrow a few others? It's not the same as hearing them live, but it might help us decide."

"Yes, there is nothing quite like seeing them performing in person," Jordan said.

"How does that work?" I asked. "Do you schedule all of their appearances?"

He nodded and reached for the computer keyboard. While he was clicking away, Esmeralda went to a cupboard above the counter and selected three compact discs from their supply. She showed them to Jordan. He nodded his approval and kept typing. A minute later, the printer on the end of the table was spitting out four sheets of paper. Each one held the name and colorful logo for the four bands in question, along with a list of venues and dates for the current year. The list also included any engagements from last December. He tucked them in a glossy portfolio and slid it across the table to a spot between us.

"Here is some information about the various acts we represent. I have no doubt that we can assist you in finding the very best in entertainment available. All of our contact information is included. And we'd be more than happy to accompany you if you'd like to hear one of the acts perform. We may even be able to sneak you into a similar venue." He offered a sincere smile and extended his hand.

I shook it as we got to our feet. "How did you get into this line of work?"

"Sideways. I worked in a saloon, tending bar while I was in college, studying business. Some of the guys I knew from high school formed a band. I encouraged the owner to give them a try. He did. They played well but had no sense of how to make money. I offered to manage them for a cut." He shrugged and grinned. "One band led to another. I've been doing it ever since."

"What ever happened to the original band?" Megan asked.

"They still perform. They're called Clutch Cargo."

"I've heard of them. They have been around a long time."

Tate ran his hand over his bald spot. "Yes, we've gone from the long-haired days to baldness, hearing aids, and arthritis. But they still know how to rock."

We thanked them for their time and headed out to the car.

Chapter Thirty

Back in the car, Megan quickly pulled the glossy portfolio open. She riffled through the sheets and withdrew the one for Scoundrel. I leaned over to read it at the same time.

"Sweet squeeze," she muttered. "Did you really call me your sweet squeeze?"

"I wanted something memorable."

"That was sickening." She jabbed a finger at the sheet. "Yes! If that place is where I think it is, we're on to something."

She handed me the list and pulled out her cell phone. Switching it to internet mode, she typed in the name of the venue. "Here it is. The Token Lounge is in Westland. That's maybe twenty minutes from where our first victim lived."

According to the roster, Scoundrel performed at the Token Lounge in early December. The first killing took place in mid-January. In January, Scoundrel was an opening act at a club over in St. Clair Shores, called Black Bart's. The first week in February, they played at The Magic Bag in Ferndale. Megan confirmed the locations.

"That's one in each county, about six weeks before each homicide. Could that be how she's picking her targets, Chene?"

"It certainly looks promising. Call Laura and see

how they are doing." I put the car in gear.

Kozlowski and Laura were still compiling background on the other band members. Megan put her phone on speaker mode. She relayed what we learned from our visit and what we surmised. Cantrell's voice popped through the speakers.

"Y'all call it, Chene."

"Megan and I are going to the Token Lounge now. We'll stop at the Magic Bag on our way across town. Koz, call Ted. He probably knows the owner or the manager at Black Bart's. You two go over there and check it out. Take pictures of the victim. Also take the pics of the band. See what you can find out."

"Got it, boss."

I heard a snicker from Cantrell at that comment. Megan broke the connection. "It's starting to come together."

"Damn straight."

****

The Token Lounge is a Detroit area institution. Since the early 1970s, this was a place for bands of all sizes to perform. With a capacity of about four hundred people, it enabled audiences to get up close to the acts. It wasn't uncommon for well-known musicians to stop in to hear a new band and to join them onstage for an impromptu jam session. It was early afternoon when we pulled into the lot. As I expected, delivery trucks were lined up, bringing supplies of beer and alcohol for the weekend. We followed a couple of guys in through the back door. One of them pointed out the manager. He was a short, stocky fellow with several days' stubble on his chin. His hair was straggly, a moss-colored brown.

"December? You guys want to know about a gig in

December? Get real! I've got enough trouble remembering what happened last night." He paused, checking off an invoice for a beer delivery and pointing the driver toward the walk-in cooler.

Megan caught my eye. She tipped her head toward the stage. I wandered in that direction. Maybe she would have better luck with this guy. When the place was busy, only pinpoint lights in the ceiling would be used. Now the regular lights were on. Two guys were busy sweeping up and preparing to mop the floors with an industrial cleaner. The air was thick with the smell of sweat, spilled beer, and marijuana.

While watching Megan talk to the manager, I tried to envision the place packed with a band and four hundred people. What I couldn't picture was Mary, the first victim, in the middle of the crowd. Around the perimeter of the room were tables. Chairs were upside down on them now. I wondered if there were specific spots that were kept vacant for a dance floor. Maybe she was kept to the side. But would she have come here alone? That triggered a thought. I was finishing the call when Megan approached, a satisfied grin on her face.

On the way to Ferndale, she filled me in. There wasn't much. Megan used her charms to persuade the manager to review their records. Scoundrel was in fact in the house in early December. They played for almost an hour, opening for another band. It's normal for the place not to be full when the warm-up band is playing. A smaller crowd would actually work in Victoria's favor.

I parked in front of the Magic Bag Theater on Woodward Avenue. The fact that this location was within a couple of miles of Victoria Samuels's residence didn't escape our attention. The exterior probably looked the same as it did in the 1950s. The girl behind the ticket window didn't seem impressed by our badges, but she did summon the manager. I was expecting a repeat of the shaggy guy from the Token Lounge. When the door swung open, it proved again how wrong I can be. An older woman waved us inside. Her curly hair was iron gray and trimmed close to her scalp. She wore black jeans, a white cardigan sweater, and a black Silver Bullet Band T-shirt. We introduced ourselves.

"I'm Maureen Ness. Is there some kind of problem?"

"We're trying to get information about a band that played here in February."

Maureen waved her fingers and led us back into the theater area. There was a movie screen visible on the stage. There were enough old upholstered seats to hold three hundred people. She leaned against the last row and folded her arms across her ample chest.

"We call it 'brew and view' on Wednesdays and Thursdays. Usually we have live entertainment on the weekends. Some of the bands are local, up and comers. They are more affordable for both us and the crowd. Occasionally, we pull in some old music legends, guys who can't draw in the big stadium crowds anymore."

"Do you book the acts?" I asked.

"Sure. We work with a couple of outfits locally. And if it's one of the legends, we deal with their agents from whichever coast they call home."

"Do you remember anything unusual about one of your acts in February?" Megan asked. "Was there anything out of the ordinary?"

Maureen raised a finger. "Let's go check the log. We rarely have any problems. We limit alcohol intake pretty closely. And since we're a smoke-free establishment, you don't have to worry about the dope."

She led us back to the office and quickly settled in behind the desk. Maureen turned the computer monitor so we could all see it. She brought up the manager's log and scrolled it to February. "Any night in particular you want to see?"

"Those with live entertainment."

We read the notes from each night. Details included the number of tickets sold, the name of the acts, the length of the performance, crowd reactions, and highlights.

"I've got three managers. We all cover different nights and events. But we make sure the information is there. That way we know if we want to book a band for a second show at a later date. We've been running this way for more than a dozen years now, and it works out just fine. Is there a particular night you're interested in?"

Megan shook her head. "No, we're just trying to get a handle on how this works. It may have something minor to do with an investigation we're reviewing."

"We run a clean business here. We don't put up with troublemakers and that goes for the entertainment too," Maureen said, her tone becoming tense.

"We appreciate your help." We headed for the door.

Maureen Ness stood in the doorway, bracing her hands on her hips. "Stop by one night and see for yourself. That's the best way to understand our business."

"We'll do that."

"You pay for your own tickets though. We don't make enough money to give away freebies to cops."

As we were getting into my car, Megan's cell phone rang. She glanced at the screen and immediately put it on speaker. It was Kozlowski.

"We just caught a serious break."

Megan propped the phone on the console. "We're ready for one. Give."

"Ted knew the owner and the manager of Black Bart's. He made a call, and the manager was ready for us. The guy pulled a rabbit out of his ass."

"How did he do that?"

"He's trying to convince the owners that live entertainment really draws the crowd. So he's got it set up to videotape the performances. He uses three cameras, gets shots of the audience as well as the band. And he keeps the videos to support his argument. He says some bands draw better than others."

"What about the night in question?" I asked.

"It shows Scoundrel on stage, with Samuels front and center. Since the cameras are digital, the manager lets them run all night long. Not only do we have Samuels at the scene, but we also got shots of her schmoozing with the victim, Stephanie Grange, and two other girls. They didn't look like groupies, but she zeroed in on her. They were at a table just beyond the dance floor, where you could see her from the stage."

"You get a copy of the tape?"

"No."

Megan nearly jumped out of her seat. "The hell you mean, no! Cantrell will have your ass if you—"

"Relax, girlie. We've got the original."

"And a signed statement from the manager as to its contents and the date of the event," Laura added with a laugh. "How did you guys do?"

"We'll fill you in when we get to the post."

Megan broke the connection and tucked her phone in her pocket.

"You hear that?" I asked.

"What?"

"If you listen carefully, you can hear the unmistakable sound of the net drawing closer on Victoria Samuels. We just need to get to Samuels before the days add up. This case needs to end. And it needs to end now."

****

Cantrell, Kozlowski, and Laura were waiting in the conference room. Pappy offered us a wink as we settled around the table.

"Y'all done some damn fine work today. We on the right track at last."

We watched in silence while Laura keyed up the video. She sped through most of the footage that focused on the band, slowing it down for shots of the crowd. There were several views of Stephanie Grange, sitting at a table with two other women. Later, Victoria Samuels joined them. At one point, Victoria was alone with Stephanie, and they were talking earnestly. I shifted my gaze to Cantrell. He snapped flame to his cigarette and slapped his palm on the table.

"Hot damn, we gotcha!"

Once the video ended, we filled in the others on the results of our visits. There was a slim chance that Victoria Samuels was somehow connected to one of those managers. I didn't want her becoming aware of our interest. As Megan finished our report, my phone rang. Donna Spears was checking in. I put it on speaker.

"Hey, boss. You were right. None of the interviews conducted by the original detectives went back more than thirty days. But I did review the credit card and bank statements like you asked. There was activity on Mary's debit card for the Token Lounge. I can't find anything on Stephanie's for Black Bart's. She may have paid cash if she went there. The bank just confirmed that Janet's credit card was used at the Magic Bag in February."

"That's great work, Trooper." I broke the connection and looked around the table. Cantrell let a stream of smoke ease from his nostrils.

"What's the plan, Chene?"

"All of this action happened at night. If we get on this now, we might find someone who saw the killer with our victims. We hit the motels where the murders took place. Koz and Laura, take the Wayne and Macomb counties. Show Victoria's picture to everyone, from desk clerks on up. If there isn't a restaurant or bar there, hit the ones nearby. You've already got the good photos on the victims. See if anyone can put them together nearby. Megan and I will go to the Oakland County motel."

Cantrell glanced at Kozlowski. "Y'all take Wayne. Ah'll take the Macomb spot. What else?"

Pappy was known to jump in when needed. He recognized that we had a lot of ground to cover in a little bit of time.

I motioned to the monitor. "Can you print a still of the three women at the table?"

"Sure," Laura said. "I'll make some copies."

"Whatcha thinking, Chene?"

"Megan and I will try to run down the other women in this photo. Maybe Evelyn Grange will recognize one of them. They may be able to give us more information on that night."

Cantrell was rolling his Zippo lighter across his knuckles. "Do it matter?"

"I don't know, Pappy. But at this point, I want to try and find out."

"Are we close enough for an arrest warrant?" Kozlowski asked.

Pappy glanced up at the clock. It was almost seven. Where had the day gone?

"Ah'll reach out to Beckwith tonight. Chances are he'll want to see what y'all got sometime tomorrow."

"I'd love to arrest that bitch tomorrow," Koz said.

Megan's face lit up. She flipped open the portfolio that Jordan Tate had given us and paged through it.

"Scoundrel is scheduled to perform tomorrow night at a club called Waverly in Pontiac. We know where she's going to be. We could have everything in place to take her there."

We could all feel the level of excitement building. We were getting close.

Chapter Thirty-One

Evelyn Grange agreed to meet us. She was at a condominium in Birmingham, not far from her office building. She was still dressed for work, although she had kicked off the high heels. I could hear someone else moving about the condo. We didn't really care who it was. Evelyn had a very large glass of wine in one hand.

"It's late. I hope this won't take long."

Megan explained why we were there, and slowly pulled the photo from an envelope. I heard a sharp intake of breath as Evelyn realized what she was looking at. Somehow, she managed to set the wine on the counter. She took the photo in both hands.

"Oh my," she whispered. "That's my baby."

"Do you recognize either of the other women?" Megan asked gently.

Evelyn didn't respond. Megan waited a moment and repeated the question.

"No, I don't know them."

In the picture, Stephanie was on the left. While the other two women were smiling widely, she looked less enthusiastic. But she did appear to be enjoying herself. I could see the photo tremble in Evelyn's hands.

"When was this taken?" she asked softly.

Megan glanced at me. I couldn't see any harm in telling her. "We think it was sometime in January."

Evelyn started to hand the photo back. A flicker of

recognition crossed her face. "This girl, the one in the middle, I think went to high school with Stephanie. But I don't know her name."

"Would you like to keep that?" Megan asked. "You could crop the photo, so it would only show Stephanie."

"Isn't it evidence?" Her voice cracked as she spoke.

"We have other copies."

Evelyn nodded and pulled the photo to her chest. "Thank you." Without another word, she turned and walked away from us. Taking our clue, we left.

****

Laura was thorough. Before she'd left the post with Kozlowski, she emailed the photos to Donna Spears. Now Megan called her and asked her to look through Stephanie's high school yearbooks. They were included with the case files. I drove from Birmingham to the hotel where our involvement with this case began. It was hard to believe that less than two weeks had passed.

I parked in the lot by the steak house where Janet Calder's car was found. The place was packed for a busy Friday night, but it looked like the first wave of the dinner rush was done. Not wanting to disturb the patrons, we got a booth in a quiet section of the dining room. It took only a few minutes for the manager to join us. I showed him the photo of Janet and the publicity shot of Victoria. He studied them closely for a moment and slid them back.

"Two weeks ago? Sorry, bro, but if it was last night, I might remember. We crank a lot of people through here every week."

"We'd like to ask your staff if anyone noticed

them."

"Hey, bro, we always cooperate with the law. I'll send them over, as long as you don't hold up service." He shot a look at our empty table. "You are gonna eat something, right? We've got great burgers, and steak, maybe a cup of chili?"

Megan piped up. "Give us two burgers, rare, with blue cheese. No fries."

The guy winked and walked away. I looked across the table at her.

"What? I'm hungry. We didn't stop for lunch and when you get close on a case, you never even think about food. You can't expect me to sit here for an hour interviewing waitresses and not eat."

"No fries?"

"These are half-pound burgers. Be thankful I didn't get bacon."

Gradually, the staff came over to our table. As we started showing the pictures of Janet and Victoria, a thought occurred to me. We explained that they were probably in here alone that Friday night and they might have been cozy. Based on the level of alcohol in Janet's system, I suggested that at least she might have been drinking heavily.

It was almost an hour later when the last of the staff appeared. Our burgers were long gone. A waitress and a bartender approached to look at the photos. The bartender was a guy in his early twenties, with thick black hair that fell to his shoulders. He was more interested in looking at Megan until she waved the pictures under his nose.

"Two weeks ago tonight?"

Megan stared at him intently. "That's right. Were

you working that night?"

"Sure. Friday is one of our best nights. I think I remember those two. We were jammed, and they were waiting at the bar for a table." He tapped a stubby index finger on Victoria's photo. "This one was in charge. She stood next to the other one, who was on a bar stool. It's like she was protecting her."

"What else do you remember?"

"She used the same trick I do when on a date. When the girl wasn't looking, she kept pouring wine from her glass into the other girl's. Makes her think she's only had one glass of wine when in reality, it's a glass and half. Only they weren't drinking wine. They were doing cosmopolitans. More alcohol, so it gets you there quicker."

"Is there anything else?" Megan asked.

"Yeah, this one didn't want anything to do with me. I tried to chat them up a bit while they were waiting, but it was obvious I have the wrong equipment. She wasn't interested in guys."

Megan got his name and address for our files. The manager stopped by as they moved away. He had checked the records and determined that most of the people who would have been working that Friday night were also working tonight. I paid the bill and made sure we left the waitress a generous tip.

The energy was coming off Megan in waves like heat shimmers in the desert. Rather than drive, we walked across the parking lot to the hotel. I doubted we would have much success here, but since this was the most recent crime, we stood the best chance of someone recognizing Victoria.

"We're getting closer, Chene. Every little step we

take brings us that much closer to nailing this bitch."

"Yeah, but I'm wondering if she's with her next victim. For all we know, she could be romancing her as we speak."

"I thought she was still under surveillance."

"Good point. But I'll be happier when we stop her."

"As Pappy would say, 'Y'all gotta lock her narrow ass up.' That will make all of us happy."

We spent the next hour interviewing the hotel staff. There was a small bar in the hotel along with the reception desk. No one recognized the photos of either Janet Calder or Victoria Samuels. I remembered the missing security video. Chances were Victoria had been cautious reserving the room. She must have swiped Janet's credit card and identification before their final date.

As we were leaving, I decided to take a run down to Black Bart's. It was getting late. When I offered to drop Megan at the post so she could pick up her car and go home, she gave me an icy look. The saloon was five miles from my place, so I had no intention of driving back to the shop. When we got to Black Bart's, the parking lot was only half full. Apparently, there was no live entertainment tonight.

Settled into a booth, Megan shot me another look. "I want a beer. We've been going full tilt all day. One beer will not kill me or affect my abilities to function. We finish up here you can drop me at home."

"It works for me."

The waitress approached and took our orders. Megan showed her the picture of Stephanie Grange and the two other women. She shook her head. I asked if she could send over the other waitress who was working the far side of the bar.

The second waitress, an older woman named Rosalyn, took one look at the shot and nodded. "Sure, I've seen her. She came in just a few times. It's been a while."

"How come you remember her?" Megan asked.

"She wasn't the type to hang out in a place like this." Rosalyn parked a hip on the table between Megan and me. "She looked like Miss Prim and Proper. Most of the girls who come in here are dressed to impress, or at least to flash. They want to be seen. They wear the push-up bras, the thong panties, and clothes so tight you'd swear they bought them before they hit puberty, or had a visit with the plastic surgeon." She reached down and tapped a lacquered nail on the photo. "This one looked like she went over the wall at a convent. She kept her goodies under wraps, if you get my meaning."

"Loud and clear," I said.

"Did she hook up with anyone while she was here?" Megan asked.

"Both times I saw her, she was with the same girls. Maybe someone she worked with. She kept to herself for the most part. She drank cola with lemon. I got the feeling she was the designated driver."

"You remember anything else from the nights she was here?"

Rosalyn considered that for a minute. She had four dangling earrings in her right lobe, each one slightly longer than the one before. She played with them, letting them clink softly together while she thought. Then with a smile, Rosalyn tapped the picture again. "That backup singer. What's her name, the tomboy? I

309

remember she kept coming over to talk with her during the band's breaks."

"Is that uncommon?"

"Usually girls like the singer go for the guys who have been drinking heavy, buy her a couple of drinks, maybe hoping to get a hummer in the parking lot between sets. But she kept coming over and flirting with this girl."

Megan slid Samuels's picture on the table without saying a word.

"Yeah, that's the one. Not the greatest voice, but she has the moves on stage to keep everyone's attention."

She certainly had our attention.

Chapter Thirty-Two

We were in the bullpen Saturday morning when Cantrell arrived. Lazily, he waved a hand at us to follow, as if he were a Pied Piper. Gathering coffee mugs and notebooks, we moved into the conference room. As I was closing the door, there was movement coming down the hall. I waited and recognized the attorney from the Macomb County prosecutor's office. He nodded as he passed me and stepped inside. Dropping his briefcase on the table, he immediately made the rounds, greeting everyone by name and shaking their hands.

Eric Beckwith was a short, stocky guy in his late forties. He had been with the county's office since passing the bar exam on the first try. With a thick head of wavy brown hair, dark brown eyes, and chiseled features, he gave the impression that he was not someone to mess with. He had a solid track record of convictions. This may have been the result of only handling strong cases. He had worked with Pappy many times since the squad was created. I think Pappy liked him because he dressed in off-the-rack suits, his shoes were always in need of polish, he got his hair cut once a month, and the fanciest thing about him was his briefcase.

Beckwith's voice was his gift. During normal conversations, he was as plain as you and me. But in the courtroom, he could crank it up like a news anchor, deep and serious tones that demanded your attention. He dropped into a chair, pulled a legal pad from his case and a cheap ballpoint pen.

"Cantrell called me last night. Anyone want to spell it out for me?"

Everyone looked to me. I gave him the summary. When the others had a point that fit into the narrative, they jumped in. Megan shared the results of our interviews last night. We looked at Kozlowski and Laura. Koz filled us in.

"We went to the motel where the first murder took place. We interviewed everyone on duty, without any success. There were two bars nearby. We went to both and interviewed all the staff there as well. Unfortunately, no one recalled seeing our victim or the suspect. But since this murder occurred in January, I'm not surprised."

Cantrell was rolling his lighter across his knuckles. "'Bout the same luck Ah had out here. Talked with everyone at the motel; ain't nobody recognized this girl. There was four bars around the corner. I went to each one. No luck there either."

Beckwith scratched down a few notes. "That doesn't help our case."

"Think about it for a minute. Two women alone in a bar, having a few drinks, maybe some dinner," I said. "That's not unusual. Our victims were all very timid. They would not have done anything to draw undue attention to themselves, or their date. And Samuels certainly wouldn't do anything to make their time there memorable."

He considered it for a moment. "You're right. She

wants to be a ghost. It's easier for her to blend in. And since the victims are all rather...plain, they wouldn't have stood out in the crowd."

"Exactly," Megan offered, "then when you take into consideration the amount of time that has passed since the first two killings, it doesn't surprise me that most people didn't remember them. We got the statements from the bartender in Bloomfield last night and the waitress at Black Bart's. Both positively identified Samuels."

"You got those on tape?" Beckwith's eyebrows went up.

She nodded. "I'll transcribe them this morning and email you a copy."

He tossed the legal pad into his case and snapped the locks. "Do that. I will talk to the judge. We should be able to get a warrant for her arrest later today."

"I want a search warrant for her home, her garage, and her car. Also get one for where she works."

Beckwith nodded. "What are you hoping to find?"

"Souvenirs from the kills, like clothing, jewelry, cell phones, purses, anything that we can add to the connection with her and the victims."

"Better include any computers and cell phone records too," Laura said.

"Yes, it's best to be thorough." Beckwith got to his feet. "I'll let you know as soon as I can."

We watched him leave. Pappy lit a smoke.

"Go do your paperwork. Git your files up to date."

****

Six o'clock Saturday night found us at Samuels's home in Ferndale. The surveillance team had followed Victoria there half an hour ago. It was late in the afternoon before Beckwith came through with the warrants. We didn't want to wait any longer. The whole squad was here. Cantrell made a courtesy call to the Ferndale Police and asked for two uniformed officers to assist. He stationed the local squad car behind Samuels's vehicle, efficiently blocking it in. The two surveillance guys, Naughton and Giles, carried a battering ram up the driveway to the back door. Kozlowski and Laura were behind them. The two Ferndale cops brought another ram to the front door. We weren't taking any chances. We were all dressed in bulletproof vests and the blue windbreakers identifying us as police. The Ferndale cops were in uniforms.

Cantrell looked at me. "Y'all do the honors." He drew his weapon from his holster and racked the slide.

"Thanks, Pappy."

"Let's go bust her narrow ass," Megan said.

Kozlowski's voice buzzed in my ear, confirming they were in position. Megan and Cantrell followed me up the drive to the front porch. I raised my fist and hammered on the wooden door.

"Police! Open up!"

Over the radio, I could hear Koz give the order. The battering ram slammed into the back door. I stepped aside as the Ferndale cops shattered the wooden door. Cantrell had already instructed them to break down the door and remain outside for support. As the door caved in, I dashed inside. Megan and Cantrell were right behind me.

The living room was just past the door. I caught a glimpse of Victoria Samuels running toward the rear of the house.

"Police! Freeze!" Megan shouted over my

shoulder.

Ahead of us, I could hear a scuffle taking place. I signaled with two fingers for Megan and Cantrell to check the hallway and the bedrooms. We didn't know if there was anyone else in the house, and we weren't taking any chances. I waited in position, blocking the path to the front door.

"Bedrooms are clear," Megan called, stepping into the hallway.

"Bath's empty," Cantrell said, moving into position behind me.

We entered the kitchen. Victoria was surrounded. The kitchen had old gray and white tile on the counters, with gray linoleum on the floor. The cupboards may have been replaced in the fifties. They needed serious attention. A tired electric stove was across from the window, next to a battered refrigerator. Victoria was bracing her arms on the counter by the sink. Her eyes were flicking around the room, trying to take everything in at once. There was no avenue for escape. Kozlowski moved up directly behind her. I was in front, with Megan on my right. Cantrell drifted to my left. Laura was to the side of Kozlowski, blocking the access to the rear exit. I expected a snarl of defiance to cross her face, but she seemed relieved. A sense of calm was spreading over her. She was dressed for the band, with another sheer blouse, tight blue jeans, and a pair of heavy-duty work boots. Kozlowski was the only one of us who didn't have his weapon drawn. Now he deftly pulled her arms behind her back and snapped the handcuffs around her wrists. We remained silent while he read her the Miranda rights.

"This isn't over," Victoria hissed.

Megan took a step closer. "You're damn right it's not. I can't wait to see you locked away for life after murdering those women."

"What's the matter?" Victoria focused her attention on Megan. "Did I strike too close to home for you?"

The color drained from Megan's face. "I'm nothing like them."

"Oh, I don't know. A little less tits, a little less ass, and a little less sass, and I think you're exactly like them!"

"Save it for the judge," I snapped, shoving my gun back into the shoulder holster. "Let's get her the hell out of here."

My gaze went to Megan. Her jaw was clenched so tightly, she could have cracked her molars. Without taking her eyes off Victoria, Megan used both hands to put her weapon back on her hip. She was breathing rapidly, as if we had just chased the killer up several flights of stairs. Movement from our captive drew my attention.

"Let's go," Kozlowski said, tugging on her wrists.

Victoria stumbled backward, her shoulders pressed against Kozlowski's chest. Then she moved so quickly, my eyes almost didn't catch it. She jumped up, using his broad chest for support, and drew her knees up to her chin. She lashed out with both feet, the heavy boots connecting solidly with Megan's sternum. One boot flipped up and caught her squarely on the chin. A howl of pain ripped the air out of the room. Megan's head snapped back. She lost her balance and dropped to the floor. Kozlowski now had his arms wrapped around Victoria's chest, and he spun around, pressing her against the wall. I rushed to Megan. She was on her back, dazed, her head rolling back and forth where she had impacted the floor. Her eyes were out of focus, and there was a thin line of blood showing on her lips.

"Get the medics!" I shouted at Laura.

Sadistic laughter poured from over my shoulder. I drew Megan into my arms, trying to keep her calm. Laura scrambled out of the room. Koz called my name. I glanced in his direction. He had one massive hand planted on the back of Victoria's head pinning her in place. The fingers of his free hand curled open and closed.

Cantrell stepped forward and jammed the barrel of his gun into her ear. "Gimme a reason," he snarled.

"Throw me your cuffs," Kozlowski shouted.

I pulled mine from the pouch on my belt and tossed them to him. Kozlowski snagged them in mid-air, then muttered something to Victoria. I saw her body go rigid. Somehow, he yanked one of her legs up and pulled the boot free. He wrapped a cuff around her ankle and repeated the process with the other foot. I could hear footsteps running toward us. Two paramedics charged in with their gear followed by Laura, Naughton, and Giles. The medics nudged me out of the way and went to work on Megan.

Cantrell stepped back. Kozlowski handed Victoria over to Naughton. "There are two uniformed troopers waiting down the street. Have them take her to the post and lock her in a holding cell. Do not remove those cuffs." He pointed at the boots. "And take those too. Log them in as evidence in her assault on a police officer."

Together, they dragged her out of the room.

The four of us stood against the far wall, watching

the paramedics work on Megan. At length, one guy climbed to his feet and approached us.

"She may have a couple of cracked ribs, and her lip is split. It looks like she took quite a blow to the chin. She knocked her skull pretty hard on the floor when she fell. We could be talking a concussion too. We should take her to the hospital for x-rays."

"What's closest?"

"St. John's. We'll put her on a gurney. It's safer than having her bouncing around. A rib could easily puncture her lung."

I nodded. "Make it happen."

****

I hate hospitals. It's so rare that anything good ever came out of my time at one. But Megan was my partner and an old friend. I followed the ambulance, lights flashing as they cut across traffic and raced to the emergency room. Pappy called and informed me that the crime-scene unit was already going through the house. He assured me that the interrogation of Samuels would not begin until I arrived. She insisted on having her lawyer present, which was fine with us. Beckwith from the prosecuting attorney's office would meet us at the post in an hour.

I stood outside of the cubicle where Megan was being examined. Nurses and doctors bustled about. Several encouraged me to take a seat in the waiting room. I didn't respond. The paramedics who brought her in were wheeling their gurney out. Both guys gave me an encouraging nod.

"I think she'll be fine," said the one I'd spoken to at the scene. "She's tough."

"Damn straight."

Eventually, the curtain parted and another gurney rolled out. This one contained Megan. She was wearing a hospital gown and had a blanket over her legs. A man in scrubs and a lab coat stepped in front of me. He introduced himself as Lane Book. I gave him my name.

"Are you related?"

"We're partners."

"Do you mean domestic partners or police officer partners?"

I studied him for a moment. He was about five foot ten with sandy hair and dark green eyes. He had an athletic build. I'd noticed his grip was strong and firm when we shook hands.

"We're both police detectives. We work together."

His features relaxed slightly. "This is the second time I've treated Megan recently. She's in a dangerous line of work."

"Sometimes it's a matter of being in the wrong place at the wrong time."

"I understand."

"What is the extent of her injuries?"

Book looked around for a moment, to see if anyone else was close enough to hear. Then he inclined his head down the hall, in the same direction Megan had been taken. "We're not supposed to reveal anything to someone who is not related."

"She's my sister."

A smirk crossed his lips. "Yeah, I can see the family resemblance."

"So tell me."

"She has two ribs that are badly cracked, and she took a nasty shot to the chin. That will leave a deep bruise for a week or so, as will the injuries to the ribs.

We're taking her for x-rays now and an MRI on her head. I'm worried about a concussion."

"Megan banged her head pretty badly the last time she was here."

He nodded in agreement. "Two serious blows to the head in such a short period can be trouble. It's just like a quarterback in football. There is only so much punishment you can take before it starts having an adverse effect."

"Something tells me you're not going to be releasing her tonight."

"You're right. We can treat the ribs, give her something for the pain, but I want to keep her for observation."

"Thanks. How long will it be before you put her in a room?"

"We should have everything in place within an hour."

I nodded and turned to go. Cantrell was waiting. Book called out before I'd gone a couple of steps.

"Did you catch the person responsible for her injuries?"

"Yeah, we did. I'll be back in a couple of hours."

He stuck out his hand. "Ask for me at the ER desk. I'll know what room your…sister is in."

"Take good care of her." I shook his hand again and headed for the post.

Chapter Thirty-Three

The public defender was in the conference room with Victoria Samuels. He was a heavyset guy in his late thirties, who had given up the battle with his receding hairline and had opted to shave his skull. His name was Root. Every time I'd seen him, he was wearing the same gray flannel suit. Either it was the only one he owned, or he had bought several at one time. Cantrell was in the corridor, talking with Beckwith.

"This is an opportunity for her to make a statement," Beckwith said. "I will explain the charges and see what reaction we get. Then we'll lock her in a cell until the arraignment Monday morning."

"Y'all include the assault on a police officer?"

Beckwith checked his notes. "Yes, that and three counts of first degree murder."

"Y'all gonna question her?"

"No need. Your team did an outstanding job, gathering the evidence, putting everything together. There are no holes in this case."

"It would be interesting to hear her motive for those killings," I said.

"We've got it. She didn't shut up on the way here even after you guys read her the Miranda rights. The uniforms did it too when they were transporting her. They made sure the dashboard camera was on, and it taped everything. The cops didn't say a word, just let her ramble. She kept claiming she didn't want those girls to suffer, didn't want them to grow old and lonely. She wanted to give them a truly passionate, romantic experience that would be the high point of their lives."

"I wonder how long she's been rehearsing that line. Sounds like she was looking for an audience." It was impossible to keep the disgust from my voice.

Beckwith grinned. "She got one."

My phone rang. Kozlowski and Laura were still at the house, overseeing the crime scene unit. I listened silently, then ended the call. Beckwith and Cantrell were staring at me expectantly.

"So far they found items belonging to all three victims, including their cell phones and wallets. It was practically hiding in plain sight. There was a small suitcase under the bed. Inside were three separate bundles, wrapped in tissue paper and tied with a thick red ribbon. There was also the clothing we assume each victim was wearing that night."

"There's your smoking gun." Beckwith pumped a fist in victory.

"There may be more. Kozlowski's making sure they take their time. Every inch of that house is going to be searched."

Beckwith was about to enter the interview room when I stopped him. Cantrell shot me a quizzical look.

"You said there are three charges of first degree murder. Since her actions resulted in setting up Myers and the subsequent death of Detective Barksdale, can we charge her for that too?"

Beckwith jabbed a finger in the air. "Damn right. She'll be charged as an accessory for his death. She may not have pulled the trigger, but she manipulated that series of events." Beckwith turned and entered the interrogation room.

Cantrell and I watched from the observation room. Victoria Samuels appeared to have run out of steam. She was slumped in her chair, her wrists cuffed to a ring that was bolted in the center of the table. Root acknowledged Beckwith and sat back with his hands folded on the table. Beckwith didn't waste any time. He read the charges and told Samuels she would be held in custody in the Macomb County Jail pending the arraignment Monday morning. Transport would take place shortly. He asked if she had anything to say. She stared past Beckwith at the glass separating us.

"Fuck off and die," she snapped.

Beckwith slapped his legal pad on the table. "You first."

****

Megan was propped up in bed. A heavy gauze pad covered her chin. Her eyes were still a little glassy. She was trying to watch a romantic comedy, but I don't think it was keeping her attention. Book led me into the room and stepped over to her bed for a closer look. I waited while he talked softly to her, staring intently into her eyes all the while. He gingerly checked her ribs, then looked up as I moved to the other side of the bed.

"Nothing we can really do for the rib injury, other than give her plenty of meds for the pain. They will heal with time, but she's going to have to take it easy. Once we get past our concerns for the concussion, we'll increase the dosage on the pain meds."

Megan managed a weak smile at him. The doctor nodded once, then slipped out of the room.

"I think he likes you."

She groaned. "Seriously? You think he's checking out my ass while I'm loopy?"

"I didn't say he was checking you out."

"So you don't think he likes my ass?"

"Every man who sees your ass likes it. Obviously, you'll survive your injuries."

"He does have nice hands. And he has a real gentle touch to go with that bedside manner." She took a slow deep breath and held it for a moment before letting it out. "Why are you here?"

I pulled over a chair and settled into it. "Where else would I be?"

Megan stuck her right hand through the rails of the bed and took mine. "Thanks. I understand we're related now."

"I always thought we were."

"How are the others doing?"

"Kozlowski will come by in a couple of hours. Then Laura will be stopping in. It wouldn't surprise me if Pappy showed up as well."

"What's the deal on Samuels?"

"She'll be arraigned Monday morning. I don't think the media will get the story until then. Pappy will probably have to hold a press conference. We'll see what tomorrow brings."

Megan was quiet for a while, watching the movie, holding my hand. She found the remote and lowered the volume as a series of commercials kicked in. Slowly, she turned her attention to me.

"I'm putting in for a transfer. There's an opening at the police academy for an instructor. I've been approached twice before about it. Figure I can teach cadets how to do the job and share real-life experiences. I'm tired of dealing with scum like Samuels. The havoc they wreak on people's lives. It's gotten to be too much."

I didn't say anything, just kept holding her hand.

"Don't try and talk me out of it, Chene."

"I wasn't going to. You deserve to have a normal life. Find somebody good, like that doctor. Fall in love, get married, have a few kids. Be happy." I got up from the chair and perched a hip on the edge of her bed. "Have a good life."

Megan's eyes were watering. "Can you really see me with kids?"

"You're gonna make a great mom. Just consider sending them to a public school." I leaned over and gently wiped her tears away.

"That doctor is kind of cute."

"You'll have to wait until you're discharged before you can date him. There's got to be some ethics issues there."

"I wonder if he makes house calls."

****

Cantrell led Squad Six into the courtroom for the arraignment at nine o'clock Monday morning. Victoria Samuels looked subdued when she was brought in from the holding cell. She was wearing a jailhouse jumpsuit in bright orange. Her wrists and ankles were cuffed and a long chain ran between her extremities and hooked to a loop on a thick belt around her waist. Her attorney, John Root, stood beside her at the defense table. Beckwith stood at the prosecutor's table. Everyone wore a solemn expression. Beckwith looked as if his breakfast had not agreed with him.

The judge listened while the charges were read. Each attorney was given the chance to speak. There was no chance for bail, not with three homicides on the slate. Root asked for special circumstances regarding jail. It was denied. He requested a psychiatric evaluation, to prove whether or not his client was sane enough to stand trial. The judge agreed. The evaluation would be done within four weeks. Samuels was remanded to custody. Still in shackles, she was guided out by a deputy.

Beckwith led us out of the courtroom. He had another case to present in twenty minutes. The expression on his face was grim.

"Did any of you talk with the media?"

"Ah haven't yet," Pappy said. "The governor will want us to put the word out that the killer's been caught."

"Yeah, well, someone beat you to it." Beckwith held up his phone. On the screen was a headline from one of the newspaper websites. There was a grainy picture of Samuels under the banner that read "Alleged Serial Killer Apprehended." He scrolled down to show the text, which included details about this morning's arraignment.

"We kept this quiet," I said, jerking a thumb at the screen. "We didn't even put anything on the radio, so we could avoid anyone picking it up on their scanners."

"Well, the word is definitely out. And once the television channels get wind of this and tie all three killings together, there could be hell to pay. This will be plastered all over the evening news."

Beckwith jammed his phone back into his pocket and moved down the hall to another courtroom.

Cantrell looked over the rest of us. With a shrug of his shoulders, he turned for the exit. We took the elevator down to the lobby and headed outside.

The early April day was warming up. After so many weeks of cold and rain and intermittent clouds, it was a pleasure to see the sunshine. Maybe part of it was realizing that we had caught the killer. Kozlowski tipped his head back, enjoying the sun on his face. Laura pulled a pair of sunglasses out of her pocket. Megan was still a bit wobbly, so she rested a shoulder against Kozlowski. Cantrell fired up a smoke. I was about to suggest going for some food when the unmistakable sound of gunfire erupted nearby.

All five of us raced toward the corner of the building. Cantrell somehow managed to get there first. He slid to a stop and peered around the corner. I took in the scene. This was the rear of the building, where prisoners were transported to and from the Macomb County jail. There was a transport van parked back there with its doors open. From here, I could see one pair of legs sprawled on the ground. It looked like someone was hiding behind the van's doors.

"Fuck me hard," Cantrell muttered. He waved two fingers at Kozlowski and indicated the opposite side of the driveway. He motioned Megan to fall in behind him. Koz and Laura quickly moved to that side.

"Better identify ourselves," I said.

"Damn straight."

I announced our presence, and we moved quickly up the drive. From the doorway leading into the building, I could see an officer down. Laura had a portable radio and called dispatch, requesting assistance. Megan and Cantrell were behind me.

Kozlowski slid alongside the transport van.

"Got a deputy down," he called out. "Looks like someone knocked him out. No blood visible, and I can feel his pulse."

Cantrell motioned to the doorway. In the distance, I could hear sirens. I pulled the access door to the building wide. Another deputy was sprawled here. He was shot in the left thigh. He was trying to keep pressure on the wound. Cantrell dropped beside him, yanking off his belt in the process. Quickly, he fashioned a tourniquet higher up on the leg. Laura elbowed me out of the way. Megan went back up the driveway to direct the other cops arriving at the scene.

"How many?" Cantrell asked the deputy.

"It's one guy. He clubbed Andrews with a bat and pulled his weapon." The deputy's face was waxy and covered with a thick sheen of sweat. But he was determined to help. "That's what he shot me with. We were getting ready to transport the prisoner."

"What's this guy look like?" I asked.

"He's a white guy, late forties, maybe older, with black hair going gray. It looks like he hasn't shaved in a few days, real crazy eyes. Not a real big guy. He chased our prisoner."

"Which prisoner?"

"Samuels, the one accused of killing those women."

Cantrell looked up at me. Laura pulled something from her pocket and jammed it into the hole on the deputy's leg. Now she was ripping a corner from his shirt to make a compress. The sirens were getting closer.

"Y'all go find this bastard."

"We're on it."

Kozlowski and I moved deeper into the building. On the concrete floor, I could see a blood trail. Obviously, this guy had stepped in the deputy's blood before moving inside. Koz motioned to the right side of the hall. This led to the holding tank where prisoners were kept awaiting their court appearances.

As we approached the door, I heard another shot ring out. But this came from down a hallway. We rushed in that direction. And there at the end of the hall, we found our quarry.

Chapter Thirty-Four

Victoria Samuels was pressed against the far wall. She was still in shackles. She had run as far as she could go. This corridor dead ended. Her orange jumpsuit was staining red along the left side from a shot to the stomach. A trickle of blood ran down her chin. Unable to reach her hand up to wipe it away, she turned her head and used her shoulder. I wasn't close enough to see her eyes, but she wasn't cowering.

Standing in front of her was Edgar Grange. He was trembling with rage as he pointed the pistol at her. Less than five feet separated them. He took a step closer.

"Grange! Lower that weapon!"

"She killed her. She has no right to live!"

"That's not up to you to decide. She's going to trial. She's going to be found guilty." I took a step closer. On my left, I could see Kozlowski taking deadly aim. But the way Grange was standing, if Koz took the shot there was a good chance the bullet would pass right through him and hit Samuels.

"Jail won't bring my daughter back!" Grange shouted.

"Killing her won't bring Stephanie back either."

"She killed my little girl! She's all I had."

"Don't do this!"

Kozlowski was trying to get a better angle. Even if he shot Grange in the leg, there was no guarantee we could stop him from shooting Samuels. As if reading my mind, Grange took another step closer to the killer.

"Get away from her."

"She was all I had," he said, "and I'll never get her back."

Grange lunged for Samuels, catching the chain around her waist and pulling her to him. Then he spun around, placing his back against the wall and using her as a shield. He had the gun jammed against the right side of her head. Blood was dripping down the jumpsuit now, making a sticky puddle on the floor. Samuels turned her head once more, looking over her shoulder at Edgar Grange. She ran the tip of her tongue across her lips, then made a smacking sound.

"She was pretty tasty. Wouldn't you agree?"

Grange's face flushed with anger. He whipped the gun around and jammed the muzzle against her chest. And before anyone could move, he pulled the trigger.

As their bodies slithered to the floor, Kozlowski and I rushed forward. He pulled the weapon from Grange's hand. In the distance, I could hear the thump of boots as other deputies and officers ran toward us. I pressed two fingers against Grange's neck, but you could tell that he was also gone. What would haunt me for years was the fact that as he was pulling the trigger, Samuels had swung her head back just enough to lock her lips on his. I straightened up as Cantrell led the charge down the hall. He took in the scene in an instant.

"Fuck me hard."

Kozlowski and I exchanged a look. "Couldn't have said it better myself," he said.

****

We were gathered around the conference table. I

had yet to do the final report, wrapping up this escapade of chaos. Outside, the sky shifted to twilight. I wondered what had happened to the day.

With the scene secured, Kozlowski and I had given our reports to Cantrell. He then worked with the Macomb County Sheriff to put together a statement. The governor had been contacted. A review of the security protocols at the courthouse would be undertaken. Video footage showed Grange arriving earlier and watching the transport entrance. There was a clear shot of him approaching the first deputy, who was caught off guard by his appearance. Grange had clubbed him with a bat, then pulled the deputy's weapon and fired it twice, striking the other deputy in the leg and grazing Samuels in the abdomen. We knew what had happened after that.

Both deputies were taken to the hospital. Laura helped Cantrell with the logistics and handling the media, who descended upon the building like buzzards. Kozlowski pitched in. Megan and I tracked down Evelyn Grange and told her of Edgar's actions and his death. She took the news without an outward physical reaction. I couldn't help but wonder again if she was really that cold.

Now Cantrell appeared. He carried a large brown paper bag. It thumped loudly on the table as he opened it. First he removed six thick plastic cups. Then he pulled out a fifth of Tennessee whiskey. He cracked the seal and poured a generous shot into each cup. Cantrell raised his. We followed his example. The extra cup was placed in front of the chair where Barksdale always sat.

"This has been one bitch kitty of a case. But y'all done me proud. Y'all never quit, even after we los'

Barksdale. It mayn't be pretty, but in the end, we got justice. So here's to justice." With that, he gulped down the alcohol and dropped into his chair.

"To justice," Koz said.

We all drank to that.

Pappy gave us the update from the press conference. He nodded his thanks to Laura for her assistance. She told us about the two deputies and their anticipated recovery. While she was on that subject, a memory clicked in my head.

"What did you put in that deputy's leg?"

She tried to give me an innocent expression but couldn't hold it. "The guy was bleeding all over. Even with Pappy's tourniquet, I needed something to slow it down." She shrugged. "I used a tampon. It just so happened that I had one with me. Hey, they can be very absorbent."

Megan and I relayed our meeting with Evelyn Grange. Cantrell nodded sagely and pulled the whiskey over for another shot. We talked a few more minutes. I glanced at Megan and wondered if the others knew of her plans. I knew she was still on pain pills and realized she'd only taken a tiny sip of the whiskey. Cantrell read my mind. He told the others of her request to transfer.

"Y'all gonna have two slots to fill on the squad. Final decision is mine, but ah'll consider anyone y'all think might be worthwhile."

I had already been thinking about a replacement for Barksdale but wasn't ready to voice it. On that note, Pappy waved us all out. Reports could wait until the morning.

Kozlowski wasted no time leaving. Laura and Megan walked out together, discussing her transfer. I watched Pappy slip the whiskey bottle back in the brown paper bag. He looked at Megan's cup, which was still half full, sitting next to me. I pointed across the table at Barksdale's. He grinned and we each picked one up. We raised them in a silent salute and drained the cups.

"You keep that around just for emergencies?"

"Nah, picked that one up on the way here. Closing this kind of case deserves it. Y'all done good, Chene."

"Yeah, but it came with a huge cost. We lost two people from the squad and that really hurts."

"Price we pay. Y'all get out of here, Chene. Go see that pretty girl and give her some good news."

I started to rise when his comment got to me. "What pretty girl?"

"Unless y'all started wearing perfume, there's gotta be a pretty girl in your arms recently."

I could only shake my head in amazement. "Damn, Pappy, do you miss anything?"

"Nope."

I walked out to the bullpen to grab my jacket. But first, I stepped over to the board and carefully took down the pictures of our three victims. After tucking them into a folder, I picked up the phone and dialed. Simone answered on the second ring.

"Can you come over?" she asked.

"Yes. We've got a lot to talk about. I'll be there in half an hour."

"Make it twenty minutes."

A word about the author...

Mark Love lived for many years in the metropolitan Detroit area, where crime and corruption are always prevalent. A former freelance reporter, Love is the author of three other novels, *Devious, Vanishing Act,* and *Fleeing Beauty* and numerous short stories.

Love currently resides in West Michigan. He enjoys a wide variety of music, books, cooking, and the great outdoors. He is currently working on another novel featuring Jefferson Chene.

http://motownmysteries.blogspot.com

Thank you for purchasing
this publication of The Wild Rose Press, Inc.

If you enjoyed the story, we would appreciate your
letting others know by leaving a review.

For other wonderful stories,
please visit our on-line bookstore at
www.thewildrosepress.com.

For questions or more information
contact us at
info@thewildrosepress.com.

The Wild Rose Press, Inc.
www.thewildrosepress.com

Stay current with The Wild Rose Press, Inc.

Like us on Facebook

https://www.facebook.com/TheWildRosePress

And Follow us on Twitter
https://twitter.com/WildRosePress